She was struck by an overwhelming sense of impending danger

Annja had been abo... ...e passages that led de... ...a feeling so strong spu... ...about to come unde... ...from her dive companions, she was...

What on earth?

On that heels of that thought came another.

Get out of here. Now!

Her instincts had rarely proved wrong.

Unfortunately, she and the rest of the dive group had far less time than she thought. She'd barely given Manuel the signal to ascend when a thundering groan filled their ears. In the next second they were struck by a massive pressure wave that rolled inexorably over them, shaking them about like corks in a stream, tossed and turned in the grip of its power, before leaving them abandoned in its wake.

Titles in this series:

ROGUE Angel

Alex Archer

TREASURE OF LIMA

A GOLD EAGLE BOOK FROM

WORLDWIDE®

TORONTO • NEW YORK • LONDON
AMSTERDAM • PARIS • SYDNEY • HAMBURG
STOCKHOLM • ATHENS • TOKYO • MILAN
MADRID • WARSAW • BUDAPEST • AUCKLAND

Recycling programs
for this product may
not exist in your area.

First edition January 2014

ISBN-13: 978-0-373-62166-8

TREASURE OF LIMA

Special thanks and acknowledgment to
Joe Nassise for his contribution to this work.

Printed in U.S.A.

The
LEGEND

...THE ENGLISH COMMANDER TOOK
JOAN'S SWORD AND RAISED IT HIGH.

The broadsword, plain and unadorned,
gleamed in the firelight. He put the tip against
the ground and his foot at the center of the blade.
The broadsword shattered, fragments falling
into the mud. The crowd surged forward,
peasant and soldier, and snatched the shards
from the trampled mud. The commander tossed
the hilt deep into the crowd.
Smoke almost obscured Joan, but she continued
praying till the end, until finally the flames climbed
her body and she sagged against the restraints.

Joan of Arc died that fateful day in France,
but her legend and sword are reborn....

1

Lima, Peru
July 1820

Viceroy José de la Serna stared out the window of his office at the city below, his thoughts churning. San Martín's Army of the Andes was threatening the capital, and with negotiations failing so miserably at this point, de la Serna had no doubt that he would soon need to either capitulate to the rebels' demands or abandon the city entirely.

He didn't consider either option acceptable in the least.

Why couldn't that bastard be happy enough with Argentina and Chile? he asked himself, not for the first time. *He hasn't pulled enough land out of Spanish hands? He has to come here and cause trouble for me?*

The bastard in question, of course, was General José de San Martín, leader of the rebel army, now just a few days' march from his door. San Martín was no stranger to confrontation, either: after liberating Argentina, he'd led his army across the Andes, no small feat in and of itself, and had then fought rather brilliantly at both the battles of Chacabuco and Maipú, liberating Chile from Spanish rule. Now he planned to do the same to Peru.

De le Serna had half a mind to abandon the city that very evening. He could reestablish the capital at Cuzco and run the defense of the province from there, if need be. It was a better location both tactically and strategically, which made it quite attractive to the viceroy.

He'd do it, too, if it wasn't for all that damned treasure!

He turned away from the window, crossed the room and practically threw himself into a thickly padded chair in front of the fireplace. In the corner stood one of the pieces from the very collection that was causing him such vexing problems.

The statue was life-size and cast entirely in gold. It showed the Virgin Mother kneeling with the infant Jesus clasped gently in her arms. Mother and son were staring at each other, seemingly lost in each other's eyes. The artist had done a marvelous job of infusing the statue with a sense of life, of emotion, and from the very first moment he's laid eyes upon it, de la Serna knew he had to have it. Thankfully, his present position of viceroy of Peru allowed him to do pretty much whatever he wanted. Appropriating the statue from the cathedral had been one of his first acts as viceroy.

The statue was just a tiny fraction of the wealth stored in the cathedral's vaults, however. For years the church had been gathering vast sums of treasure through donations from the rich and poor alike. The bishop had recently estimated the value of the vaults' contents to be somewhere in the neighborhood of one hundred and sixty million sols! If the church's treasury were to fall into San Martín's hands, he could finance hundreds of revolutions and still have plenty of wealth left over to live a long and prosperous life.

De la Serna could not allow that to happen.

Which meant he had to find some way to get the treasure out of the city before San Martín and his men reached the city gates.

He's been pondering the problem for several days now and knew that his options were weak, at best. Pulling a group of his own men off the line would quickly be noticed by the enemy. Once that happened, any attempt to move the treasure overland would more than likely be sniffed out and intercepted by the enemy. Besides, it was more than a thousand kilometers to Cuzco, over mountainous terrain, and San Martín's army wouldn't be the only danger his men would have to face along the way. Everything from brigands to the weather could pose a threat, and there was more than one lonely stretch of road where they could be ambushed, their cargo stolen with no one the wiser. Travelers disappeared from those mountainous roads all the time, often never to be seen again.

No, overland was out.

That left the sea. The port of Callao was less than ten kilometers to the west. If he could get the treasure aboard a ship he could send it north, to his Spanish allies in Mexico, who would no doubt be happy to secure it for a reasonable fee until things had settled down enough here for him to reclaim it.

It seemed like a reasonable answer, until he remembered that the last vessel flying a Spanish flag had left port several days earlier when it became apparent San

Martín's army was headed their way. Right now, the only ships in the harbor belonged to the French, English and Dutch. None of them could be called allies, but then again, they weren't outright enemies, either. For the right price, he might be able to persuade one of them to handle his cargo for him.

He considered the ships he knew to be in port, reviewing what he knew about the captains of each. After some time, he came to a decision.

Clapping his hands sharply twice, the viceroy summoned one of his servants. When the young man appeared, de la Serna said, "Send a message to the *Mary Dear* and invite Captain Thompson to dinner this evening."

The servant bowed. "Sir," he said, then, straightening, turned for the door.

"Wait!"

When the man stopped and turned back, the viceroy said, "If Thompson declines the invitation, go to the *Majestic Wind* and make the same invitation to Captain Barbossa next, but only if Thompson declines. Understood?"

"Yes, sir."

"Good." A wave of his hand. "Get!"

The viceroy went back to gazing out the window, searching the horizon for the storm that he knew was on its way.

"A FINE MEAL, Viceroy," Captain Thompson said several hours later. "A fine meal indeed!"

De le Serna nodded his thanks, careful not to let his irritation show on his face. Of course it was a fine meal—he had one of the best cooks in all of Lima at his disposal, and the man had gone out of his way to prepare dishes the Englishman would enjoy. Thick steaks from the finest Peruvian cattle. Rice-stuffed squab. Potatoes baked in garlic and butter. Never mind several bottles of fifty-year-old French wine to wash it all down.

The English sea captain drained his glass and then held it out for de la Serna's steward to fill it again for what had to be the umpteenth time. The steward looked in the viceroy's direction, but de la Serna simply nodded for him to proceed. Wine was the least valuable thing they'd be discussing this evening.

With his glass topped up, Thompson settled back in satisfaction. "While I appreciate the hospitality, Viceroy, something tells me that this is more than just a social call."

De la Serna forced himself to smile. "You are an astute man, Captain."

"So what can I do for you?"

"I'd like to hire your ship."

At the word *hire,* a change seemed to come over the man. In the space of an instant, the ruddy-faced drunkard who had consumed two of his best bottles of wine all on his own was replaced by a steely-eyed man who was all business.

"What's the destination?"

"Acapulco, Mexico."

De la Serna was sending the treasure to the Spanish ambassador in Mexico City; Acapulco was the closest port to that landlocked city.

"Cargo?"

"Six passengers and roughly thirty to fifty crates."

Captain Thompson caught his gaze with his own. "The contents of these crates?"

"I'd rather not say."

The Englishman smiled and rose from the table. "Well, then, I suspect we are through, Viceroy. Thank you for dinner but I must—"

De la Serna broke in. "That's it? But you haven't even asked what the fee is for your services."

Thompson shrugged. "You leave me no choice, Viceroy. A dead man cannot spend his fee, no matter how exorbitant it might be."

"Even one as exorbitant as one hundred thousand sols?"

The Englishman laughed. "Especially one like that. You see, Viceroy, mysterious cargos tend to bring mysterious enemies out of the woodwork like termites around fresh wood. It is hard to defend a hold full of goods that I know nothing about. Therefore, reason dictates that I should say no."

De la Serna thought he heard a note of hesitation in the other man's voice. "But?" he asked hopefully.

"But reason doesn't always keep the ship repaired and the men fed. Tell me, Viceroy, does your need to move this particular cargo have anything to do with the army amassing to the south of the city?"

"You know it does, Thompson."

"Then it would seem that your fee is a bit low, given the hazardous nature of the task. General San Martín will not look kindly on those who assisted the monarchy when he 'liberates' the city."

De la Serna bristled at the insinuation that his men would fall before San Martín's troops, but he held on to his temper lest he ruin his chances before they even got off the ground. "San Martín's troops will not set foot in this city, but your point about the dangerous nature of shipping a cargo out from under his very nose is well taken. I am willing to double my fee. Two hundred thousand sols."

The viceroy knew the price was insignificant when compared to the cost of the treasure itself. He was willing to pay twice—no, three times—that if it meant the treasure would be safely transported to Mexico City.

Despite the viceroy's poker face, Captain Thompson must have picked up on a little of what he was thinking, for he extended his hand with a smile on his face and said, "Three hundred thousand sols and you've got a deal."

De la Serna tried to look pained as he shook the other man's hand, but inwardly he was more than satisfied. A deal had been struck; now all he had to do was ensure that Thompson carried out his half of the agreement.

2

Later that night Captain William Thompson stood on the command deck of his vessel, the two-masted, square-sailed brig named the *Mary Dear*. He looked down upon the long line of horse-pulled wagons making their way along the dock toward the place where his ship was moored. He eyed the approaching cargo carefully and then turned to the grizzled old sailor standing attentively at his side.

"That's a pretty heavy load," he said to Jones, his first mate. "Get a crew to shift some of the ballast aft before we begin loading that cargo. Don't want to stress the old girl unnecessarily."

"Aye, Captain," Jones replied and moved off, shouting orders.

Thompson remained where he was until the caravan drew close and then headed back to his cabin to await the newcomers' arrival. Other captains might have met their passengers on deck, but Thompson was a stickler for protocol aboard his ship and there was no way he was going to stand around waiting to receive the viceroy's men like a common sailor. He'd have Jones bring them to him when they arrived and with that one gesture make it clear to all just who was in charge. He might be carrying cargo for the viceroy, but he was still his own man, through and through, and on this ship he was king.

He was standing by the table in his cabin, a lantern shining light on the sea charts spread out in front of him, when there was a knock at his door.

"Come," he called.

The door opened and Jones led three men into the room—two priests, one young and one old, with a grizzled old soldier to guard them.

"Fathers Alvarez and Blanco, Sergeant Ruiz," said Jones, "may I present Captain William Thompson."

Thompson smiled. "Gentlemen, please, come in."

The older priest, Alvarez, was of medium height and build, but he carried himself as if he owned the place, a trait that made Thompson instantly dislike him. The younger priest was cut from the same cloth—five minutes after meeting him, you wouldn't be able to pull him out of a crowd, so bland were his features. But he had yet to take on that mantle of self-importance that his superior had in spades.

Give him time, Thompson thought, *give him time. The apple doesn't fall far from the tree.*

Sergeant Ruiz, on the other hand, was exactly what Thompson expected him to be, an obvious veteran of several wars who carried an air of hard competence about him like a cloak. This was not a man to toy with lightly.

Of the three, Thompson would regret killing Ruiz the most.

Handshakes were exchanged all around and beverages were offered but declined. With the social niceties out of the way, the older priest, Alvarez, stepped forward and handed a sealed letter to the captain.

Thompson glanced down at it, noting the viceroy's mark in the middle of the wax seal, and then broke open the packet to remove a single sheet of paper. He stepped over to the lantern to see it better as he read.

Captain Thompson,
Reports arrived on my desk this afternoon indicating that Lord Cochrane is headed up the coast with a fleet of ships at his disposal, intending to block Callao in order to force those of us here in Lima to capitulate to the rebels' demands. Time is clearly of the essence; if you are caught in port when Cochrane and his fleet arrive, I have little hope that your national sovereignty will save you from humiliation at the rebels' hands, especially given the cargo you now carry.

I urge you, therefore, to make haste and put to sea as quickly as possible. My representatives, Father Alvarez and his assistant, Father Blanco, are familiar with those at your destination and will help smooth your passage once you reach Mexico.
Godspeed and God bless.
Viceroy José de la Serna

When he finished reading it, Thompson carefully folded the letter and then fed it to the flame of a nearby candle until the heat got too close and he tossed it into a nearby bowl to burn itself out. If Cochrane did catch him, he wanted no proof of his collusion with de la Serna left on hand.

"Thank you for delivering that, Father," he said to Alverez.

The older priest smiled. "Good news, I hope?"

Thompson shrugged. "Too soon to tell, I fear, but one can always hope."

"We will pray for it to be so," Alvarez replied, which threatened to pull an explosion of laughter out of Thompson before he got a handle on it.

"I'd appreciate that, Father," he told the other man instead. With a straight face, no less. He glanced over the priest's shoulder and nodded at Jones.

"Jones here—" indicating the first mate "—will show you to your cabins, gentlemen."

Ruiz spoke up for the first time. "My men and I will bunk down in the hold to keep watch on the cargo."

"As you wish, Sergeant. I can have Jones arrange some bread, meat and cheese for supper, if you'd like."

The old veteran nodded. "That would be appreciated. Thank you, Captain."

"My pleasure," Thompson said. "Now, if you gentlemen will excuse me, I have a voyage to plan."

ONE HOUR LATER the ship got under way with a minimum of fuss. The harbormaster would normally have given them some grief about leaving at this hour of the night, but with rumors of the city's fall swirling about like smoke around a campfire, he didn't begrudge those who wanted to get out before the hammer came down and let them go with nary a word.

Thompson had given orders that they head north for several kilometers and that was precisely what they did, cutting through the darkness like a knife through butter as a decent breeze filled their sails and guided them forward on their journey. Satisfied that the pilot had things under control, Thompson turned the ship over to him and retired to his cabin.

Half an hour after he'd left the deck, the door to his cabin opened and Jones slipped inside.

Thompson looked up from the charts he was studying. "Well?" he asked.

Jones gestured behind him and two of Thompson's other crew members stepped into the captain's cabin. Between them they carried a large sea chest, and from the way they were handling it, it was clear that it was rather heavy.

"Bring it here, boys," Thompson told them, indicating they should put it on the table before him, and then, once they had, dismissed them back to their other duties.

He glanced inquiringly at Jones once the others had left the room.

"We swapped one of ours for one of theirs during the loading process."

It was a standard sea chest made of iron-banded wood, with a lock built into the lid itself—not like that was going to stop Thompson, however. He drew the dirk from his belt, inserted the blade between the lid and the chest itself just an inch or so away from the lock, then pushed down sharply on the hilt.

There was a moment of silence, as force fought with metal, and then a sharp *ping* sounded through the room as the interior of the lock gave way and the lid popped open.

Both men stared at the sea of gold coins that filled the chest.

"That devious son of a…"

Now the viceroy's willingness to meet his price made sense to Thompson. He had no doubt that the rest of the cargo was equally valuable. He'd seen the wagons weighted down under the load and knew that the other chests probably contained as much gold, if not more, than this one did.

"Sweet Jesu, there's a fortune in that one chest alone!" Jones whispered, awed by thoughts of just how much treasure they might be carrying.

Thompson barely heard him, his mind whirling with the possibilities that had suddenly presented themselves. De la Serna was trying to move the treasury out from under the nose of General San Martín. That was clear. What was equally clear was the fact that the viceroy would need to keep the operation secret: the more who knew, the greater chance that word would reach San Martín and the treasure would be intercepted by the rebels. De la Serna hadn't even been willing to tell him what was in the shipment and it was his ship that was carrying it!

If the shipment were to conveniently disappear, Thompson thought, only a handful of people would know it had ever gone missing in the first place.

With the exception of de la Serna himself, most of those people were right here on this very vessel.

Temptation reared its head and Thompson embraced it eagerly. A plan coalesced fully formed in his head.

Turning to Jones, he explained to his first mate exactly what they were going to do to ensure that they would be set with riches for the rest of their lives.

Jones eagerly agreed.

After that it was a simple matter of waiting for their guests, priests and soldiers alike, to fall asleep before sending men to slit their throats while they slept. Once they were dead, the bodies were hauled to the side of the ship and tossed overboard as food for the sharks.

With the spies out of the way, Thompson, Jones and four handpicked men returned to the hold to determine the extent of their booty.

It was an impressive haul, by anyone's standards. After all the chests had been broken into and their contents cataloged, Thompson stared at the list with something approaching wonder.

113 gold statues, all of a religious nature
200 chests of jewels, including rubies, cornelians,
topazes and emeralds
1,000 cut diamonds
273 swords and daggers, all with jeweled hilts
150 gold chalices
4,000 Spanish doubloons
5,000 Mexican crowns
4,265 uncut gemstones
2 gold reliquaries
2 life-size statues of the Virgin Mary and child
cast in solid gold, her clothing decorated with
jewels

All of which was currently sitting in the hold of his ship, waiting for him to decide what to do with it.

They couldn't keep it aboard, that was for certain. The *Mary Dear* was a simple two-masted brig: it wouldn't stand a chance against the man-of-wars lurking in these waters if de la Serna had him declared a pirate. No, they needed to get the treasure off the ship and stored somewhere safe for the time being and then lay low until after the revolution was over. At that point, they could return and cart off the treasure in small chunks with no one the wiser.

The question was, where? Where could a man hide millions in gold?

After a few moments of thought, he realized he knew just the place.

It was perfect!

"Jones, tell the pilot to set course for Cocos Island."

"Aye, Captain!"

3

Annja Creed fell into darkness.

Down.

Down.

Down she fell.

Deeper and deeper with every passing second, until it seemed that the only thing she'd ever known was this darkness, pressing in on her from all sides.

She could feel her eyes straining to see something, anything, even the slightest glimmer of light, but finding nothing but this total darkness. She could feel her heartbeat speeding up, her pulse accelerating, and she told herself to relax; there was nothing to worry about.

Nothing but what might be lurking out there in the dark.

As she was telling the voice in the back of her head to shut up and be quiet, her feet touched bottom. She bent her legs to absorb the impact, what little there was, and then stood up straight again. The weight belt around her waist would keep her anchored, but still, she was careful not to push off with her legs as she did so.

She took a deep breath off her regulator…and hit the switch on the high-powered handheld spotlight that she was holding.

The grotto directly ahead of her lit up spectacularly, just as Manuel had said it would, and she was caught in spellbinding wonder as brilliantly colored stalactites hanging from the ceiling of the grotto were revealed. A dozen shades of red, blue and yellow hues danced in the light, transforming the underwater cavern into a cathedral of color. It was breathtaking and Annja felt her pulse quicken in admiration.

The cenote she was diving in had been formed thousands of years before when the naturally acidic groundwater seeped through cracks in the limestone bedrock, gradually wearing away the softer stone beneath, creating a pocketlike chamber with a thin limestone roof. At some point in the far past that roof collapsed and the empty chamber gradually filled with the groundwater seeping in through the surrounding soil. The result was a natural well hundreds of feet deep.

Even better in Annja's eyes was that fact that this particular cenote connected with a series of caverns extending more than a mile underground, making it a perfect dive location through which to experience Costa Rica's subterranean world.

The cable television show that Annja worked for, *Chasing History's Monsters,* was devoted to exactly what its name suggested. For the past week she'd been here in Costa Rica filming segments on one of the more notorious Portuguese pirates of the 1800s. Benito "Bloody Sword" Bonito had raided shipping and seaside towns up and down the west coast of the Americas for a number of years before being captured and hanged by the British. According to legend, his ghost still haunted the Spanish Main, complete with spectral pirate vessel, and that was more than enough for her producer, Doug Morrell, to send her here to chase down those who claimed to have seen it and perhaps get lucky enough to see it for herself.

Normally Annja might have objected to such ridiculousness—she was an archaeologist by training and preferred the episodes she hosted to have a bit more of a factual basis, but a week enjoying the green jungles and gorgeous beaches of Costa Rica was something she just couldn't pass up. When the crew had called it a wrap two days ago, she'd phoned Doug and let him know she was taking a few days of vacation to relax in the sun and enjoy herself for a change. She'd even changed rooms to mentally mark the difference between the time she spent here for work and the time she was taking for herself. It was silly, yes, but it made her feel better and that was all that mattered.

She'd gotten to know the resort dive instructor, Manuel Fernando, pretty well during the course of their shoot and enjoyed spending time with him, so when he'd invited her along on the dive expedition earlier that morning she'd readily agreed. There were three other resort guests on the dive, all beginners. Due to her previous diving experience, Manuel had let her go down ahead of the others so that she'd have the chance to view the grotto uninterrupted, just as he had the first time he'd dived the well. Gazing at it now, she was thankful that he had; it was a glorious sight!

Other lights broke the gloom above her and she knew

the rest of the divers were on their way down. She moved closer to the side wall, noting the stronger current along the cenote's edge as she did so, and waited for the others to reach her. The guests came first—Julie and Steve, a couple in their mid-twenties spending their honeymoon in Costa Rica, and Rick, a heavyset male in his early forties here on a business trip—with Manuel following directly behind them to be certain they made the descent without problem. The three guests had completed a weeklong dive-instruction course just the day before and today's dive was sort of their graduation exercise. Annja remembered her first time making a major dive and felt a slight thread of envy; for the three of them, it was all new territory, and boy, did that feel good.

Once they were all gathered together on the bottom, Manuel checked with each of them to be sure that they were okay. Annja gave them a thumbs-up when his attention turned to her. His eyes smiled at her through his mask. *Bear with us,* he seemed to be saying, and she smiled inwardly in return. She'd noticed Manuel eyeing her when he thought she wasn't looking and she was pretty sure that he was working up the nerve to make a pass at her, something she wouldn't mind in the least. Fact was, if he didn't get up the nerve relatively soon, she'd probably make a pass of her own. Not only was he fun to be around, but he was damned good-looking, too, with raffish good looks and a body to rival that of a professional fitness instructor. It was all that swimming, she knew. *Gave him abs to die for.*

She chided herself. The sun, sand and sea were starting to get to her, it seemed. It was hard being alone in the midst of so much beauty and it was only natural that she'd want a little male companionship given her surroundings, wasn't it?

Damn straight.

At five feet ten inches tall, with chestnut hair, amber-green eyes and an athlete's share of smooth, rounded muscle, Annja got more than her fair share of male interest, but her schedule normally didn't allow her to take advantage of it. She was always jetting off somewhere new, following the latest mystery, searching for the answers to some age-old puzzle, and her social life was practically nonexistent as a result. It took a vacation to remind her that life shouldn't be lived alone. Or, at least, not all the time.

She shook off thoughts of Manuel and concentrated on the grotto into which he was taking them, letting them drift among the rock formations and marveling at the uniqueness of each stalactite and stalagmite that hung down from the ceiling above their heads or grew upward from the floor beneath their feet.

Annja was about to take a look down one of the adjoining passages that led deeper into the cave system leading off the cenote proper when she was struck by an overwhelming sense of impending danger. It was so strong that she literally spun about in a circle, certain that an enemy was looming nearby and that she was about to come under attack, but aside from her dive companions, she was alone.

What on earth?

On the heels of that thought came another.

Get out of here. Now!

Annja had learned to trust her instincts. She didn't question them. She didn't second-guess herself. She just turned herself about, searching for Manuel and pointing frantically upward, knowing that whatever was coming wasn't going to be good.

Unfortunately, she and the rest of the dive group had far less time than she thought. She'd barely given the signal to ascend to Manuel when a thundering groan filled their ears and in the next second they were struck by a massive pressure wave that rolled inexorably over them, shaking them about like corks in a stream, tossed and turned in the grip of its power, before leaving them abandoned in its wake.

For a moment, it was all they could do to hang there in the water and get their bearings. Annja recovered first, moving to where Steve and Julie clung to a nearby stalagmite. She used hand signals to confirm that they were both okay. Once she had, she looked about and saw that Manuel was doing the same with the other guest, Rick. They were all shook up, and no doubt scared, but fortunately none of them had been seriously injured, thanks in part to the fact that their position in the grotto had partially shielded them from the full force of the earthquake.

That was what it had been, an earthquake; Annja was certain of it. Costa Rica had more than its fair share of quakes and she'd been through enough of them to recognize the phenomena, even this far underwater. She also knew that there would likely be more to come, if only from the series of aftershocks that were likely to follow. In fact, they had a limited window in which to get out of the danger zone before the ground betrayed them a second time.

It was time to get out of there.

Annja caught Steve's and Julie's attention and signaled for them to head for the surface. Thankfully, they did as they were told, grabbing hands and kicking hard for the sunlight high above. She nodded approvingly as she watched them go; they stayed in the center of the shaft and rose quickly but carefully.

The newlyweds had risen about a hundred feet toward the surface when the first of the aftershocks hit. The frenetic shaking of the cenote's walls carved off chunks of limestone that fell downward into the water below like unguided missiles. Annja watched one such projectile fall toward her and just managed to get out of its way; it might not strike with bone-breaking force because of the resistance of the water, but it would certainly be heavy enough to carry her to the bottom and pin her there if she were unlucky enough to be trapped beneath it.

Seeing her charges continuing upward in the wake of the aftershock, Annja turned her attention back to her own level, wondering why Manuel and Rick hadn't joined her yet. She saw the answer quickly enough; the aftershock had apparently spooked Rick into action and he was now headed for one of the tunnels rather than back up the main shaft toward the surface.

As Annja looked on, Manuel went after him, catching up with him before Rick could get more than a few feet down the length of the tunnel. The dive instructor got his charge turned around in the right direction and followed in his wake, headed back to the main shaft of the cenote where Annja waited.

That was when the second aftershock hit.

The world bounced and shook and careened around

her, the pressure wave throwing her against the wall of the cenote with bruising force. To Annja, it seemed that this aftershock was stronger than the first by a factor of two or more; it was nearly as strong as the initial quake itself. Debris thundered down around her, rocks the size of softballs competing for space with those the size of refrigerators.

The water, crystal clear just moments before, rapidly became obscured with dirt, silt and rock kicked up by the action of the quake, reducing her visibility to just a few feet. She caught a glimpse of Rick cutting away his weight belt and using the sudden increase in his buoyancy to rise swiftly out of reach, and he headed for the surface high above their heads.

Annja waited for Manuel to follow suit, but the dive instructor didn't appear. With every passing second she grew more concerned that something dire had happened to him, until she couldn't stand it anymore and set out to find him.

It was a good thing she did.

After searching about for several moments, she finally spotted his brilliant blue wet suit pressed up against a pile of rubble. Swimming over, she discovered that he was conscious but unable to move, his left leg trapped beneath the remains of a stalactite that had broken free from the roof of the tunnel.

Aware that another tremor could strike at any second, Annja mimed to Manuel that she was going to try to move the stone. It was too big to lift, but she thought she might be able to roll it away. She got down next to it, put her shoulder against the stone and, using her legs for power, pushed as hard as she could.

It didn't budge.

She glanced at Manuel, saw him trying to wave her off. Through a series of hand signals, he told her to head for the surface and leave him behind, but she shook her head, ignoring his request. There was no way she was going to abandon him, not while they still had plenty of air and she was physically capable of making the effort.

Annja backed away and eyed the stalactite. She had been trying to push it backward, but saw now that it was wedged up against several other rocks that had been shaken loose by the quake. If she reversed direction, perhaps she could create some leverage beneath it and roll it forward instead.

She swam around the side of the stone and found a suitable spot that was partially hidden from Manuel's view. Satisfied that he wouldn't be able to see exactly what she was doing, she mentally reached into the other-where and drew forth her sword. It slid smoothly into existence, appearing at the speed of thought, fully formed and ready for use. The hilt fit her hand like a glove and at times Annja thought it had been made for her and her alone, despite her knowledge of the blade's history.

The broadsword had once belonged to Joan of Arc. It was plain and unadorned, the kind of blade that was barely worth a second glance from those who admired such things. But the reality of the situation was quite different. This sword was something special.

It had been broken on the morning of Joan's execution, shattered into dozens of pieces by a savage downward blow from the booted foot of the English commander in charge of her execution. Hundreds of years later, when all of the pieces had been brought back together for the first time, the sword mystically re-formed in a flash of light and bonded itself to its new bearer. When Annja wasn't using it, the sword dematerialized, existing as a thought in some in-between place she'd come to call the otherwhere. She could summon it at a moment's notice, simply by willing it into her hand, and could release it in similar fashion. After all this time she still wasn't sure why the blade had chosen her to be its bearer, but it had become such a part of her life that she couldn't imagine what things would be like without it.

Right now, she was going to use that sword to help save Manuel's life.

Annja wedged the blade deep between the stalactite and one of the rocks behind it, wiggling it around to get it as deep as possible. When she was satisfied, she put her hands on the hilt and pushed down with all she had.

The tempered steel of the blade bent slightly, but not so much that Annja was worried about it breaking. She began to apply more pressure, forcing the blade downward, hoping that it would be enough.

She felt the stalactite shift slightly.

Got you! she thought and then really leaned into it, forcing all of her body weight down onto that point of the system.

The stone rocked once, twice and then rolled off Manuel's leg as if it had never been trapped in the first place.

Annja wanted to shout for joy.

That was when her internal alarm bells went off for the second time that day.

This time, she didn't stop to think. She didn't stop to

analyze the consequences or the possible repercussions of her actions; she just moved, throwing herself bodily over Manuel's injured form as she released her sword back into the otherwhere. She landed across him just as the ground beneath them began to buck and shake, tossing them about in a terrifying reminder of Mother Nature's strength and her casual indifferences to the creatures that called her home. Annja gripped Manuel tightly, not wanting the two of them to become separated in the maelstrom.

While still fairly powerful, this latest aftershock was weaker than the previous two and was over almost before it had begun. When it had passed, Annja found herself pressed up against the wall of the cenote, still holding tightly to Manuel. Their masks were close enough together that she could see him watching her through the glass.

You okay? she signed.

He nodded, then pointed upward.

This time she obeyed. Still holding on to him, she kicked for the surface.

A RESCUE TEAM from the resort was waiting for them when they surfaced, summoned by a call for help on Steve and Julie's cell phone.

The water level was substantially lower when they surfaced than it had been at the start of the dive, so Annja had to wait for new ropes to be tied off and thrown down to them before she could get them out of the water. She tied one rope around Manuel, secured another around herself and then gave the line a sharp tug to indicate that they were ready. Minutes later the ropes were pulled taut and the two of them began rising into the air.

Annja helped Manuel spit out his regulator and remove his mask, before doing the same herself. When she was finished, she looked up to find him watching her, an unusual expression on his face.

"What's wrong?" she asked, concerned.

He continued to stare at her, then seemed to find his courage.

"Down there, in the water," he asked, "was that a sword?"

Annja's pulse kicked up a notch. How much had he seen?

"A what?" she asked, buying time.

"A sword."

The hesitation in his voice told her that even if he had seen her conjure her sword out of thin air, his rational side was trying to find some other explanation for it all.

Annja laughed. "A sword? What would I be doing with a sword in the middle of a cave dive?"

He frowned. "It sounds silly, I know, but I could have sworn…"

"Silly, yes, but not entirely unexpected. You were banged up pretty good down there, after all." She grinned, as if to show she didn't think ill of him for seeing things, and breathed a sigh of relief when rescue workers reached them.

Ten minutes later a doctor had pronounced them fit to travel and they were loaded into a waiting SUV. The quake had been worse deep underground than it had been topside; there were a few buildings with minor damage to them and a fair number of palms that had been uprooted, but the general area appeared under control. Since the resort was on the way to the hospital, the driver stopped long enough to let Annja and the other guests get out before continuing on to the hospital with Manuel and a few others who had suffered minor injuries in the quake.

As she was getting out of the truck, Manuel reached out and caught her arm. "Thanks for saving my life," he told her. "I owe you one."

"Nonsense," she said. "You would have done the same for me. That's why they call it buddy diving, right?"

"Right, but still, the least you can do is let me buy you a drink."

She agreed and they made plans to meet later that evening, provided Manuel was allowed to come back from the hospital. As the truck drove away from the resort, Annja grinned.

Once again, her intuition had been right.

Annja stayed behind to assist with unloading the dive equipment from the truck since Manuel couldn't do it, then helped the rest of the crew purge and refill the tanks with clean air so that they'd be ready for the next group in the morning.

She was standing in the shade at the back of the dive shack, hanging the neoprene wet suits that had been used during the afternoon's adventure, when she spotted a blond-haired woman talking earnestly with two members of the Policía Turística, or Tourism Police. Officers from that particular branch of the Ministerio de Seguridad Pública, or Ministry of Public Safety, were in charge of ensuring the safety and well-being of those who travelled through Costa Rica, whether for business or pleasure.

It wasn't the officers' presence that caught her attention; their deep blue uniforms were a common sight at resorts like this, for it was in the government's best interests to protect the tourist trade as much as possible, given that it accounted for over 20 percent of the foreign exchange within the country. No, it was a combination of the earnestness with which the woman was speaking to them matched with their seeming indifference that made her pause as her gaze traveled over them.

The woman looked to be in her early thirties. She was tall, probably close to six feet, and had blond hair, which she wore pulled back in a ponytail in much the same way that Annja wore hers while on a dig. She was dressed in a tank top and shorts, with hiking boots on her feet.

As the woman spoke, she gestured generously with her hands. From Annja's perspective, she seemed to be making some rather emphatic statements, if her hand motions were any indication of her words. Each time she did so, however, the police would simply shake their heads and shrug, as if saying, *Sorry, I can't help you.*

Annja found herself wondering what was going on, but before she could wander over and satisfy her curiosity, the woman threw up her hands in disgust and stalked off. The police watched her a minute and then went their own way, the incident no doubt already forgotten in their minds.

It should have been the same for Annja. After all, she had enough to deal with in the wake of the afternoon's events, but something kept bringing the woman to mind long after she had disappeared from view.

Something was wrong there. Annja could feel it in her bones.

4

Annja was just finishing her dinner when she glanced across the restaurant and saw the same blond-haired woman she'd seen earlier now sitting off by herself at a corner table. She didn't think anything of it at first, but something about the woman's posture, the way she was holding herself, brought Annja's attention back to her again and the second time Annja realized what her intuition was trying to tell her. The woman was crying.

Leave it alone, she told herself. *It's none of your business. Probably nothing worse than a marital spat or boyfriend trouble.*

But the memory of the woman talking to the police officers earlier in the day would not leave her, nor the knowledge that more than one tourist had met a bitter end far from home while vacationing somewhere they considered safe.

Annja watched the woman for a few seconds and then made up her mind. She stood and walked across the room, not quite sure what it was she was going to say until she was next to the woman's table and found the words flowing out of her mouth.

"Excuse me, but are you all right?"

The woman started and looked up to find Annja

standing there. "I'm sorry...what?" she said as she wiped at the tears on her face and looked around for a few seconds in confusion.

When the woman's attention came back to her, Annja smiled reassuringly. "I asked if you are all right."

The woman nodded her head. "I'm fine. Fine."

Right.

Annja didn't need any supernatural help in hearing the lie in the woman's words; one look was all it took. *You've come this far,* she thought. *Why stop now?*

"May I sit down?" she asked.

Annja didn't wait for an answer; she just pulled out a nearby chair and sat. She smiled at the woman again, to show she wasn't a threat, and said, "I was sitting over there—" she nodded toward her table across the room "—and couldn't help but notice that you were upset. I know what it's like to be in a foreign country alone, so I thought I'd come over and be certain that you were okay." She put out her hand. "I'm Annja."

"Claire," the blonde said, wiping at her face again with her left hand even as she shook Annja's with her right. "Claire Knowles."

"So let me ask you again. Are you all right? Were you or someone you know injured in the quake earlier?"

Claire shook her head. "No, nothing like that. Really, I'm fine."

The woman's remark was accompanied by a smile as fake as a three-dollar bill. Annja didn't say anything in response; she just looked at the woman and waited.

Claire's smile faltered. "Actually, no. No, I'm not all right."

Annja felt a whisper of excitement run through her

veins. She'd come over here on a whim, following nothing more than a fluttering sensation in her gut that told her there was something going on, something that she should be involved with, and now that sensation was sparking to life, confirming her hunch.

"It's my husband," Claire said. "He's gone missing."

A thousand different questions ran through Annja's mind. She went with the obvious one.

"Have you gone to the police?"

"Yes, but they said they couldn't do anything."

Annja frowned. *Odd.*

"Perhaps you'd better start at the beginning."

Claire smiled weakly in her direction. "I think you're right."

She composed herself and then began her tale.

"My husband, Dr. Richard Knowles, and I came down here three weeks ago as part of an investigative expedition. Richard is head of the Antiquities Department at the University of Chicago." Claire paused, looked down and then said, "Antiquities is the branch of science that studies—"

Annja interrupted, "I know what the antiquities department does," she said with a smile. "Go on."

"Right. Sorry. Well, Richard's been interested in this region of the world and its unique history for a long time. He's an expert on the ancient cultures of Central and South America, particularly the Inca. Are you familiar with them, as well?"

Annja nodded.

Claire went on.

"A few years ago my husband became fascinated

with a particular legend involving a large treasure that went missing in the final days of the Peruvian revolt."

"The lost Treasure of Lima!" Annja exclaimed.

Claire looked at her with surprise. "Yes, that's the one. You're familiar with the legend?"

Annja grinned sheepishly. "I'm a bit of a fan when it comes to stories of lost artifacts and ancient civilizations. The Treasure of Lima is perhaps one of the most notorious in this part of the world."

The other woman laughed. "I understand. Richard's like that, too."

"Don't tell me he came looking for it."

"He did indeed. Like many people before him, Richard believed that the treasure was hidden on Cocos Island, about three hundred miles west of here. He was able to persuade the Costa Rican government to authorize an expedition and to let him try to find the gold."

Annja was surprised. Cocos Island was not only a Costa Rican national park, but it was also a UNESCO World Heritage site, which meant just about everything on the island was protected. She knew people who had been trying to obtain permission to explore the island for years, decades even, without success.

"How on earth did he manage that?" she asked.

Claire waved her hand as if shooing away a fly. "It had something to do with convincing the authorities that he wouldn't be doing any damage to the local environment because he would be using a new kind of ground-mapping radar program. Don't ask me to explain it—way beyond my meager science capabilities—but it basically allows them to explore likely places where the treasure might have been buried without disturbing so much as the top soil in any way. Completely non-damaging to the local plant and wildlife."

Clever man, Annja thought. She'd used such technology in the past and it *was* non-damaging to the environment. Until you started digging to recover what the radar found, that is.

"The expedition got under way without difficulty. They made landfall around midafternoon the first day and camped just off the beach near Chatham Bay. At dawn they headed inland, following what Richard believed to have been the route the pirates, thieves, whatever you want to call them, had taken when they secreted the treasure there originally."

Claire paused. Her expression drifted inward. Annja had seen that look before; her companion was reliving some painful experience from the past. To break the spell, Annja reached forward and touched her wrist.

"What happened?" she asked when Claire started and came back to herself.

"The morning of the third day, Richard called by satellite phone to tell me that they'd found a sea chest that had been partially exposed during a rockslide. The chest contained a number of clerical vestments and a handful of gold and silver chalices. Richard was convinced that it was a part of the missing treasure, since much of it had come from churches across Peru, and told me that they would be staying in that location for another day or two while they investigated further. He agreed to call me later that day to let me know what they had found. He never called."

"How long has it been since you've heard from him?"

Claire bit her lip nervously, then said, "A week."

Annja sat back, her thoughts churning furiously. A week was a long time to be out of touch. If something had happened, it might already be too late for help to do any good....

"Did he have any other communication equipment with him besides the satellite phone?"

"Richard is a firm believer in redundancy. Besides the two satellite phones, they also had a standard wireless-radio set. They were also testing one of those new solar-powered laptops."

Annja smiled reassuringly, but inside she wasn't happy. If Dr. Knowles had followed standard procedure, he would have distributed the communications equipment among several people in the group. That way they wouldn't lose their ability to communicate with the outside world if one of them were lost to injury or accident. Of course, there was the chance that he hadn't followed the usual procedures, but everything she'd heard so far made him sound like a very careful man.

"I saw you speaking with the police earlier this afternoon. Was that about Richard?"

"Yes. I have men and equipment lined up and ready to make the trip to Cocos Island, but trying to get official permission to go is like pulling teeth. My permits are all tied up with red tape and it looks like it will be weeks before it gets all sorted out. I thought the police might be able to help me make my case, but they've been unwilling to interfere in what they see as a noncriminal matter."

Bureaucratic red tape was something Annja was intimately familiar with. Claire was right; it could take weeks before it was resolved. If her husband was in danger or, heaven forbid, seriously injured, help would arrive far too late to do him any good. They needed to act now.

"It seems fate has put us together for a reason, Claire," Annja said. She explained about her background in archaeology, starting with her first dig at Hadrian's Wall in England, and her history of finding objects and civilizations that most thought to be myth or legend. She told Claire about her work with *Chasing History's Monsters* and how that had brought her in touch with quite a few people over the years.

"I'm sure that my contacts in the Costa Rican government can help expedite your paperwork, but it's likely that one of the requirements of doing so will be my presence as part of the expedition."

Claire eyed her steadily. "Just what is this going to cost me?"

"Ten percent of the salvage if the treasure is recovered. Basic expenses—food, transportation, any gear I might need—if it isn't."

It was a fair deal, Annja thought. International law required them to turn the treasure over to its rightful owners—either the Peruvian government or the Costa Rican government, depending on how you looked at it—in exchange for a 20 percent salvage fee. Treasure hunters had been estimating the value of the loot at something in the neighborhood of sixty million dollars, but Annja knew those estimates were always pure guesswork. *More important,* she thought, *it gives me the chance to take part in one of the biggest treasure hunts of the twenty-first century.*

Claire paused, appeared to think it over and then

stuck out her hand. "Deal," she said. "I'll have my attorney draw up a contract to that effect. With my husband missing, I'll use my power of attorney to retroactively agree on his behalf. If he's found the treasure, you'll be a rich woman."

Annja took Claire's hand in her own and shook on their agreement.

"My priority is finding your husband," she said. "We can worry about the lost Treasure of Lima later."

She glanced around, spotted a waiter and waved him over.

"It's not too late to make a few calls this evening, so I'll do so and get back to you in the morning if I hear anything. Here's my cell number," she said, grabbing a paper napkin from the waiter as he arrived and writing her number on it for Claire. "Call me if you hear anything new."

Claire took the napkin with a bit of a self-deprecatory laugh. "I can't believe I started to explain to you the role of an antiquities department," she said. "How ridiculous."

Annja shrugged it off. "No problem. It's actually nice not to be recognized for a change," she said with a laugh. "Don't worry. We'll find out what happened to your husband. I promise."

5

After dinner, Annja returned to her hotel room to make some phone calls. She hadn't been entirely honest when she'd told Claire that she had contacts in the Costa Rican government. She didn't; but she bet she knew one or two others who certainly did. She was confident that she could get them to grease the wheels for her and convince those in charge to issue the permits they needed for their rescue mission to Cocos Island. Especially when she told them what else they might find there.

Her first—and only—call, as it turned out, was to Roux.

Annja and Roux had what could only be described as a unique relationship. After all, it wasn't every day that your sometime partner, sometime mentor was a four-hundred-plus-year-old French knight once charged with defending Joan of Arc from the English!

Annja and Roux had met in the countryside outside Paris several years ago. As usual, Annja was on assignment for *Chasing History's Monsters,* doing an episode on the werewolflike creature known as the Beast of Gévaudan, which had once terrorized the French countryside. Roux, on the other hand, had been searching for something even more mystical—the last remaining piece of Joan's shattered sword. Roux was convinced that it was the sword that was responsible for keeping him and his squire, Garin Braden—also present on the day of Joan's execution—alive through the centuries, and he'd been working to restore the blade to its original condition. As it turned out, it was Annja who had discovered that final, missing piece—a discovery that would bring them all together and change all three of their lives in unexpected ways.

More than a few people, including both Roux and Garin at various times, had tried to take the sword away from her after it had miraculously restored itself, but she refused to allow that to happen; she was as bound to the sword now as the sword was to her.

Over time, Roux had become both a mentor and sometime business partner. She'd used his knowledge to chase down more than one artifact in the past, making them both a tidy bit of money. Not that Roux needed it; more than two hundred years of investments, both in Europe and abroad, had made him a very wealthy man. It wasn't the money but rather the thrill of the chase that excited Roux, and while he would sometimes accompany Annja on one of her expeditions, for the most part he lived a bit vicariously through her adventures and exploits.

The network of contacts Roux had built up over the years was more than impressive, as well. For a man who disliked the spotlight and did most of his business dealings from behind the protective covering of shell companies and layered corporate connections, he certainly knew a lot of people in a lot of places, something that Annja was counting on now.

It was just after 9:00 p.m. in Costa Rica, which made it just after five in the morning in Paris. Annja knew that Roux was an early riser, however, and so didn't hesitate to place the call.

The phone was picked up after only two rings.

"Good morning, Miss Creed."

It was Henshaw, Roux's majordomo and butler. He took his duties seriously; in all the time she'd known him, she didn't think he'd ever used her first name.

"Good morning, Henshaw," she replied in the same formal tone, trying not to laugh as she did it. "Is he in?"

"He is indeed. Shall I get him?"

"If it wouldn't be too much trouble."

"No trouble at all, Miss Creed."

Roux was on the line moments later.

"What do you need, my dear?"

Annja frowned. "What makes you think I need anything? Perhaps I just called you up to say hello and chat for a bit."

Roux chuckled. "I can see your ability to lie hasn't improved in the slightest. You really need to work on that verbal tic of yours."

"Verbal tic?" Annja asked, a bit indignant at the suggestion.

Besides artifact hunting, one of Roux's other major pleasures in life was gambling. He would spend weeks at a time at the high-stakes poker games in places like Monte Carlo and Las Vegas, routinely winning and losing fortunes that would make other people weep.

A "tic" was just gambling slang for an unconscious

behavior that a cardplayer displays that gives away knowledge of his hand to the other players. It could be something as obvious as a player wetting their lips when they get a good hand to something more obscure, like that slight twitch of their eye muscles when they are about to bluff. Tics were as varied and as unique as the players themselves, and spotting one wasn't always easy.

Roux, however, had elevated the process to an art form.

"Yes, a verbal tic. You have a tendency to ask rhetorical questions whenever you're lying. So I'll ask again, what do you need?"

It was easier to just let it go than argue further. Besides, she *did* need something, verbal tic or not.

"I need some help getting an expedition permit approved by the Costa Rican government."

She could also feel Roux sitting up straighter in his chair, his interest now piqued.

"And what, might I ask, is this expedition looking for?"

"A missing archaeologist."

"Oh." Roux's enthusiasm audibly deflated.

"That and the Treasure of Lima."

There was a moment of silence on the line and then Roux asked her to repeat what she'd just said.

"You heard me just fine, Roux."

She went on to explain what she knew of the situation, how Knowles had gone missing just after he thought he'd found some actual evidence of the treasure and how his wife was being prevented from going to the island due to bureaucratic red tape.

Roux didn't give two hoots about Dr. Knowles's situation. Annja knew that. Roux came from another age, when death was common and life was cheap. But being a part of the team that located and salvaged the Treasure of Lima? That was something he would have a hard time passing up, which was precisely why Annja had pitched the problem the way she had.

"As a matter of fact, I do have a few acquaintances in the Ministry of Culture and Tourism," Roux said. "Let me make a few phone calls and I'll get right back to you. What hotel are you at?"

Annja gave him the name of the hotel and her room number. Roux had already hung up by the time she got to goodbye. She didn't take offense; that was just Roux.

While she waited for Roux's return call, Annja fired up her laptop and dug into some research, wanting to refresh her memory on the history of the treasure.

According to her sources, the majority of South America was under Spanish colonial rule at the start of the nineteenth century and governed via the viceroyalty of Peru in Lima, established back in 1542. At the height of its power, almost all of the goods headed to Spain from the territories of Peru, Bolivia and Argentina were first sent to the port of Callao, just west of Lima, and then sent on to the old country. As a result, the city of Lima became a repository for the wealth collected on behalf of the empire, especially the wealth collected by the church.

The wars for independence broke out in 1810, and by 1820 the republics of Chile, Argentina and Bolivia had all declared their independence from Spanish rule. The rebels then set their sights on Peru and several of them, including the Argentinean general José de San Martín, Chilean naval commander Lord Cochrane and Bolivian leader Simón Bolívar, worked together to pressure the royalists from several sides. By July 1820 it was clear that the city of Lima would fall to the rebels. Before that could happen, Viceroy José de la Serna made plans to protect the treasure until the insurrection had been put to rest.

The viceroy hired William Thompson, captain of the English brig the *Mary Dear,* to transport the treasure to de la Serna's allies in Mexico, where it could be stored safely until it was either returned to Lima or shipped on to Madrid. Unfortunately for the viceroy and his plans, that much money, equal to something in the neighborhood of sixty million dollars in today's currency, was too much of a temptation for Captain Thompson. On the first night of their voyage, he and his men slaughtered the six soldiers and two priests that the viceroy had sent along to accompany the treasure and tossed their bodies overboard. They then set sail for Cocos Island, off the coast of Costa Rica, where they planned to bury the treasure and lie low for several months before returning for it.

The best-laid plans of mice and men, Annja thought.

The *Mary Dear* ran into a British man-of-war and after a brief chase were forced to surrender. Captain and crew were tried for piracy on the high seas, with only Thompson and his first mate managing to avoid the death penalty by agreeing to show the British captain where they had hidden the treasure. The rest of Thompson's crew were hung from the masts of the British ship before it, in turn, set sail for Cocos.

Historians differed on what happened next, Annja discovered. Some said that Captain Thompson led the British commander to the treasure, at which point it was dug up, loaded aboard the man-of-war and transported to England, where it still sits in the Royal Treasury today. Others that Thompson led the British to the treasure as promised, but killed them all before they could dig up even a single gold coin. In a third version, Thompson never encountered the British at all, ending up marooned on the island for several years with only his first mate for company when his ship was wrecked by a rogue wave in the midst of a tropical storm.

Annja knew the truth probably lay somewhere in the middle, in that place where all the stories intersected with one another. It was this approach that had allowed her to find other ancient sites and artifacts when most believed they were no more than myth or legend. She intended to do the same thing here. First she'd find out what had happened to Dr. Knowles and then she'd find the treasure, she told herself with a smile.

Pleased with what she'd accomplished so far, she picked up the phone and ordered a snack and a cup of hot chocolate from room service. She'd just replaced the phone in the receiver when it rang beneath her hand.

It was Roux.

"That didn't take long," she said after they'd exchanged hellos.

"No reason it should. The tourism minister owed me a favor. I persuaded him to put a little pressure on the bureaucrat who was holding up the paperwork and, wouldn't you know it, the permits were suddenly pushed through with alacrity."

Annja breathed a sigh of relief. If the permits hadn't been forthcoming, she'd planned to go without them—after all, a man's life might be at stake—but having them would make things much easier in the long run.

Roux, however, wasn't finished.

"There is, however, a small price attached."

Annja tensed. If there was money involved, Roux wouldn't have even mentioned it to her; he'd have simply paid it and taken it out of their share when they recovered the treasure. Which meant it was something else.

"I'm listening," she said.

"In the course of our conversation, I happened to mention you to my friend César. Turns out he's a big fan of the infamous Annja Creed and he requested that you have dinner with him as the price for his assistance."

Great, she thought. *Guy can't get a date on his own so he has to bribe Roux into making one for him.*

"This is the tourism minister, right?"

"That's correct."

She pulled her computer closer so she could reach the keyboard. "What's his name again?"

Roux told her.

She quickly searched for him. The picture that came up on the screen was a surprise. She wasn't exactly sure what she'd been expecting, maybe an elderly Hispanic man with a leer in his eye, but what she got was an image of a well-dressed man in his early thirties, with a neatly trimmed goatee and dark hair.

Maybe dinner wouldn't be so bad after all, she thought. Still, she had her priorities.

"I don't have time to be gallivanting about on dinner

dates when Dr. Knowles might be in serious danger," she said sharply, hoping that might settle it.

Roux, however, was prepared for just such a response.

"I quite agree. Which is why I agreed that you'd have dinner with him when you returned from Cocos Island. The permits will be waiting for you at the front desk in the morning. Au revoir, my dear."

Annja opened her mouth to protest, only to find herself talking to the dial tone.

She glanced once more at César's picture, sighed in resignation and went back to her research. There was a lot she needed to familiarize herself with if they were going to head out in the morning.

6

Annja was waiting in the lobby the next day when the official courier arrived at the hotel with their expedition permits. She checked them over to be certain they were correct and then signed in receipt of them. The permits allowed them to travel to the island and spend a week searching for Dr. Knowles and the rest of his team, noting that the island was a World Heritage site and that care should be taken to have as little negative impact on the local ecology as possible.

That was fine with Annja; she wasn't there to excavate anything, anyway. At least, not unless they found the treasure, she thought with a grin. She used the housephone to call Claire, give her the good news and suggest they meet on the patio for breakfast to go over the remaining details. Claire agreed.

By the time the other woman arrived twenty minutes later with a burly, tattooed man with a thick handlebar mustache in tow, Annja was halfway through her breakfast. The newcomer was introduced as Marcos Rivera, leader of the four men who had been hired to help Claire get to the island and assist with the search once they'd arrived.

Rivera was in his mid-thirties and said very little

during their meeting, but Annja didn't miss the way the man's eyes were constantly moving, taking in their surroundings and storing away the information for later reference. She'd been around enough soldiers to recognize such behavior and there was no doubt in her mind that Marcos had served at some time in the past, perhaps even recently. That meant the men under him were apt to be ex-military, as well. Annja didn't have any problems with that; soldiers were generally good at taking orders. She just needed to be sure to make it clear who was the one with the authority to give them and they should get along just fine.

With the pleasantries out of the way, the trio got down to business. Supply lists were reviewed and adjusted slightly where necessary; Claire had a good eye for the kinds of goods that were needed for the expedition, but had a tendency to underestimate what they were going to need to get through the week. Cocos might be a tropical paradise from an environmentalist's perspective, but to the unwary it could be particularly deadly. Without access to local towns where they could replenish their supplies on a regular basis, Annja and her team were going to have to carry in everything they needed on their backs. Food, water, shelter, medical supplies—the list went on. To make matters worse, they had no idea what condition Dr. Knowles and his team would be in when they found them, so they had to plan for that, as well. In the end, Annja was glad for the extra bodies; there were a lot of supplies to bring with them.

A boat had been chartered to take them to the island and most of the supplies had already been loaded aboard. The rest, including those things that Annja had just added to their list, could be secured in the next few hours and packed at departure time. If all went according to plan, they could depart for Cocos later that morning.

ANNJA HAD BEEN expecting a tired old fishing trawler with just enough space on the deck to accommodate them and their equipment, so she was pleasantly surprised, delighted even, to discover that the *Neptune's Pride* was a much more substantial vessel.

The captain, a portly man in his mid-fifties with a jovial smile but the hard gleam of a businessman in his eyes, caught her expression and smiled in return as she came up the boarding ramp.

"You like, yes?" he asked in heavily accented English.

"Yes. Yes, I do," she said, and meant it, too.

"Excellent!" He was practically beaming as he extended an arm. "May I give you the tour?"

Annja slipped her arm through his. "By all means, please do!"

As it turned out, the *Neptune's Pride* had been built in 1993 for the Japanese government as a fisheries training vessel, Annja learned. She had put in fifteen hard years of training work before running aground during a storm. Not wanting the expense of repairing an older vessel, the Japanese government had auctioned her off to a refitting company, who refurbished the vessel and then leased it out on a regular basis for short-term expeditions. Claire had hired the boat and had then gone in search of a captain with the skill to handle that size boat and knowledge of the area surrounding Cocos Island, eventually settling on Captain Vargas as her man.

Vargas had taken to the boat like a mother hen to a newborn chick and Annja quickly understood why. She was a marvelous ship—one hundred and twenty feet in length and boasting three full-size decks, two above and one below. Her hull was made of modern steel, providing both the durability and sleekness necessary for long-range cruising, and her single diesel engine could deliver a steady twelve knots. Best yet, the entire ship could be operated by a crew of less than five, a situation Vargas liked as much as Claire.

The captain was rightfully proud of his new command and was more than happy to talk a person's ear off about it if they let him. Which Annja did. She wanted to know as much about the vessel as she could, for you never knew what little piece of information might save your life when you were in a bind. She received the full tour, top to bottom, and when it was over she had to admit the refitting company had done a marvelous job. The guest staterooms were wide and spacious, with so many modern amenities that Annja felt as if she was aboard a cruise ship rather than an expeditionary vessel.

Along with the usual pair of motorized skiffs, the ship was also equipped with a high-powered winch capable of moving several hundred tons and a small helicopter pad on the rear portion of the upper deck.

"Alas, no helicopter, though," Vargas told her. "Someday."

Annja knew how he felt. The things she could do with a ship like this at her disposal…

Her tour ended at the galley on the lower deck, where

she found Claire and the rest of her team on a coffee break. They'd arrived after their morning meeting with Annja to supervise the loading of their supplies. Annja had already met the mustachioed Marcos Rivera. Joining him was a short, wiry fellow named Hugo Morales and a young, athletic-looking man they called Michael Reyes. Cursory introductions were made and then the men got back to work, leaving the women to coordinate their next steps.

"Why don't we go up to the bridge and I'll bring you up to speed on what I know about my husband's movements before he lost contact?" Claire said to Annja.

"Sounds like a plan."

The decks were connected by short, ladderlike stairways, and the two women quickly made their way up two levels to the bridge. Vargas and his crew were busy elsewhere, but that didn't stop Claire from walking over to the plot table in the center of the room. Once there, she opened a drawer, removed a map and spread it out in front of her for Annja to see.

"Our destination," she said with a smile. "Isla del Coco."

Annja studied the map, letting the details sink in slowly. The island was roughly rectangular in shape, but a rectangle that had been partially canted to one side. It was divided into two general regions—the southernmost portion comprised of the area surrounding Mount Yglesias and the northernmost portion around an unnamed ridgeline that stretched perpendicularly across the island.

Much of the shoreline was nothing more than cliffs rising practically right out of the water, but on the north and northeast face of the island were two bays that would provide access. The first, Wafer Bay, was protected by a long isthmus that ran east-west and provided shelter from the waves that crashed against the northern shore. The second and smaller of the two, Chatham Bay, was on the northeast face of the island and was supposedly the place where Captain Thompson and his pirate crew had come ashore to hide the treasure.

A glance at the legend and some quick mental calculations told Annja that the island was roughly eighteen square miles, which made it roughly fourteen times larger than Central Park in Manhattan. Most of the land area was covered with dense tropical forest, and the lack of human habitation, with the exception of a single park ranger stationed there year-round, kept it in pristine condition. Pristine, in this case, meaning very difficult to navigate through, and the order not to damage the local environment would only increase that difficulty tenfold. Add to that the varied nature of the wildlife sure to be present under that forest canopy and you ended up with a formidable environment in which to operate. Sure, it didn't hold the same degree of outright danger as the heights of Everest or the depths of the Atlantic Ocean, but help was a bit more than a phone call away, and that might mean the difference between life and death if it came to it.

"The charter Richard hired to carry his team to the island docked here, in Chatham Bay," Claire told her, pointing out the location on the map even though Annja had already seen it for herself. "The expedition had permission to be there for two weeks but couldn't afford to keep the boat on station for that long. So the captain waited overnight, giving the team time to unload their gear and establish a camp on the beach, and then he headed back to the mainland the next day."

"Did Dr. Knowles have a prearranged time that he expected the boat to return or was there some means by which he was going to contact the captain?"

Claire reached into the pocket of her cargo shorts and pulled out a satellite phone. "Richard carried a sat phone just like this one. The plan was for him to call Captain Swanson two days before Richard and his team broke camp, so that the boat would be waiting by the time they needed it."

Annja knew that it was roughly a thirty-hour journey by boat from Puntarenas, where they were now and from where Richard's expedition had set out, as well, to Cocos Island. Two days before breaking camp was more than enough time for the boat to arrive.

"Was that call ever made?" she asked.

Claire shook her head. "Richard only made a few calls from the island and all of them were either to our home number in Baltimore or to my cell phone."

"You know that for certain?"

This time the other woman nodded. "I'm listed on the same account, so it was easy enough to check," she explained. "The last call on record was the one he made to me prior to trying to excavate the chest they'd found."

In Annja's view, it seemed likely that Dr. Knowles had suffered some kind of injury while the team was investigating the find, but it could be a simple matter of equipment failure.

"Was there a backup plan in case the satellite phone was lost or damaged?"

"Yes. Richard's second in command, David Mathers, also had a satellite phone. I tried calling that line as well, but it goes straight to voice mail. I've left several messages and now all I get is a 'mailbox full' reply when I try to do so."

That didn't bode well, Annja knew. The chance that both phones were malfunctioning at the same time were minimal, particularly since they were specifically designed to work anytime and anywhere, be it the backyard or from a remote corner of the world. Geographic interference was unlikely; Mount Yglesias was barely twenty-five hundred feet, after all.

Something must have shown on her face because Claire said, "I know. It's not a good sign, is it?"

Annja tried to smile reassuringly. "We could come up with a thousand different scenarios and still not even come close to the truth, so speculating doesn't do anyone any good. Try to relax. We'll be there soon enough."

She just hoped they were in time to help.

7

The boat left Puntarenas and took a little over thirty hours to reach Isla del Coco. The first part of the journey passed without incident. Annja spent several hours reviewing the topographical maps of the island, tracing the route Claire had indicated her husband had taken inland before vanishing and trying to anticipate the obstacles that they might face, in turn, when they followed suit.

Thinking that perhaps Dr. Knowles had sought assistance from the Costa Rican park ranger that lived on the island year-round, Annja wandered back up to the bridge and asked permission to use the shortwave radio. Her earlier research had given her the ranger station's frequency and call sign; it seemed only common sense to make use of them. If the ranger didn't know Dr. Knowles's current location, perhaps he could shed some light on what might have happened.

Unfortunately, she was unable to raise the station.

She had just replaced the microphone and was turning away from the radio station when her gaze fell across the radar plot. As if on cue, two blips suddenly appeared at the edge of the radar screen north of their position. Annja watched them and waited for the information from their transponders to come up on the screen, but it never did. The small boxes designed to display such information remained blank.

Whoever they were, they were coming on fast.

Annja glanced over and found the captain frowning at the screen in unconscious imitation of her own expression.

"Trouble?" she asked.

Vargas shook his head. "I'm sure it's nothing to worry about."

But his expression remained thoughtful and a few seconds later he ordered a slight course change to take them out of the path of the incoming vessels.

No sooner had the *Neptune's Pride* changed course, however, than the two blips on the radar screen changed course as well, putting them squarely back on a direct intercept.

An uneasy feeling rolled through Annja's gut.

There were probably half a dozen legitimate reasons why another boat might approach them so quickly, but two? It just didn't seem right and she could feel herself tensing up as the two blips drew closer to their position on the radar screen.

Vargas moved over to the radio position, standing almost exactly where Annja had been. Picking up the microphone in one hand, he used the other to double check that Annja had returned the set to the standard nautical frequency, which she had. Satisfied, he flipped a few switches and then brought the microphone to his lips.

"Attention approaching vessels, this is the Panamanian vessel *Neptune's Pride*. Do you need assistance? Over."

Vargas repeated the message in Spanish and then released the mike and waited for a reply.

None came.

He tried a second time, once more in both English and Spanish.

"I repeat, *Neptune's Pride* to approaching vessels. Do you need assistance? Please state your intentions. Over."

Still nothing.

The other two vessels were now roughly two miles away and closing in fast.

Vargas reached up, changed the frequency on the radio to an emergency channel and tried again. The lack of response must have been getting to him, for this time he was a bit more abrupt in his message.

"*Neptune's Pride* to inbound vessels. You are on a collision course. I say again, collision course. Bear fifteen degrees to starboard immediately to avoid contact."

If the other vessels could hear him, there was no sign of it. Their course remained exactly as it had been moments before. At this rate of speed, they would be on each other in less than five minutes.

Vargas swore in gutter Spanish, tossed the microphone onto the radio table and snatched a pair of binoculars from a stand to his left. He moved over to the window at the front of the bridge and brought the binoculars to his face, searching back and forth across the horizon for any sign of the incoming vessels.

Annja stepped up beside him.

"Anything?"

"No. Nothing yet."

The minutes ticked slowly by.

Beside her, Annja felt Vargas stiffen. Then he handed her the binoculars, pointing slightly to the right. "There," he said.

Putting the binoculars to her eyes, Annja adjusted the lens until the scene in front of her swam into view. At first all she saw was open water, but then the spray from the oncoming boats caught her attention and she focused in on her targets.

What she saw did not relieve any of her unease.

The radar blips turned out to be two interdiction-style patrol boats, similar to those used by the Port Authority Police in New York Harbor. Roughly forty feet in length, with a three-quarter wheelhouse sitting just aft of a bow-deck gun mount that, thankfully, seemed to be missing on this particular model, the boats were capable of extreme speeds over a fairly decent range.

Neither boat was flying a flag, which was another bad sign; if they were legitimate patrol craft, they would definitely have colors flying high, if for no other reason than to indicate their authority to those they were approaching. The boats were coming directly toward them and so Annja was unable to see if there were any markings or identification numbers on the hull of either craft, but she suspected there were not.

She could see that the boats were carrying at least half a dozen men each. It might even be more; she had no way of knowing yet how many were behind the wheelhouse itself. Those she could see lined the rails on either side, their attention focused on the ship before them. Something about the way they were standing bothered Annja, but they weren't close enough yet for her to make out what it was.

Judging from how fast they were coming on, that wouldn't be a problem for long, she knew.

Vargas hurried back over to the radio station and changed several settings on the control panel. This time, when he spoke into the mike, his voice was broadcast out across the water through the loudspeakers mounted on top of the bridge.

"*Neptune's Pride* to unidentified vessels. Reverse course immediately or suffer the consequences. You have been warned."

As before, the message was repeated in Spanish.

Vargas glanced over at Annja. "Anything?"

She brought the binoculars back up and looked out at the approaching patrol boats, now less than a quarter of a mile away. She could make out individual faces at this point and what had been bothering her about the way the men aboard the patrol boats had been standing was immediately obvious at this distance.

Each and every one of them was armed.

She could see several automatic weapons—a couple Russian Kalashnikovs and an Israeli Uzi—and a smattering of handguns. Those without firearms were carrying makeshift weapons of all kinds, from clubs with nails driven through them to machetes, their blades gleaming in the sunlight.

As if the presence of the weapons weren't bad enough, several of the men carried coils of rope looped over their shoulders, and from where she stood, Annja could see that at least one of those ropes ended in a steel grappling hook.

Annja finally understood the unease she'd been feeling.

These men were pirates and they were going to try to board the *Neptune's Pride*.

8

Aboard the Neptune's Pride
One hundred miles offshore

Annja was just about to let Vargas know what she was seeing when she spotted a man in the lead boat raise his automatic rifle and point it in the direction of the *Pride*'s bridge.

"Get down!" Annja shouted, throwing herself at Captain Vargas and tackling him to the floor just as the gunman opened fire.

Bullets struck the bridge windows, blowing them inward in a shower of shattering glass and blazing-hot lead. Annja curled up against one of the bridge consoles and tried to make herself as small a target as possible. She wasn't worried about the gunman being able to hit her—she was below his line of sight, after all—but a ricochet could be just as deadly and she didn't want to take any chances. Nearby she could see Captain Vargas doing the same.

Unfortunately, not everyone who was on the bridge had heeded her warning. One of Vargas's crewmen—Annja hadn't even had time to learn his name since she'd come aboard—took a bullet right through the throat and was dead before his body hit the floor. She could see him from where she lay, his eyes open and staring but not seeing anything.

Soon the shooting stopped.

Annja stayed where she was, waiting, even going so far as to yank Vargas back down to the ground when he started to get up. If the gunman had simply run out of bullets, he might start shooting again as soon as he swapped out the gun's magazine, and she didn't want either of them to be caught in the open when he did.

When nothing but the roar of the motor launches' engines reached their ears, Annja scrambled to her feet and let Vargas do the same. Keeping as much of herself below the edge of the bridge controls as possible, she peeked out the now-shattered window.

The pirates' boats were to the port side of their bow and would be on them shortly. The men aboard were cheering and brandishing their weapons, no doubt thinking they'd already won the battle.

Annja intended to show them there was lot more fight left in this opponent than they'd ever imagined.

"Keep your head down," she barked at Vargas, when, glancing around for a particular item she knew had to be here somewhere, she saw him starting to get to his feet.

A quick burst of gunfire crashing through the now-open bridge windows convinced him of the wisdom of listening to her.

"What do they want?" he asked in a quavering voice.

"At a guess I'd say the ship."

"My ship? They wouldn't dare!"

They would dare and, in fact, had already done so. And if someone didn't get out there and stop them before they could take things to the next step, they were in a whole heap of trouble.

Stealing the ship made sense, in a warped and twisted kind of way. Selling something like the *Neptune's Pride* would be a challenge, Annja knew, but so would simply letting it sit and rot on the tide. At the very least they could strip her of useful equipment and then carve her up into smaller pieces, selling both the equipment and the scrap metal for a profit.

If they were smart, they might even do one better: they might keep the boat for themselves. A quick paint job and a few changes to the identification numbers would give them a ship that could be used to further their piracy efforts, particularly if they could get the vessel legitimately registered through some foreign nation that didn't look too closely at where the vessel had come from.

That wasn't what sent a shiver of apprehension up Annja's spine, however. No, that was a result of the fact that she knew she and the rest of the crew, Captain Vargas included, would either be killed outright or kept alive just long enough for the kidnappers to receive a ransom, at which point they'd be killed, anyway. In order to survive this thing, they had to keep from getting captured.

That meant keeping the pirates off the ship for as long as possible.

All this flashed through her thoughts in an instant, helping her make up her mind. She turned and headed across the room toward the door.

"Wait! Where are you going?" he whispered frantically as he saw her getting ready to leave the bridge.

"Someone's got to stop us from being boarded, right?" she replied, then slipped out the doorway onto the narrow walkway just outside. The sound of the engines was growing louder; it would be only moments before they were alongside. She could even hear the men aboard shouting to one another, but couldn't make out what was being said. She hurried over to the steep set of stairs—almost a ladder, really—leading down to the main deck and raced down them as fast as she dared.

Just as she reached the main deck, she ran into Claire and Marcos coming up the stairs from below.

"What's going on?" Claire exclaimed upon seeing Annja racing toward them.

"Pirates," Annja told her. She didn't have time to explain anything beyond that, for the patrol boats were closing in.

Thankfully, Claire didn't need anything more. Annja could see the woman was practically bursting with questions, but Claire managed to hold on to them all with the exception of the most important.

"What do we do?"

"Keep them from getting on board," Annja said. "No matter what. If they do, we're all in even more danger than we're in right now."

"How?"

Excellent question. Just how were they going to keep the men from boarding?

"Are you or any of your men armed?" she asked.

Claire shook her head. "We're carrying a pair of rifles as part of the expedition's gear, but both of them are packed away with the rest of the supplies. There's no way for us to get to them in a hurry."

Annja had her sword, and she wouldn't hesitate to use it when the time came, but it wasn't going to do them much good against armed opponents. They needed something to keep the pirates at a distance; if they were close enough for Annja to need her sword, then she and the others aboard the *Neptune's Pride* had already lost.

As the sound of the approaching motorboats filled her ears, Annja's gaze fell upon the glass-fronted case mounted on the side of the ship. Inside was a long-handled ax and yards of coiled hose, both designed to be used in case of a fire on board the boat.

For Annja, the sight of them was like water to a man dying of thirst.

"Help me! Quickly!" she exclaimed, racing over to the case, Claire and Marcos on her heels.

Annja didn't have time to locate the key, so she lifted one booted foot and kicked out sharply, driving her heel through the front of the case and shattering the glass. Reaching inside, she grabbed the ax and tossed it to Claire, who snatched it out of midair. Annja then grabbed the front of the fire hose, handed it to Marcos and ordered him over to the side of the boat with it in hand.

Marcos didn't ask any questions, just did as he was told, trusting that she had a plan. They hauled the hose free of its moorings and, with Claire crouching by the lever that controlled the flow of water, hunkered down below the waist-high edge of the boat, waiting for the right moment.

The plan, if you could call it that, was simple. Annja intended to wait until the pirates were getting ready to throw the grappling lines she'd seen in their hands.

Just before the lines were thrown, she and Marcos were going to pop up into view, holding the fire hose between them, and hit them with a blast of high-pressure water. Given that the stream of water would have more than two hundred pounds per square inch of pressure behind it, it should be powerful enough to knock the pirates right off their feet.

She hoped.

Only one way to find out.

The thrum of the *Pride*'s massive engines sounded in weird counterpoint to the throaty roar of the patrol boats' smaller ones. Annja chanced a quick look over the side, knowing that they had to time this right if it was going to work.

Her glance showed her one of the patrol boats sliding in toward them while the second hung back by fifty feet or so. The pirates standing in the bow of the first boat were spreading out slightly, their weapons slung over their shoulders or resting on the deck at their feet as they prepared to use the boarding lines in their hands.

It was now or never.

Annja shouted, "Now!"

Claire threw the lever, releasing the hundreds of pounds of water held in the reservoir hidden behind the bulkhead at her back. At the same time, Annja and Marcos popped to their feet, the thick canvas fire hose supported between them, and pointed at the pirates standing exposed in the bow of their boat.

The stream of water shot out from the deck of the *Neptune's Pride* and hit the pirates at about knee level, knocking them right off their feet. Several of them were thrown backward along the deck into their waiting companions but at least two were knocked right overboard without even knowing what had happened to them.

In response to the unexpected attack, the patrol boat carrying the would-be boarders veered sharply away from the *Pride*'s hull and Annja wanted to cheer. She knew it was only a temporary respite, that the pirates had been caught by surprise and would certainly try again, but it was a good feeling just the same. Claire grasped the lever controlling the water flow and it shut off again, allowing Annja and Marcos to drop back down below the waist-high bulkhead beside them, out of view of the pirates. Annja shot a grin at Marcos, who returned it with equal fervor.

Score one for the good guys.

The pirates weren't going to give up easily, however, and they let the defenders aboard the *Neptune's Pride* know it seconds later. Bullets thundered into the thick steel of the waist-high bulkhead next to Marcos and Annja and along the back wall, against which Claire crouched near the hose controls, sending sparks and hot pieces of steel ricocheting in various directions.

In truth, the position the three of them—Annja, Claire and Marcos—had taken was precarious, at best. All the attackers really had to do was keep the trio pinned down with constant gunfire while the grapplers threw their hooks and pulled themselves up the ropes to the deck above their heads. With bullets filling the air around them, the defenders would be unable to get the hose back into position and take another shot at them without revealing themselves to the danger of getting shot and the pirates would be able to reach the deck unimpeded.

Any decent tactician would have seen it.

Thankfully, the men in the boats were nothing more than common thugs who probably relied on simple violence or the threat thereof to get what they wanted. Tactics was not something they were schooled in, something they proved by emptying their guns at the spot where Annja and Marcos had been hiding.

The pair were no longer there, however.

As the bullets whipped and whined overhead, Annja signaled that Marcos should follow her, and the two of them crawled on hands and knees about fifteen feet or so away from their last position, leaving Claire to continue controlling the water flow.

As soon as the shooting stopped, Claire hit the water controls, the duo popped up a second time and again hammered the pirates with a stream of high-powered water.

This time, they knocked the man off the roof of the wheelhouse and even managed to shatter the glass in the wheelhouse windows before the boats veered off a second time.

It was at that point that the pirates made what Annja hoped would prove to be a fatal mistake.

9

Annja heard one of the pirate boats rev its engines. Glancing over the side for a split second, she saw it race away from the other boat, headed toward the prow of the expedition ship. With the engines capable of producing almost three times as much horsepower as the *Neptune's Pride,* the patrol boat was quickly able to match and then overcome the *Pride*'s speed. It shot ahead of the larger vessel and then crossed over in front of it.

Come on, Vargas, run her down, Annja thought, but she knew there was no way the *Neptune's Pride* could ever do such a thing. At a ponderous twelve knots, the expedition ship was practically standing still compared to the sixty-five to seventy knots that the patrol boat could manage. The smaller vessel would have to be practically still for the larger one to do what Annja was dreaming of.

Still, it never hurt to hope.

She realized that the pirates were splitting their forces, hoping to come at them from two sides. By doing so they might succeed in getting men aboard in one location or the other before Annja and her compatriots could stop them.

She wouldn't let that happen.

"They're headed for the opposite side," she said to Marcos. "Can you hold them off here?"

"Provided they don't get smart and coordinate their climbing and firing efforts, yeah. What about you?"

"I'll hold them off on the other side. Hopefully by then the captain will have called in the coast guard or something."

"Out here?" Marcos scoffed. "Good luck with that."

Claire, who'd been listening to the conversation, broke in and asked, "Where is Vargas? Is he all right?"

Annja pointed to the bridge above them. "He was when I left him. Can't say the same for one of the other guys, though." The memory of the man falling before her, hands to his throat, flashed through her mind but she shoved it aside. She'd have time for regrets later. Right now she had to keep them from being boarded.

Staying as low as she could, she raced down the length of the boat until she came to one of the corridors that ran perpendicularly across the vessel. Bullets pinged off the door as she hauled it open, and she felt one of them burn its way across the back of her calf but then she was through, the heavy steel bulkhead door closing behind her as protection.

She ran pell-mell down the corridor, praying none of the crew suddenly showed up and opened a door in her path as she raced for the one at the far end. Thankfully, none did.

Reaching the other side, she hauled down on the lever to open the door but kept it from doing so with her other hand. She didn't want to yank open the door and instantly give away her position to the pirates, who had no doubt reached this side of the ship by now, as well. Instead, she slowly opened the door a few inches, peering out through the crack.

The patrol boat was just now coming up alongside the ship, moving in the same direction as the larger vessel. Annja quickly realized that it must have swung across the *Pride*'s bow and then come about in a wide circle that allowed it to approach the ship from the rear. Its greater speed had allowed it to catch up easily and in just moments the pirates would likely make another attempt at getting aboard.

It was up to Annja to stop them.

But with what?

There was probably a fire hose on this side of the vessel, too, but as powerful as it was, it took two people to hold it steady against the flow of the water, so repeating what they'd done on the other side of the ship was out of the question for her alone. Like the rest of the crew running around *Neptune's Pride,* she didn't have a firearm handy, so there was no way she could keep them from getting close to the ship.

No, she would have to wait until the pirates were all but aboard the ship and then take the fight to those she could reach. It wasn't the best of plans, but it was the only one she had.

So be it.

Annja summoned her sword to hand, feeling it materialize in her grip with just a simple thought. As always, its presence was reassuring; she felt she could conquer just about anything when she had the sword in hand. So far, that had always proved to be true, but she was enough of a realist to know that at some point she was probably going to run into an enemy that was faster, stronger and smarter than she was, sword or no sword. Today, however, was not that day.

She peered out through the opening, noticed the patrol boat pull up alongside the *Neptune's Pride* almost directly opposite her present position.

She watched as the men in the bow of the boat readied their ropes and flung them up and over the side wall of the *Pride*.

In her head, she started counting down from five.

On one, she burst out the door, her gaze locked solidly on the hooks clamped to the *Pride*'s bulkhead, her sword raised high.

Shouts rose from the deck of the patrol boat and Annja knew she had seconds, at best, before the startled pirates opened fire.

It was going to have to be enough.

As the first of the pirates pulled the trigger of his weapon and bullets began to pepper the wall where she'd only just been, Annja brought her sword down against the rope attached to the first of the grappling hooks.

The edge of the weapon, honed to razor sharpness through the same mystical process that allowed it to exist in the first place, slashed through the thick hemp rope as if it wasn't even there.

Annja heard a muted cry reach her from over the side of the ship as the pirate who had been climbing up the rope suddenly found himself falling unexpectedly toward the water rushing by below him.

Annja barely noticed; her attention was already on the second rope ahead of her.

She slashed through that one as well, heard an equally surprised cry followed by a splash from below.

As before, Annja paid it no mind. One grappling hook remained.

By now the pirates had gotten over their surprise at her appearance, however, and their shots were much more accurate. Bullets whipped through the hair hanging alongside her neck, missing her flesh by a half inch or less. Sooner rather than later one of those bullets was going to find its mark, she knew.

Still, she raced forward.

Annja's heart was pounding and she could hear her own breathing, drowning out the shouts of the pirates, the sound of their weapons, even the roar of the patrol boat's engine. Nothing mattered but that final grappling hook.

Another five steps separated her from it.

The pirates took aim at her running form. A bullet ricocheted off the blade of her sword, sending vibrations racing up and down her arm and threatening to knock the blade from her grasp, but she tightened her grip, refusing to lose it at this point.

Three steps.

The blare of the ship's horn filled the air with its thunderous roar. Annja didn't know if Vargas had triggered the device to distract the pirates or signal for help but didn't care. All she knew was that she had to cut that rope.

Two steps.

Instinct screamed at her to get down and she did just that.

A hand came over the edge of the outer rail, followed

half a second later by a male face. The pirate had long, tangled hair and a tribal tattoo covering one side of his face. As he sensed motion to his left, he turned to look at her and his eyes went wide as he saw her sliding toward him, sword already on its way down.

Speedy reflexes saved his neck. He yanked his head back just as the sword came whistling past. Even a fraction of an instant later and he would have taken the blade through the back of the neck.

But Annja hadn't been aiming for his neck, but rather the hand that held him securely to the side of the ship.

Down came the blade and the man's fingers proved no more difficult for its edge than the two ropes before them had. The blade slashed right through them, sheering them off as if they'd been amputated by a professional surgeon. The blade's downward arc also took it through the rope attached to that final grappling hook. The pirate didn't even have time to scream before he dropped back over the side and disappeared from Annja's view.

She'd done it!

The gunfire stopped as the patrol boat arced away from the *Pride,* but she knew they'd be back. They'd gained a few moment's respite, no more.

Knowing she could retrieve it in the blink of an eye, Annja released her sword back into the otherwhere. She didn't want a crew member stumbling on her while she was carrying it, though if one did she would simply claim she'd picked it up from one of the pirates who had gotten too close for comfort. Their attackers were carrying plenty of bladed weapons of their own, so the explanation should stand up to scrutiny.

From the far side of the boat, she heard cheers and

knew that Marcos and Claire, perhaps with the help of the others, must have succeeded in repelling the attempted boarding, as well.

It suddenly struck Annja as highly ironic that they were being attacked by pirates while on an expedition to recover pirate treasure. She wondered how prevalent piracy was in this part of the world; she was used to hearing news reports about pirates operating off the coast of Africa and Indonesia, not Central America. Leaked to the wrong individuals, news of Dr. Knowles's expedition could provide quite a fair bit of incentive for piracy on the high seas.

The more she thought about it, though, the more Annja realized that news of the expedition wasn't necessary in this case. A ship like the *Neptune's Pride* was prize enough on its own, as she'd noted earlier. Getting a few captives was just a bonus.

The roar of the patrol boat drew closer again and Annja chanced a quick glance over the side, trying to discover just what they were up to this time.

The gunfire started the minute her head popped up, and she was forced to dive for the deck without really seeing anything.

So much for that tactic.

She was going to have to find some other vantage point from which to spy on their activities.

Annja rose to a crouch, preparing to try to make a run for a door about ten yards from her current position, when the crack of a rifle sounded from close by. Not knowing where the shot had come from or who was doing the firing, Annja threw herself to the deck and hugged the exterior bulkhead while glancing wildly about in an attempt to find the gunman.

It didn't take long. Behind her, at the far end of the walkway, one of Claire's other hired hands, the steely-eyed one named Reyes, was leaning around the jamb of an open bulkhead door, using a rifle to fire upon the approaching patrol boat. He took two more shots in rapid succession and then shouted to her.

"On the count of three, run for it. I'll cover you."

Annja didn't know him from a hole in the wall. Dare she trust he was a good enough shot to do what needed to be done?

"One."

She glanced over the side, saw the patrol boat closing in once more. Saw the menacing looks on the faces of the pirates standing boldly in the bow, brandishing their weapons and yelling for her blood. She'd taken out three of their number and they weren't the type to forget.

"Two."

She bent down, facing Reyes, still not certain what she was going to do. What if he couldn't shoot worth a damn?

"Three!"

Her body decided for her, pushing off and charging forward before she'd realized she'd made up her mind, her powerful thighs driving her on as she raced for the safety of the door behind her.

Michael began firing, and at the sound, Annja's indecision about his ability vanished. He was shooting rapidly but with complete control, and she had no doubt that his shots were hitting precisely where he wanted them to go. Almost every step she took was punctuated by the crack of the rifle and the little bit of sporadic fire that came in her direction was off the mark and ineffectual.

Reyes stood in the doorway, firing past her head, and for a moment their eyes met.

Time seemed to stop as Annja registered the utter coldness in the man's gaze. In the space of that heartbeat he could just as easily shift that rifle barrel a half inch to the left and drill her right through the skull with his next shot as easily as he could stand there and fire on the pirates trying to take over the *Pride*. Reyes didn't care; it was all the same to him.

His final shot whipped over her shoulder, bringing forth a choked scream of pain from somewhere behind her, and then she was racing past him and into the safety of the steel-lined corridor in which he stood.

The minute she passed, he stepped away from the doorway, pulled his rifle back inside the corridor and threw the bulkhead door shut in front of him.

"What are you doing?" Annja cried, her usual steadiness rocked a bit by what she'd seen in his gaze seconds before. "We need to see what they're up to!"

"Not here," Reyes replied. "We'll have a better view, and a better chance to disrupt their activities, if we go down one level. That will put us near the waterline. We can take out their boats rather than get in a pissing contest with rifles."

It sounded good to her. If they could take out the patrol boats, the pirates would have no means of following them.

But as she opened her mouth to say so, the deck beneath her feet lurched abruptly, throwing both her and

Reyes to the floor. As she pushed herself back up on hands and knees, it occurred to her that she didn't hear the thrum of the *Pride*'s engines anymore.

Either the pirates had crippled them or someone up above had shut them down; either way it didn't matter. One thing was certain.

They couldn't outrun the pirates now.

10

Reyes led the way, moving quickly through the narrow corridors, trying to get to the far side of the vessel before the pirates could spread out and cut them off. Annja raced along in his wake, ready at any moment to call her sword to hand should she need it.

Her companion had either spent time memorizing the layout of the ship or had an excellent sense of direction, for he didn't hesitate at any of the junctions they came to, his decisions swift and sure. They cut across a couple of passageways, slipped through a supply room that turned out to be a shortcut to the other side of the boat and headed down a ladder to the deck below where they'd started.

They were hurrying along the last corridor that led to the dive station at the back of the boat when a door ahead of them suddenly opened and a man stepped out. He was dressed in a torn T-shirt and blue jeans and, at the sound of their footfalls, spun to face them.

In his hand was a large-bladed knife.

Reyes skidded to a halt, bringing the rifle up as he did so.

The two men stared at each other. Annja waited for the sound of the shot, knowing it would echo in the narrow corridor and give away their position to anyone else who might be nearby, but thankful that at this distance Reyes couldn't miss.

The shot never came.

Instead, Reyes relaxed and lowered his weapon, glancing back at Annja as he did so.

"It's Jimenez," he said. "From the engine room."

Reyes waved the other man forward and the two clasped hands, exchanging greetings in Spanish as they did so. Reyes had just started questioning the other man about what he'd seen when Annja heard the quiet click of a door closing behind them.

Spinning around, she saw another man enter the passageway through the door at the far end that they'd just used. The newcomer was young, couldn't have been more than twenty-five in Annja's view, with dreadlocks that spilled down to surround a lean face with a sharp nose. His eyes lit up when he saw them, and he licked his lips as he brought the machete in his hands up so Annja could get a good look at it.

"We've got company," she said to Reyes, interrupting him, and both he and Jimenez turned to look.

Dreadlocks gave a shout and began to run toward them.

Annja flattened herself against the corridor wall, giving Reyes a clear shot.

Reyes brought the rifle up, sighted down its length and then stiffened, a groan escaping his lips.

Annja stared, uncomprehending, until Jimenez took a step back, away from Reyes, and the knife in his right hand was revealed, dripping blood—*Reyes's blood*—onto the deck at his feet.

Reyes tried to hand her the rifle, but he didn't have the strength, Jimenez's blow having punctured not only a lung but his heart, as well. The rifle clattered to the deck and he collapsed forward, falling atop it.

Jimenez grinned and stepped toward her, knife in hand.

Time seemed to slow as Annja assessed and evaluated the situation. With two opponents bearing down on her from opposite directions, she needed to eliminate one of the threats as quickly as possible. Doing so would prevent her from having to split her attention and would also increase her chances of getting out of this in better shape than her companion had.

Since Jimenez was closest, she decided to deal with him first.

The crewman-turned-pirate no doubt expected her to run, or at least panic, but Annja did neither of those things. In fact, when he smiled at her a second time, brandishing his knife, she smiled back.

That confused him. His steps faltered, then stopped as he stared at her in surprise.

Annja knew he must have been wondering what she had to smile about, why she wasn't quavering in fear, and so she decided to show him.

She called her sword to hand and plunged it into his chest while he stood there in shocked surprise.

That's for Reyes, she thought as she yanked the weapon free.

Jimenez stood there for a second, a thin stream of blood slipping free of the side of his mouth, and then his eyes rolled back in his head and he toppled over backward.

If he wasn't dead, he soon would be.

Annja dismissed him without another thought and turned to face his partner in crime. Dreadlocks had covered more than half the distance between them in the few moments it had taken her to deal with Jimenez, and seeing how close he was, Annja slipped into a defensive position, legs braced and sword out in front of her, ready to beat back his charge.

But Dreadlocks's reflexes were better than she expected and he managed to skid to a stop a few yards away, his own weapon raised, as well.

His gaze flicked to Jimenez and then back to her.

"I'm going to kill you for that," he told her.

Annja grinned. "You can try."

Dreadlocks gave a shout and came for her, his machete slashing back and forth.

Annja parried with her sword, conscious of the advantage that the other man's shorter weapon gave him. Due to the narrow corridor and low ceilings, her range of motion with the sword was limited; overhead or wide, slashing blows were out of the question. If she tried them, all she'd wind up doing was get her sword caught against the wall or ceiling and leave herself vulnerable to Dreadlocks's attack.

Dreadlocks slashed at her, leaving his rib cage open

to attack, and Annja took advantage of the opportunity, jabbing with the point of her sword. Her opponent was quick and light on his feet, however, and he managed to twist his body away from her strike far enough that all he received was a shallow cut along the outside of his torso.

Shallow though it might be, Annja knew it still must have hurt, and the way he began favoring that side confirmed it for her. She pressed the advantage, hoping to overwhelm him, driving him several feet back down the corridor as a result.

For a split second she paused, catching her breath, and that was when he made his move. He leaped toward her with a savage cry, slashing with the machete as he did so. As before, she countered with her sword, dashing the machete blade to one side.

She didn't see the short, narrow-bladed knife he now held in his other hand, the one he'd drawn midleap, and was very nearly skewered on it as he thrust it toward her gut. It was only the fact that he glanced downward toward his target that gave his strike away and allowed Annja to bring her knee up and knock the blow to the side.

Not one to miss an opportunity, she used the same leg to drive a powerhouse kick into the outside of his front leg, just above the knee. She smashed it in the wrong direction, eliciting a howl of pain from her opponent as he backed off again.

Annja knew she couldn't let the fight go on too long, for reinforcements were no doubt already on the way. If she didn't break free soon, she'd be trapped by the new arrivals and her chances of getting out of this alive would be significantly reduced.

Dreadlocks must have been thinking the same thing, for he suddenly pressed another attack. Every thrust she made in counterattack to his own was parried with the machete in turn, and she soon found herself on the defensive, backing away from the flurry of blows he tried to rain down upon her.

Her heel struck something on the floor behind her and she realized that Dreadlocks hadn't been trying to break through her defenses with his whirlwind attacks at all. Instead, he'd been intentionally driving her backward in hopes that she'd trip over Reyes's body and leave herself vulnerable for a killing blow!

Annja refused to let that happen. She'd been watching for a pattern in his strikes and she thought she'd found it. As Dreadlocks came in with another right-to-left thrust, Annja blocked the blow with her sword but this time let the blade of the machete travel down the length of her sword until it struck the hilt. The move took her inside Dreadlocks's guard and it allowed her to pin the machete against the wall with her sword held in her right hand and pivot one hundred and eighty degrees. Putting her back to him, she swung her left arm around in a wide arc and slammed her elbow into his face.

The blow was enough to stun him, and as he stumbled back a step or two, trying to widen the gap between them so he could find time to regain his breath, Annja completed the turn, thrusting forward with the blade to take her opponent through the throat.

Mere moments had passed since the fight had started,

but that was long enough. Annja could hear people running on the deck above her, no doubt drawn by Dreadlocks's yells, and she knew she had to get out quickly before they managed to surround her.

Willing her sword back to the otherwhere, Annja stepped over the bodies and slipped through the doorway through which Jimenez had emerged.

She found herself in the engine room. It was unusually quiet, the *Pride*'s diesel engine having been stopped from the bridge above, and a glance told her that the room was currently empty. A large tool locker filled one wall of the room and she was tempted to hide inside it, but knew the presence of the bodies in the hallway outside would let them know she'd be nearby. Her pursuers would be likely to search the room, and if they did so, the tool locker would be an obvious hiding spot. She'd have to find someplace else.

But where?

Her gaze fell upon a small maintenance hatch in the wall closest to the outer hull. Annja hurried over to it and, with a small amount of effort, managed to pry it open and look inside. The hatch led to what seemed like a very narrow maintenance corridor, between the inner bulkheads and the outer hull of the ship. A glance showed her that it ran both forward and aft, which would allow her to slip away from her current pursuit and emerge elsewhere when the time was right. She didn't waste any time considering it, just climbed inside and pulled the hatch shut behind her.

She was lucky.

Through the steel mesh that made up the surface

of the hatch, she saw three pirates burst into the room from the corridor outside.

"She can't be far," one of them said. "Spread out and find her!"

Annja didn't wait around to hear anything more.

As quietly as she could, she began to crawl through the shaft.

11

Annja followed the maintenance shaft forward for several minutes. It was slow going; there was just enough space for her to creep along. There were too many obstacles in her way, like support beams, pipes and tubes for running electrical wires, for her to move very fast. She passed up the first and second hatches she came to, thinking they were too close to the one through which she'd entered, but by the time she reached the third, she figured she'd gone far enough.

She pushed the steel mesh serving as a hatch outward until it popped free, and she slid out of the tunnel and into a storage room. A glance told her she was in the forward equipment locker. That put her about halfway down the length of the ship on the starboard side, if she remembered the quick tour Captain Vargas had given her earlier.

She stepped quietly over to the door and put her ear against it, listening.

She didn't hear anything.

Annja slowly opened the door a crack and peeked outside.

All she saw was an empty hallway.

Satisfied, she opened the door, stuck her head into

the hallway and glanced in either direction. Not seeing anyone, she stepped out of the supply closet and shut the door behind her.

So far, so good.

That was when the loudspeakers all over the ship suddenly came on, broadcasting a message meant for only one person but heard by all.

"I'm growing tired of this nonsense, Miss Creed," the speaker began.

Annja recognized Captain Vargas's voice easily enough, though the happy-to-please persona he'd previously cloaked himself in was gone. Now he was all business.

"Your friends are currently my guests here on the bridge. How long they remain so depends on whether or not you know how to follow orders. Can you do that, Miss Creed? Follow orders?"

Annja preferred the old eager-to-please Vargas better, as men with overly large egos had a tendency to annoy her. Especially when they thought themselves to be smarter than she.

"I have no intention of chasing you all around this ship, Creed," Vargas continued. "You will surrender yourself to the next one of my people that you see and join us here on the bridge in the next ten minutes or I'm going to start shooting people, starting with the lovely Mrs. Knowles. I trust I've been clear."

Annja wanted to hit the bulkhead in frustration. She had no doubt that Vargas would do exactly what he said he would. His pirates hadn't hesitated to kill Reyes and she knew he wouldn't hesitate to kill the rest of Claire's team, either. It didn't take a genius IQ to know that Vargas didn't require Annja for anything special; he just wanted them all in one place to make it easier for him and his men to get rid of them.

Permanently.

All the more reason she shouldn't comply with his request, but that was precisely what she intended to do, anyway. It was, after all, the simplest way she could think of to get close to him.

She'd figure out what to do after that when the time came.

Annja continued down the corridor in the same direction she'd been going moments before, but didn't worry about trying to be stealthy any longer. In fact, she made a point of making more noise than necessary, not wanting to suddenly come upon one of Vargas's people and end up getting shot because she'd surprised the fool.

She turned the corner from one corridor to another and found herself face-to-face with a young guy who had a knife scar bisecting his left cheek and long, dark hair pulled back behind his head in a ponytail.

He stood stock-still in front of her, gaping in surprise, and Annja knew she could have taken him out then and there if that had been her objective. It was almost too bad that it wasn't. A step forward, a slash of her blade, and that would have been all she wrote. Or if getting away had been her objective, she could have done so easily.

For a moment, nothing happened. Neither of them moved. Then Annja shrugged and said, "Okay, you've got me. I surrender."

The sound of her voice galvanized the man into action. He staggered back several steps and yanked a pistol from the front of his belt. With shaking hands he pointed it in her direction and shouted, "Don't you move!"

Annja stared at him, dumbfounded. Hadn't she just said she was surrendering?

Sighing, she said, "Look, you heard Vargas…"

That was as far as she got. He took two steps forward while screaming, "I said don't move!"

Annja froze. The stress of the attack had clearly set the guy on edge. With that much adrenaline flooding his system, there was no way of knowing what he was going to do at this point. Better to do what he said. No sense getting shot for nothing, she reasoned.

The guy wiped an arm across his face in an attempt to control the sweat that was suddenly pouring down into his eyes and then he took several deep breaths.

"Okay," he said. "Okay, good." He muttered several things in Spanish but his accent was too heavy for her to understand what they were. That was okay, though. He was calming himself down and that was a good thing. She didn't care if he did the hula if that was what it took to get himself under control.

"Turn around," he told her.

Annja complied.

"Hands together behind your back."

Again, she did as she was asked. Again, nothing happened and she was considering looking over her shoulder to see what her would-be captor was doing when she felt coarse rope being tied around her wrists, securing them in place.

She was fine with that; it would add to the illusion that she was under control and not someone the others need worry about. By the time they knew that was far from the case, it would be too late.

Once her hands were secured, the man relaxed. He waved the gun around a few times, made the predictable boasts about catching her single-handedly and how that was going to make El Jefe see him differently, and generally patted himself on the back.

Annja didn't say anything; after all, what would be the point?

Eventually, when her would-be captor had finally stopped congratulating himself, he pulled out a handheld radio, keyed the switch and told whoever was on the other end in thickly accented but still understandable Spanish that he had her.

The response wasn't intelligible to Annja, but she got the gist of it when the guy put his hand between her shoulder blades and gave her a push.

"Move!" he said.

Annja stumbled forward but caught herself before she fell. Looking back would just earn her another shove, so she didn't bother doing so. Instead, she kept her gaze forward and walked down the hall at a steady pace, headed for the bridge and her meeting with Vargas.

Behind her, the man followed. Every ten feet or so he would reach out and give her another shove.

Since there was no advantage to be gained by pushing her so frequently, she knew that he was just doing it because he could. It was like a little kid pulling the legs off a grasshopper just to watch it squirm.

It didn't take long to tick her off.

She wouldn't give him the satisfaction of knowing that, however, and ignored his petty activities for the time being. The guy was her ticket to getting close enough to Vargas to turn this thing around, and she wasn't about to throw that away because one of Vargas's cronies was an annoying twerp.

So she gritted her teeth and reminded herself that she'd make him pay.

As it turned out, she didn't have long to wait.

They climbed up to the main deck and started across it to the ladder that would take them to the bridge. Glancing around, Annja saw several pirates working to lay out the bodies of their comrades in a line on the deck, and she had to resist a smile when she saw how many of them there were. The pirates might have taken the vessel, but it had been a costly victory just the same. At least ten, maybe even a dozen, bodies were lying there in the sunlight, and Annja didn't regret killing a single one of them.

They were trying to kill me, after all.

The guy led her through a set of doors on the other side of the deck directly below the bridge. Annja found herself in a small antechamber that led to a final set of doors. Beyond those doors was the stairwell leading directly into the bridge above.

If she was going to act, it had to be now.

She was ready.

Besides, she was tired of being pushed.

She intentionally slowed down, as if reluctant to continue, and true to form, he saw her hesitation as another excuse to lay his hands on her.

"No stopping now," he snarled as he stepped forward, one arm outstretched to give her a hearty shove.

As he did so, Annja dropped her wrists slightly to allow for the proper angle and then mentally reached into the otherwhere and drew her sword physically into the here and now.

The sword appeared in her hands, blade extended upward and back, just as she'd willed it, and all she had to do was give a hard shove upward with both hands.

There was a gurgling from behind her and a sudden weight that dragged the sword downward.

She released the sword and turned to watch the man sag to the floor as he stared uncomprehendingly at the wound in the left side of his chest. He blinked once, twice and was gone, the blade of Annja's sword having ruptured his heart.

His pistol turned out to be a Browning Hi-Power 9 mm, a gun Annja had passing familiarity with at least. She checked the magazine and saw that it was about half-full. It wasn't ideal, but it was the best she had available, so there was no use complaining about it.

No one around to listen to me, anyway.

Annja waited to be certain no one above had heard anything, and then, when there was no shouted cry of alarm, she started up the ladder, intent on taking her ship back from the pirates.

12

Annja kept her body close to the ladder as she went up, hoping to assess the situation first and make a move of her own before becoming a target again.

As she neared the top, she slowed down and let just the top of her head come up over that last step and only far enough that she could see what was going on in the room ahead of her. She wasn't worried about being seen; the last step was shrouded in darkness and would keep her from being spotted.

The bridge was square, about twenty-five feet in width, and reminded Annja of an air-traffic controller's tower with its windows on all four sides. A large U-shaped console running beneath the front window and down either side contained the majority of the ship's control systems, though the pilot's station in the middle of the room not only held the captain's wheel but also a secondary set of engine controls. A stand-alone plotting station for use by the navigator was to the left of the pilot's station and closest to Annja's current position.

From her location, Annja could see Hugo, Claire and Marcos lined up on their knees on the floor in front of the main console, their hands tied behind their backs.

Both Marcos and Hugo were gagged, but Claire's gag had been pulled down over her chin, allowing her the ability to speak.

A guard stood on either side of the trio. The one on the left, who she recognized as the first mate, Jenkins, held a rifle, and the one on the right, the ship's navigator, Nelson, was carrying a fireman's ax, of all things.

Captain Vargas stood in front of Claire, with his back to Annja. She didn't have to worry about straining to hear him; he was talking loud enough to wake the dead.

"Where is it?" Vargas asked.

"Where's what?" came the reply.

Vargas stared down at her. The expression on his face must have been less than charitable, for Claire shifted a bit beneath his gaze but refused to say anything more.

The captain-turned-pirate was not amused. He turned to Jenkins and said, "Get her on her feet."

The other man jumped to comply, dragging Claire to her feet and standing her in front of Vargas, who leaned in close to stare directly into her eyes.

"I don't know what kind of scam you're trying to run here, but I for one have had enough. This will go much easier for you if you tell me what you did with the treasure."

"And I told *you,* I don't have any idea—"

That was as far as she got. Vargas's right fist slammed into her stomach with enough force to drop her to her knees. He stared down at her. Claire was gasping and wheezing at his feet. He gestured to Jenkins.

"Get her up again," he ordered.

As Jenkins bent to do what he'd been told, drawing the gaze of the others in the room, Annja slipped the rest of the way up the ladder and rushed over to the navigator's station, using its bulk to hide her presence. Staying close to the ground, she peered around the edge.

Claire stood shakily before Vargas, trying to catch her breath. Even in her present condition, defiance was etched into every line of her body, and Annja knew that Vargas could go on hitting her all night long and she wouldn't give up the information he wanted.

Apparently Vargas recognized that, as well. He made a soft tsk-tsk sound with his mouth, shaking his head in mock resignation, and then drew a knife from his belt.

It was an old World War I trench knife, or more likely a replica of one, with a narrow blade several inches in length and brass knuckles attached to the hilt, so that the bearer could stab, slash or punch without putting down the weapon or changing grip.

Vargas made a show of sliding his fingers through the brass knuckles and curling his fingers around the hilt of the knife.

"Now I'm going to ask you one last time to tell me where I can find the treasure. If you tell me what I want to know, I'll keep my hands to myself. But if you don't…"

He waved the knife back and forth in front of her.

Claire spit in his face.

Vargas casually wiped her spit away and said, "Wrong choice." He started to pull back his hand, readying another blow, but Annja had seen enough. She slipped out of her hiding place and put the barrel of the gun she'd appropriated to the back of Vargas's head.

"Move another inch and I'll put a hole through your skull," she said.

The captain chose discretion over valor and froze where he stood. The two guards followed suit, uncertain of what to do with their leader under Annja's gun.

If they'd been smart, Annja knew, they would have grabbed one of the hostages and created a standoff situation where both sides would have had equal power.

Then again, if they'd been smart, they wouldn't have resorted to piracy in the first place.

"Drop the knife," Annja said to Vargas.

There was a moment's hesitation but then the weapon clattered onto the deck.

Thinking she had things under control, Annja took a step back to give herself room to maneuver. She dismissed Vargas as no longer being a threat now that he'd given up his weapon and turned her attention to the guards.

"Same goes for you two. Drop your weapons and get down on your knees, hands on your heads."

The briefest of glances passed between them as they tossed aside their weapons. As he lowered himself to his knees, Jenkins seemed to slip and put out a hand to steady himself.

It was all an act, of course. While everyone looked to Jenkins, Nelson went for the pistol hidden in his belt.

As soon as she'd seen the glance, Annja had known they were about to try something and she was waiting for just such a move. The seconds spilled out around them, but to Annja it all seemed to take forever as time slowed, her mind moving into combat mode—judging the threats and dealing with them in the order of importance to protect her own life.

As Nelson's hand wrapped around the butt of the pistol, Annja swung her pistol a few inches to one side and pulled the trigger, putting a bullet through the man's chest. The force of the shot sent him flailing backward to bounce off the console behind him.

On the other side of the prisoners, Jenkins tried to make a move of his own, but was leaped on immediately by Marcos, who carried him to the ground beneath his weight.

Out of the corner of her eye, Annja saw Vargas climbing to his feet, swinging something large and red in his hands toward her.

"Annja! Look out!" Claire screamed, but for Annja, lost in the hyperreality of combat, Claire's voice sounded as if it was coming from a long distance away.

Still, it was enough.

Annja raised her hand with the pistol and pointed it directly at Vargas. The move stopped him in his tracks.

Wisely, Vargas let the shaft of the ax fall to the floor.

"Untie her," Annja said to him, nodding at Claire.

"Or what?"

"Or I shoot you in the gut and let you lie there in your own blood until you die in horrible agony," Annja said, smiling. "Your choice, really, but the second option doesn't sound like all that much fun to me."

Apparently Vargas didn't think so, either, for he quickly moved to untie Claire.

Hugo, Marcos and Claire secured the other two men

and Vargas. Once this was done, they dragged Vargas over to the microphone and held it in front of him.

"Tell your men to surrender or we'll kill you."

Vargas scoffed. "They aren't going to care."

"Then for your sake, I suggest you convince them."

After seeing the look on Annja's face, Vargas did just that.

13

In the aftermath of the siege, decisions had to be made. They had been attacked; men had died. Normally that would call for some kind of law-enforcement investigation.

But if Annja, Claire and the others submitted themselves to an investigation, their chances of finding Dr. Knowles dwindled exponentially with every passing minute as weather and time destroyed any clues that might have been left behind. Even worse was if Dr. Knowles was in need of medical attention.

His best chance of survival was for Claire and the rest of her team to continue to Cocos Island as planned and not get bogged down dealing with things here. After a bit of discussion, they decided to maroon the pirates at sea and report their location to the authorities, which Annja thought was more than a bit ironic and a particularly fitting punishment for the crime involved.

The pirates were stripped of their weapons, their hands were bound behind their backs and then they were marched down to the main deck, where they sat in a group under the watchful eyes and guns of Claire and Annja.

While they were waiting, Marcos and Hugo were

busy aboard the patrol boats, dismantling both the radio and the engines on each with the help of a couple handy fire axes.

A rescue beacon would be attached to each boat and Claire would report their position to the Costa Rican authorities once they were on their way.

As they were outside the twenty-mile limit usually considered by international law to mark the boundaries of sovereign territory, there was a chance that the Costa Rican authorities would simply ignore the information and not do anything, but Annja was betting that wouldn't happen. The *Neptune's Pride* wasn't the first vessel these pirates had targeted; their efforts were too coordinated for that. So bringing them to justice would allow the authorities to close several cases, no doubt, and reap the benefits of some good PR at the same time. It was a win-win situation and she didn't see the authorities passing up the opportunity.

Besides, she thought, maybe a few days adrift at sea would teach some of them to take up another profession.

Annja keyed the handheld radio she carried and said, "How much longer?"

"Heading back now" was Marcos's reply, and soon the two patrol boats nosed up next to the *Pride.*

One by one the pirates were loaded onto the patrol craft. Several tried to resist, but after the first few were knocked unconscious and dumped aboard the boats, the rest were more compliant.

When it was his turn, Vargas couldn't resist getting in the last word.

"I will hunt you down for this, Annja Creed," he told her and followed it up with a long string of curse words.

Annja waited patiently until he was done and then leaned in close.

"Please do," she told him. "It will give me an excuse to feed you to the sharks." She smiled, a rather unpleasant smile to show how much she would enjoy it, and Vargas abruptly shut his mouth.

When Annja and the others were back aboard the *Pride,* the patrol boats were cut free and set adrift.

Claire made the call to the Costa Rican authorities, who agreed to pick up the pirates and hold them for trial provided Claire and the others delivered their statements to the police once they arrived back in Puntarenas. Claire agreed that they would and then hung up the satellite phone.

"Hope that's the last we see of them," she said.

Annja nodded her head, not trusting herself to speak. Saying that she hoped this was the last that *anyone* ever saw of them might just give her employer the wrong impression about her, after all.

Hugo had a little experience piloting a vessel the size of the *Pride,* so that duty went to him. They had several hours still to go before they reached the island, so Claire, Marcos and Annja took on the task of getting the ship back into shape.

Decks were washed, bloodstains hosed away as best they were able, and Reyes's body was wrapped in a tarp and stored in the ship's freezer for proper burial when they returned to the mainland.

When they were finished, they ate a communal meal

on the bridge with Hugo and then worked out a shift rotation that would allow them all to get some sleep before they reached the island early the next morning.

With that settled, Annja headed down to her cabin to get some rest.

MORNING BLOOMED BRIGHT and clear, and they reached the vicinity of Cocos a few hours after sunrise.

Normally at this time of year the waters surrounding Cocos Island would be full of scuba divers. Marine life abounded, particularly large marine species like hammerhead sharks, rays, dolphins and whales, and divers flocked to see them.

This season, however, the waters surrounding the island were as off-limits to visitors as the island itself. Annja wasn't exactly certain what had caused the temporary closure, something to do with dangerously high concentrations of marine bacteria or some such, if she remembered correctly. Still, she was thankful for the situation just the same. A ban on diving meant she didn't have to worry about maneuvering the *Pride* around the smaller vessels that divers habitually used, nor having anyone nosing around the boat while they were searching the island for Claire's husband.

As a result of the ban, Annja wasn't expecting to run into any other vessels near the island as Hugo steered the *Pride* along the shoreline, so the sight of a large yacht in Wafer Bay took her by surprise. So much so, in fact, that she had to rub her eyes to be sure she wasn't imagining it.

When she checked again, it was still there, bobbing gently in the surf about twenty yards offshore.

"That can't be right," Claire said from behind her, and Annja turned to find the other woman looking out at the vessel, as well.

"What can't be right?"

"I think that's the *Sea Dancer*," Claire said. "Marcos! Bring me the binoculars."

The big man quickly emerged from the wheelhouse with the requested binoculars in hand, and Claire used them to study the other vessel as they cruised past the inlet. For a while she didn't say anything, just stared through the glass at the other boat, but just as it was about to pass from view, she abruptly handed the binoculars to Annja.

"I'm right. It *is* the *Sea Dancer*," Claire said. "We have to go back."

She sent Marcos to pass the news to their pilot and the boat began a ponderous turn to port that would bring them back around in a circle so they could enter the bay.

"What's so important about the *Sea Dancer?*" Annja asked as she brought the binoculars up to her own eyes to take a look.

"It's the ship that brought my husband to the island."

Annja frowned. "You mean the boat your husband was supposed to call for a pickup, if necessary?"

Claire nodded grimly. "The very same."

That wasn't good.

Annja examined the boat through the binoculars as they approached. Claire was right; she could see the ship's name, *Sea Dancer,* emblazoned on her side in large letters. It was a sleek yacht-size vessel that had obviously been retrofitted for exploration work, if the crane jutting out over the stern was any indication.

There didn't appear to be anyone aboard, at least no one Annja could see. She scanned the entire ship, from stern to bow, but didn't notice any movement.

As Hugo brought the *Pride* about, Annja moved to the other side of the ship in order to keep the *Dancer* in sight. She hoped to see signs of life, but there was nothing.

An uneasy feeling began to settle into her gut.

What were the chances they'd find Dr. Knowles's support ship drifting offshore?

She didn't see any anchor lines, though she supposed they could be on the far side of the vessel, which she couldn't see from her current position.

"What do you think it's doing here?" Claire asked.

Annja shrugged. "Probably picked up another charter while waiting on your husband. It's not all that unusual."

She didn't know the captain of the *Sea Dancer,* but then again she didn't need to in order to understand him. A boat like this was expensive to operate, and every minute it spent sitting at dock was another minute he wasn't earning the money he needed to keep her afloat. Working smaller, one- or two-day charters in between his larger- and longer-paying customers was just common sense. Annja wouldn't be surprised at all if that was what was happening here.

But if you're right, where are they? that inner voice asked, and she didn't have an answer.

They anchored a dozen yards away from the *Sea Dancer* and used one of the *Pride*'s two motor launches to approach the other vessel. As they drew closer, Marcos cut the engine and let them drift in while Annja stood in the bow and tried to hail anyone aboard.

"Ahoy, *Sea Dancer!*"

When no one answered, she tried again.

"Ahoy, *Sea Dancer!* Anyone home?"

They waited, longer this time, but still nothing. With the launch's engine off, Annja knew her voice was loud enough to be heard throughout most of the boat, and the lack of a response had her nerves jangling.

Maybe they all went ashore, an inner voice said, but she didn't believe it. There was a sense, a feeling of being deserted, and Annja was convinced that when they boarded her, they'd find that she was right.

Still, no way to know until they did so.

When the boats drifted close enough, Annja jumped from the launch to the deck of the *Dancer.* A line was tossed over to her and she quickly made it fast, tying the two vessels together. Once she had, she was joined on the other boat by Marcos and Claire.

"Did your husband say how many crew members were aboard the ship when it dropped him off on the island?" Annja asked Claire.

"The captain and four or five others, I think," the other woman replied.

Annja nodded; that was about what she'd expected. There should be something here to tell them where they had gone, what might have happened.

After all, five people don't just vanish into thin air, do they?

Her inner voice was noticeably silent on that issue.

Deciding to start with the bridge, the trio made their way there along the most direct route they could. They called out as they went, hoping to hear a reply, but they didn't encounter anyone along the way.

On the bridge, things were no better.

All the ship's systems were up and running, the various consoles glimmering with lights and flashing screens. The GPS was also working, showing the current and proper location of the boat. The radio was intact as well, the dial set for the emergency broadcast station, though that in itself wasn't a sign that they'd run into trouble. Ships routinely left it on that station after leaving port, Annja knew, so they could quickly call for help if the need arose.

She saw that the anchor was still in its housing, which meant the boat was adrift. Not wanting the vessel to end up beached, Annja triggered the control. A loud clanking sound came from the front of the boat as the anchor was played out and dropped behind them to secure them in place.

They split up and searched the entire vessel. Every door was opened, every room entered. They even made a point of checking the closets and cupboards big enough to stash a body in order to be as thorough as possible.

Annja and Marcos met back on the main deck fifteen minutes later.

"Anything?" Marcos asked.

Annja shook her head. She'd been right; there was no one aboard.

Nor had she found any indication of where the crew had gone or what might have happened to them. There were no notes left behind. No commentary in the ship's log. Not even an open map on a table somewhere that might give them a clue.

"The motor launches are still in their moorings at the

back of the boat," Marcos said, jerking a thumb over his shoulder in that direction.

"The scuba tanks are in the dive lockers, as well. Five lockers. Five tanks."

Where on earth had these people gone? Annja wondered.

That was when Claire screamed.

14

They found her in the galley, staring at an object on the tabletop that was partially covered by a piece of tarp. She spun around at their approach, her eyes going wide and her hands coming up defensively before she realized who it was.

Claire pointed at the object on the table behind her and said, "That...*thing*. What is it?"

Annja cast a quick glance at Marcos, confirming that he was ready to back her up if she needed it, and then crossed to the table. Reaching out with one hand, she drew back the tarp, revealing what lay beneath.

It was a mask, crudely made and, by the color of it, fashioned from native clay. It was humanoid in shape, with the usual features: eyes, ears, nose and mouth. But that was where the similarities ended. The eyes were far too big for the face, appearing to bulge wildly at the viewer. The nose was nothing more than a pair of slits between those oversize eyes, giving the face a decidedly simian look. Its mouth spouted both jagged teeth and two sets of upward-curling tusks, and its ears were large and sticking out from the sides of its neck. Last, but not least, two large, curving horns jutted from either side of its brow.

Oddly enough, Annja recognized it. She'd seen similar depictions before, and while this one wasn't a perfect copy, the result was similar enough to make her believe they were one and the same.

But what on earth was it doing here? And what connection did it have to the *Sea Dancer*'s missing crew?

Claire repeated her original question. "What is it?"

"It's Supay. Or at least a representation of him."

Claire and Marcos stared at her blankly.

"Supay's the Incan god of death."

Marcos must not have heard her correctly. "There's an inky god of death?" he asked, confusion on his face.

Annja laughed. "Not inky, Incan."

To be certain he knew what she was talking about, she said, "The Inca were a pre-Columbian tribe that ruled the west coast of South America, from Columbia and Ecuador, down through Peru, and into Argentina and Chile, during the 1400 and 1500s.

"They were quite an advanced people for their time and would probably have continued to flourish if it wasn't for the Spanish invasion and the coming of the conquistadors, most notably Francisco Pizarro, who had the last Incan emperor strangled in public to show his disdain."

"Lovely," Claire said, and Annja couldn't disagree. There had been much to admire about the Inca. Unfortunately, the same could not be said about the Spanish conquest of South America.

But that was neither here nor there. Nor did it help in any way to explain what the Supay mask was doing in the galley of the *Sea Dancer*.

She picked up the mask and examined it more closely,

looking for something that might indicate where it had come from or who it might belong to. If it was real, it might be worth thousands of dollars, maybe more. If it was a tourist bauble, maybe they could figure out what store it had come from.

But the mask wasn't about to give up its secrets that easily. There was nothing on the mask, front or back, to indicate where it might have come from. No artist's signature, no museum's tag or number. The hardened clay from which it had been formed was of a uniform gray color, but the painted features on the front were bright and vibrant, nearly sparkling in their intensity. Due to their richness, Annja was having a hard time believing the mask was more than a few months old, at best, which would clearly indicate that it wasn't original. Yet at the same time it had a certain authenticity about it that had her inner archaeologist practically squealing with delight.

Claire said something that Annja didn't hear.

"Say again?"

"What does it mean?" Claire said, pointing at the mask in Annja's hands.

Annja shrugged. "It might not mean anything. I don't know how old it is, so I can't say if it's valuable or not. It might just be a souvenir one of the crew picked up during a previous charter."

"You don't really believe that, though, do you?"

Annja glanced over at Marcos, gauging how to best answer his question. After a long pause, she finally said, "I don't really know. It feels like some kind of warning to me, but who's to say I'm not just reading into it given my familiarity with what I know about Supay and what he represented?"

"Which is?" Claire asked.

"His nickname is Unsavory Death God, so it doesn't take much imagination to think a mask representing his face might be a warning of some kind."

"A warning against what?"

Another shrug. "I honestly don't know," Annja told her.

And she was telling the truth; she didn't know. She suspected it had something to do with the treasure hunt in some fashion, but she wasn't about to tell Claire that.

Of course, Claire was no fool.

"Do you think it has something to do with my husband's disappearance?" she asked.

Annja was wondering that very thing.

"I'm not sure," Annja said. "It might. Then again, it might not."

It was another true statement; there was no doubt about that. But the silence filling the empty boat around them seemed to mock her attempts at being noncommittal.

She knew it was a warning, could feel it down deep in her bones.

But a warning about what?

"It was those damned pirates!" Marcos said suddenly, nodding his head as if to reinforce his words. "They probably hit the *Dancer* in the past couple of days and then towed the boat here for safekeeping. Dump the bodies, wash the decks and leave the mask to scare off any poachers who might come upon the boat before they could get back to it."

It sounded reasonable until you started to wonder why modern-day pirates would use a sixteenth-century carving to scare off anyone who came aboard. At that point the entire idea fell apart quicker than a house of cards in a sandstorm.

In the end, short of suddenly coming upon one of the *Dancer*'s crew members—alive and well—there was no way for them to know what had happened here. They found no evidence of foul play. No sign that the crew had gone ashore. Nothing beyond the fact that the boat had been adrift for who knew how long and that someone had left behind a mask that resembled an ancient Incan deity.

Without anything to work from, they had no choice but to abandon the *Dancer* right where she was and get on with the reason they'd come here in the first place. They left her anchored in place, not wanting the boat to drift with the tide, and climbed back into the motor launch for the short trip back to the *Pride*. Once aboard, Claire put in a call to the maritime authorities back in Puntarenas, letting them know the location of the *Dancer* and asking them to attempt to contact the captain by whatever means they had available.

With that accomplished, it was time to find Dr. Knowles.

15

After returning to the *Pride,* they continued the remainder of the short distance to Chatham Bay and anchored the *Pride* just inside the protection of its reef walls. Annja and the others had a hearty breakfast and then set about the task of loading the expedition's gear into the two motor launches and making it secure. The last thing they needed was to hit a fair-size break and have a week's worth of food go flying over the side and into the ocean.

For Annja, the work was old hat; she'd done this kind of thing too many times to count. To her surprise it proved to be the same for the other three, as well. They packed the launches quickly and efficiently, so much so that they were ready to go by shortly after nine that morning.

The bay was a natural deep-water inlet that allowed them to literally take the motor launches right up to the surf line. Annja waited in the prow of one boat until they were in only a few feet of shallow water; she then jumped out, grasped the towline and pulled the launch up onto the sandy beach. Beside her, Marcos was doing the same for the other boat.

Annja turned and peered at the island, as if scoping out an opponent.

It really was the picture of a tropical paradise.

The beach on which she stood was crescent-shaped and the waves rolled in with the gentle rhythm and soft sound of a lullaby. The sand was light gray in color and so fine that it felt almost man-made, its perfection nearly but not quite working against its beauty. Several yards from the water's edge, the tropical forest that covered 98 percent of the island's mass began, rising up from the waterline in a gentle slope that was hidden beneath the dense green canopy. Birds chirped and called from beneath those leaves and the sun shone down on everything like a blessing.

If she didn't know any better, Annja might have been swayed by it all, lulled into an easy nonchalance that could cause her to overlook something simple.

Trouble was, it was often the simple things that got you killed.

Annja did know better; she had no intention of letting her guard down at all. As pretty as the island was, it had swallowed Dr. Knowles and his entire expedition without a peep. She wouldn't forget that, particularly since finding him and what he'd been looking for was her primary objective.

"Quit your daydreaming and let's get to work!" a voice called, and Annja turned to see Claire with her hands on her hips and an amused expression on her face.

"The faster we get the supply cache taken care of,

the quicker we can go looking for Robert," the other woman said. "And the treasure."

That was all the incentive Annja needed.

Claire hadn't wanted to be caught unprepared if the search turned out to take longer than expected, so she'd brought an extra week's worth of food and water as well as a subset of duplicate equipment that could be cached near the beach for easy access should they need it. The equipment was sealed in waterproof bags to protect it from the elements and then packed in crates that they buried a few yards above the waterline at the edge of the tropical forest. Hoisting the whole load into the trees might have been quicker and easier, but that would have left the supply cache at the mercy of the monkeys that were even now gibbering from the forest behind them, and Annja had no doubt that the clever little creatures would have found some way of getting at the goods inside, so underground it went.

As the men were doing what they could to camouflage the area where they'd buried the cache, Annja and Claire discussed what they knew about the route Robert had taken.

"Robert believed the directions that were left behind by John Keating, a friend and confidant of Captain Thompson, were reasonably accurate," she explained, "and he was using them as a starting point for his own search."

Annja was familiar with both the story—that Keating and Thompson had met after the captain had somehow managed to elude the British commander who had captured his ship and hung his crew—and the directions themselves. She'd run across both during her research and had even memorized the latter.

"'Follow the coastline of the bay till you find a creek where, at high-water mark, you go up a stream that flows inland. After passing the Three Sisters, step out seventy paces, west by south, and against the skyline you will see the gap in the hills. From any other point, the gap is invisible. Turn north and walk to a stream. You will see a hole large enough for you to insert your thumb. Thrust in an iron bar, twist it around in the cavity and behind you will find a door which opens on the treasure.'"

Claire laughed. "Very good! Robert memorized all the old accounts, as well. He was determined to find the 'loot of Lima' as he called it."

Annja could certainly understand the mind-set. Finding something that had been missing and presumed lost for centuries was an experience unlike any other, and the high you got from it could last for weeks; she knew from firsthand experience. And unlike the high from any drug, this one never got old. She was just as excited and breathless each and every time it happened. She had an archaeologist's soul and she wouldn't change it for the world.

Claire went on. "Robert had a pair of Zodiacs that his team used to take them upstream. I wasn't able to add any to our inventory, so we'll hike up the stream instead. It will take us longer but it will also guarantee that we don't miss any signs they might have left in their wake."

Annja didn't see any issues with the plan, so they pulled on their packs and set out along the shoreline toward the stream mentioned in Keating's journal. It wasn't a difficult task, for they'd seen the mouth of the stream while approaching the island. Less than fifteen minutes of walking brought them right to it.

At that point Claire turned the responsibility for taking point over to Annja, who had far more experience in jungle navigation than Claire, Hugo and Marcos did combined.

Annja stayed on the stream's north shore; it was an arbitrary decision and mainly based on the fact that she didn't see any reason for them to cross the stream in the first place. That arbitrary decision would prove beneficial to them, however, for less than ten minutes after they began their travel they chanced upon a game trail running parallel to the river and used that to make better time. It wasn't a big trail by any stretch of the imagination, but it was mainly free of undergrowth, and that made all the difference.

It was darker beneath the trees, the sunlight all but cut off from reaching the ground by the overlapping carpet of leaves hanging above their heads. Annja knew they would lose a good hour or two of hiking time due to the issue, but there wasn't much she could do about it. They were all carrying high-intensity headlamps like those worn by mountain climbers and cavers, but she knew she was unlikely to order anyone to use them. Moving about in the jungle with lights blazing was just asking for trouble, in Annja's view, for it would attract a large variety of wildlife, most of which they were better off not encountering.

Can't be helped, so stop worrying about it, her inner

voice said. *Cross that bridge when you come to it. For now, concentrate on what's in front of you.*

The air was filled with the rich scent of the tropical forest, and the humidity soon had them all sweating heavily. Annja reminded herself to check the group's water intake and adjust accordingly; it wouldn't be hard to dehydrate themselves in these temperatures.

The river ran reasonably straight and on a heading that was almost due south of Chatham Bay, so Annja wasn't worried about anyone getting lost. Still, she kept them in a tight group for security reasons if nothing else, with her in front, followed by Marcos, then Claire and then Hugo. In case they ran into some unexpected wildlife, both of the men carried rifles slung over their shoulders, and Annja, of course, had her sword, though she would only use it if absolutely necessary.

They had been following the stream for just over an hour when Marcos spotted something along the river-bank about twenty yards ahead of them. Leaving the trail behind, the foursome hacked their way through the undergrowth to reach the bank and then hiked along it for the few extra minutes it took to reach the boats.

Zodiacs were rigid inflatable boats designed to be both durable and portable, making them ideal for expedition work. They could carry several people and a fair degree of supplies and were useful on anything from shallow jungle rivers like this one to the open ocean. This particular pair of boats was made of bright orange synthetic rubber, which was why Marcos had been able to spot them so easily.

They had also been torn to ribbons.

Annja and company stared at what was left of the

watercraft in disbelief. Something had slashed through the rubber body, not once, not twice, but more than a dozen times. The cuts were long and narrow, but that told them very little about what had been used to do the deed. Had they simply fallen victim to a large predator or had some human agency been behind the work? The motors were both intact and still attached to each boat at the stern, leading Annja to think the animal theory fit best.

A human, after all, would make certain that the engines were disabled as well, wouldn't they?

She wasn't sure.

And that bothered her.

As she stood there, staring down at the ruined boats, the skin on the back of her neck began to crawl.

Annja looked up and down the river and then turned and surveyed the thick jungle behind them. She did her best to look through the dense undergrowth, for patterns instead of individual objects, knowing her mind would automatically try to make sense of any symmetrical objects her gaze washed over. It was why camouflage had been invented—to break up those patterns and disrupt the eye and keep the mind from doing its job.

She didn't see anything out of the ordinary on the river or in the trees around them, but still…something was making her uneasy.

She turned her attention back to the boat and found Marcos standing a few feet away, watching her. He glanced in the direction she'd been looking and then back at her.

"See something?" he asked

Annja shook her head. "No. Just on edge, that's all."

She realized after saying it that she hadn't been lying, either. She *was* on edge. Had been since they'd found the Supay mask aboard the *Sea Dancer*.

What did it mean?

"What do you think happened?" Claire asked, her gaze still on the ruined boats in front of her.

"Los cocodrilos," Hugo said, pointing, and even Annja didn't need that one translated for her.

Crocodiles.

Annja followed his finger to where it was pointing at a spot close to the water's edge. Moving closer, she could see a set of four-toed tracks leading from the water up the bank toward the boats. Hugo was right; crocodiles had certainly been here.

Annja wasn't quite convinced that they were responsible for the destruction of the boats, but she kept that to herself. No sense worrying the others.

Instead, she said, "There's no sign of blood or anything heavy being dragged down into the river, so I'd say the boats were empty when the damage was done. Nothing to worry about, Claire."

Claire nodded. "Yes, yes, you're right. Robert would have said something to me when we spoke on the phone that first night if someone had been hurt."

She glanced at the others, saw no disagreement and said, "Onward, then."

Knowles had told Claire before his disappearance that they had abandoned the boats because the water had become too shallow and they had struck out overland, continuing to follow the river as he searched for the Three Sisters.

Annja and the others did the same.

They began to see small signs that people had come this way before them—riverbank grasses trampled under a heavy boot, branches of overhanging trees snapped and broken at waist height and above, even a shoe print left in the soft earth near the waterline. When the bank became too narrow and steep to walk upon, they followed a path where the underbrush had previously been cut through to return to the game trail that they'd been on before. Where the two intersected, a *K* had been carved into the trunk of a nearby tree.

Apparently Knowles wanted to be certain that he had a means of retracing his steps if his GPS and other high-tech equipment failed. Annja didn't blame him; she would have done the same thing. She pointed out the marking to the others and told them to keep their eyes open for more of them as they continued forward.

Ten minutes later they found a clearing carved out of the trees just off the trail, and the moment she stepped into it and saw what it contained, Annja knew that she had found them.

The Three Sisters.

It was an apt name for a rock formation, Annja supposed, if one were inclined to name rock formations in the first place, which she wasn't. But to each his own; the individual who had discovered this one had apparently felt the need, and the Three Sisters really wasn't a terrible choice. The rocks were roughly the height of the average adult and were arranged so that the two larger, vertical stones stood on either side of the smaller, and shorter, third stone of the trio. Annja had to admit that it did look like three sisters huddled together over a fire. Or rather, it could, if you squinted a little, cocked your head slightly upward while turning it just a bit to the left…

Laughter from behind her caused Annja to self-consciously straighten up. Okay, so maybe it didn't look all that much like three sisters, but it was the only thing they'd seen so far that even remotely qualified, and Annja was willing to make a judgment call in favor of having found the right spot.

"So now what?" Marcos asked.

Without turning around, Annja said, "'After passing the Three Sisters, step out seventy paces, west by south, and against the skyline you will see the gap in the hills.'"

She stepped into the clearing, walked past the Sisters and then made a forty-five-degree turn to her left, which would point her in a southwesterly direction.

Step out seventy paces…

She glanced back to see the other three still standing by the edge of the clearing.

"Well, are you coming or aren't you?" she called.

She chose not to wait for an answer and immediately began counting with every step.

Annja only made it as far as fifty-eight, for it was at that point that she stepped between several trees and suddenly came face-to-face with a life-size statue of Supay, the Incan god of death. He looked remarkably similar to the mask they'd found aboard the *Sea Dancer*.

With one addition.

Someone had slapped a baseball cap on the statue's head.

16

Annja stared at the baseball cap sitting atop Supay's head. In all her years of exploring ancient cultures and lost civilizations, she didn't think she'd ever seen a more incongruous sight.

Which was probably the prankster's whole reason for doing it.

The statue stood about six feet tall, though the twisted horns rising from its forehead probably added at least another foot to the overall height. It stood with its feet braced and its arms outstretched, as if to catch something running toward it.

Something or someone.

The top half of the statue had been cleared of vines and other overgrowth—recently, too, judging from the looks of it. The lower half, Annja saw, was still mainly obscured behind the foliage. Like the Supay mask they'd found on the *Sea Dancer,* the statue had once been brightly painted as well, but years of exposure to the elements had stripped it of all but the faintest evidence of its original color scheme. Still, it was an incredible piece of artwork and one that would fetch quite a hefty sum in any museum in the world.

And some jokester had slapped a baseball cap—a Boston Red Sox cap, no less—on its head.

Sacrilege, Annja thought. Anyone who was anyone knew the Bronx Bombers were the only team worth watching.

"You have got to be kidding me," Claire said from behind her, then marched forward to snatch the cap off the statue's head.

The statue would probably have been rather terrifying if she'd come upon it in the dark without the cap, but since she'd seen the two items together, it just wasn't all that sinister anymore.

Claire flipped the hat over and read the name inked into the headband.

"P. Sawyer. I knew it!"

"Do you know him?"

Claire nodded. "He was one of the graduate students Richard worked with over the past few years. Big bloke, always pulling pranks on the other members of the team. And a big Red Sox fan."

Clearly didn't learn anything in grad school, then, Annja thought with a smile. Then to the others she said, "Obviously we're on the right track. Dr. Knowles and his team made it this far. Why don't we—"

"Mira! La mochila!" Hugo said, pointing as he hustled around the statue. Open ground led just beyond, to where the object in question, a dark blue backpack, lay propped against a tree trunk half a dozen yards away.

Open ground?

There were a few bushes here and there and some short tufts of jungle grasses growing around the edges, but the center was mainly exposed topsoil with a dark gray coloration, almost as if someone had poured water over it recently.

Annja glanced at the backpack, then at the snarling face of the statue of Supay and finally to the open ground that Hugo was racing across.

Ground that seemed to shift and bounce about under each footfall, as if it weren't really solid at all but just a thin layer of carpet floating atop a sea of water.

Water...

Annja was hit with a sudden sense of foreboding sharp enough to make her gasp.

She shouted at Hugo, trying to make him stop.

"No, Hugo, no! Leave it alone!"

But it was too late. Hugo had crossed half the distance to the backpack when his left leg came down squarely and disappeared up to his knee in the earth beneath his feet. His momentum forced him to take another step to keep from falling over and that foot, too, sank right into the soil on which he stood. Within seconds he was stuck fast.

Recognizing that Hugo had unwittingly stumbled into a quicksand pit, Annja shouted at him to stay still. "Don't fight it, Hugo. Just relax and stay still. We'll get you out!"

Hugo either didn't hear or didn't understand, for he began to thrash about, trying to yank his legs free through sheer force of muscle. But the activity only caused him to sink even deeper into the muck.

If they didn't do something quickly, he was going to exhaust himself and end up in more trouble than he was already in.

Annja knew that quicksand was really nothing more

than loose sand or earth mixed with water. As the water seeped into a particular stretch of ground, it forced the sand particles away from one another, making them less capable of supporting any significant weight. That in and of itself wasn't a terrible thing. If this was all that happened, it wouldn't be too bad. Hugo would get dirty, but he wouldn't be in any real danger.

The real problem was that the water acted as a kind of vacuum at the same time. As the weight of the object sank into the quicksand, it forced the water away from it, creating an air pocket that acted like a vacuum. It sucked the object even deeper into the muck before the water flowed back in to repeat the cycle all over again. The more a person struggled, the more vacuum action was generated by their movements and the deeper they sank.

Marcos shouted something to Hugo in rapid-fire Spanish and started forward, shedding his pack as he went. He clearly intended to go in after his companion and help.

Annja grabbed Marcos's arm and spun him around, getting up in his face so that he gave her his attention.

"You can't go in there!" she said. "You're even heavier than he is. All you'll wind up doing is sinking even deeper and then I'll have two of you stuck and one less person to use to help you break free. I need you here, with me."

"But he's going to—"

She didn't let him finish. "Not if you do as I say. Now help me! Quickly!"

Annja slipped off her backpack and pulled a coiled rope from its interior. She handed one end to Marcos.

"Tie it off around that tree over there," she told him, pointing to a thick banyan tree a few feet away.

As he did so, Annja turned to Claire and said, "See if you can get Hugo to calm down. Tell him to stay still and we'll pull him out."

Claire's insistent tone finally got Hugo's attention, and by the time Annja was ready to throw him the rope, he'd calmed down considerably. Of course, he had already sunk almost to his armpits by that point, so getting him out was not going to be easy.

Annja's aim was spot-on; the other end of the rope splashed down right next to Hugo and he snatched it up like a man afraid he'd disappear at any moment. Annja knew that wasn't really a concern, for quicksand didn't kill by drowning—despite the way Hollywood had tried to convince moviegoers—but through exposure to the sun and dehydration instead. It trapped you and held you there, leaving you at the mercy of the elements.

Thankfully, Hugo wasn't alone.

Marcos came running back to where Annja and Claire were waiting.

"Rope's secure," he said.

"All right, grab hold of the line like this," Annja said, demonstrating to Hugo how to hold the line with two hands and to brace himself with his feet for maximum pulling capability.

Annja called out to Hugo, "Relax and let us do the work. We're going to drag you out."

He nodded and gave her a thumbs-up without releasing his death grip on the rope.

She turned to her two companions. "Slow and steady," she told them. "No quick, hard jerks on the line. That quicksand he's in is as strong as cement. If you yank on it, all you'll do is pull his arms out of his sockets. He'll be just as stuck but injured and unable to help on top of everything if that happens."

After nodding to show that they understood, Marcos and Claire grabbed the rope a few feet behind Annja.

She glanced back at them.

"Ready?"

"Ready," they said in chorus.

"All right. Slow and steady, remember. Okay, go!"

The three of them began to pull on the rope. Annja kept her gaze fixed firmly on Hugo, watching to be certain they that weren't hurting him. The slack in the rope was quickly taken up and then the pressure against the suction holding him in place began.

"Keep pulling," Annja said to the others as the resistance became stronger. They strained against the muck, trying to pull him free. If they could just get a little traction…

Hugo let out a short cry and Annja could see the pain etched across his face as he fought to hold on to the rope. The pressure against his arm sockets must have been intense, but he gritted his teeth and held on.

"Keep pulling…"

Annja dug in with her feet and leaned back, straining against the rope. There hadn't been any give at all yet; it was like trying to pull a ten-ton block of granite with a golf cart.

Marcos let out a string of expletives in Spanish behind her, grunting with the effort he was expending, and still nothing happened. When Hugo let out a anguished cry of pain from the pressure against his arms, Annja called it quits.

"Enough! Enough!" she yelled, and they eased off the rope before they accidentally injured their comrade. Marcos and Claire looked stunned; they no doubt thought the three of them could haul him free, but were just now recognizing the truth that Annja already knew.

This was going to be harder than it looked.

"Hugo, you all right?" she called.

He grimaced against the pain but nodded in response.

"What on earth are we going to do now?" Claire asked, and Annja could hear the resignation in the other woman's voice. Claire apparently thought they were done, that there wasn't anything else that they could do to free their companion, but Annja was just getting started.

She surveyed the area around where Hugo was trapped, weighing the variables, but in the end she knew she really didn't have any choice.

She was going to have to go in after him.

17

She said as much to the others.

"You can't be serious," Claire said, but Annja was.

Quite serious, in fact.

"Look," she said. "It's obvious that we can't pull him out. If we try again we'll probably dislocate one or even both of his arms. He's strong but not that strong. He can't take that kind of pressure. We have to try something different."

"I agree, but why should you go?" Marcos asked. "I'm stronger than you."

"It's not a question of strength. Have you ever been in quicksand before?"

Marcos shook his head. "No, but I don't see—"

Annja cut him off.

"I have," she told him. "I know how to deal with it and, more importantly, how to get out of it. And I can get him out, as well. But I'm going to need both of you."

Ten minutes later she was ready.

They had retrieved the rope, cleaned it of the muck that had gathered along its length as best they could and then tied the free end around Annja's waist. They left the other end anchored around the tree.

Annja explained what she was going to do as she set out toward Hugo.

"Quicksand is twice as dense as a person's body," she said. "In theory, it's actually impossible to drown in it, for it will support your weight if you can spread it out evenly.

"I'm going to get into the pool with him and help him get his legs up onto the surface of the quicksand. If we can manage that, he should be able to just crawl across the surface to safety."

She knew the plan was a sound one; she'd survived a quicksand pit in the past doing that very thing. But the question remained as to whether she could get Hugo's legs free of the suction holding them and how she would prevent her own legs from getting as stuck as Hugo's now were.

She cautiously began walking toward the spot where Hugo was trapped. The ground beneath her feet was solid at first and she crossed half the distance between the two of them before she began to see damp pockets here and there where underwater springs brought water up near the surface. She slowed down, avoiding the areas she was certain were dangerous and keeping a watchful eye on the ground beneath her feet, looking for that telltale wobble that would indicate water beginning to pool beneath the surface.

As she drew closer, Annja could see that Hugo was trapped in the middle of a quicksand pit that was about fifteen feet across. It was just sheer bad luck that he'd been moving so quickly that his stride had taken him away from the edge before he realized he was in danger. His subsequent thrashing about had only made things worse, but surveying the situation from this distance gave Annja a bit more hope than she'd had before. Hugo was only six feet or so from what looked to be the edge of the pit; if they could get his legs free he should be able to cross that far with ease.

Annja looked back at the others standing with the rope in hand.

"Remember, if I give the sign—" she raised her hand to show what she meant "—then start pulling me back, okay?"

"Got it."

"All right, going in."

Annja carefully got down on her hands and knees near the edge of the pit and began to crawl forward. It only took a foot or so of forward movement before she began to feel the ground quiver beneath her weight, like pressing down on a bowl of jelly.

Inching her way forward, she slid out onto the quicksand. Her hands dipped beneath the surface of the muck, but because she had her weight distributed across a wider surface she didn't sink more than a few inches into it.

Little by little, she made her way toward Hugo.

The mud of the pit began to accumulate on her arms, legs and torso, and it grew harder to move the farther she got, as if she were pressing her way through wet cement.

Hugo watched her coming toward him, eyes wide. She knew he was expecting her to fall through the crust at any moment and must have been wondering what on earth he was going to do about it when it happened.

She wanted to tell him not to worry; that was one appointment she had no intention of keeping.

Eventually, after what felt like an hour but was probably no longer than ten minutes, Annja was less than two feet away from Hugo. She could have reached out and touched him if she'd wanted, but she kept her hands to herself, worried that in his panic he might grab her and drag them both down deeper into the mire.

Instead, she smiled at him, trying to ease his tension even a little, and said, "Hi, Hugo."

His smile in return was a bit more self-deprecating than hers. "Got us into a fine mess, didn't I?"

"Yes, you did, but that's okay. We're going to both get out of here without any problem."

He looked at her a bit dubiously, but answered well enough. "You're the boss. I'd guess you've got a plan?"

"Of course I do. We're going to crawl out."

He nodded. "I'm a bit heavier than you, Miss Creed. I can't crawl. I sink."

Annja laughed. "Trust me, Hugo, it has nothing to do with my weight. I'm going to get you loose and then we're both going to crawl to the edge over there," she said, pointing toward the solid ground ahead of them where the backpack still rested.

"If you say so."

"I do. But you're going to need to trust me."

Another self-deprecating smile. "Not like I've got much of a choice, do I?" Hugo replied.

That was certainly a true statement.

Annja could feel the ground shifting beneath her like a nervous horse shying on its rider and she knew they needed to get moving.

"Rule number one," she said, "is to move slowly and carefully. The more you thrash about and stir up the muck, the harder it will hold you down. Understand?"

"Yes. Slow and easy."

"Good. Like I said, the plan is to get you up on top of the quicksand like I am. Once we do, we can crawl over to the edge and climb out."

"But my legs are stuck. I can barely move them."

"I know. That's why I'm here. I'm going to try to keep the muck away from your legs long enough for you to work them free. Once I do, you need to lift them up and spread your weight out so you don't sink all over again. Can you do that?"

"Yes."

"All right, then, no time like the present."

Annja laid down on her side and let her arm sink into the quicksand close to Hugo's body, following his leg downward as far as she could reach. It was like forcing her arm into a bucket of sand, heavy and tight, and she knew she wouldn't have energy to do this for long. They had to get it right the first time.

Once her arm was as deep as she could get it, she said, "Start trying to lift your leg again, but slowly."

The hope was that with her arm up against his leg, it would create some space between the mud and his limb, allowing it to move a bit more readily. She wasn't looking for it to pop free in a single motion, but she'd take an inch of movement in the right direction, that was for sure.

Hugo must have felt the same way, for he nearly shouted for joy when his leg moved upward half an inch.

"Good. Now hold still for a moment."

When Hugo stopped moving, Annja slowly dragged her arm a bit higher from the muck, using his leg for interference the way he'd used her arm.

In that fashion, inch by inch, they managed to free both of Hugo's legs from the quicksand. With the two of them belly-down in the muck, they crawled across the top of the shifting mire toward the solid ground a few feet in front of them.

Annja reached it first because she was not yet as tired as Hugo was, but he wasn't all that far behind. They dragged themselves forward and up onto dry land, where they rolled over onto their backs, exhausted, like two drowning victims recently pulled from the ocean.

Marcos and Claire were shouting something from the other side of the clearing, but Annja didn't have the energy to figure out what they were saying. She managed to raise a hand over her head to show them they were alive and that seemed to do the trick.

At least it made the shouting stop.

She caught her breath and then forced herself to sit up. Glancing down, she found everything from her neck to her toes covered in a thick layer of grayish-brown mud that was starting to harden in the heat.

Annja leaned over and smacked Hugo on the leg. "Come on, get up. We've got to get this junk off us."

As Hugo groaned in objection, Annja staggered to her feet, nearly falling over from the weight of the mud caked to the front of her body. The quicksand was bad, but so was the mud. The extra weight of it would make them clumsy, never mind the massive amounts of chafing that would result. Even more dangerous was the tendency for the stuff to gather in the armpits and groin areas, causing the victim's flesh to erupt in angry infections and boils.

The clothes had to go.

She glanced over at Hugo, who still hadn't sat up yet.

"Come on, Hugo, up and at 'em. We have to get these clothes off."

For a moment she didn't think he'd heard—maybe his ears were clogged with grit?—but then he slowly forced himself to sit up.

"Take our clothes off?" he asked wearily, with no sign of enthusiasm whatsoever for getting undressed alongside a single woman, which Annja found amusing.

"I'll try not to take your lack of enthusiasm personally, but yes, you heard me correctly. Take your clothes off and quit wasting time." She gave him an abbreviated explanation of how miserable he would be after prolonged contact with the muck that they'd just slogged their way through. That was more than enough to get him up and moving.

Annja was trying to figure out a way to take her mud-encrusted T-shirt off over her head when Marcos and Claire emerged from the jungle to her left, having taken the long way around the clearing to be safe. In hand were Annja's and Hugo's packs.

Annja clumped over, took her backpack from Claire and held up a mud-covered finger. "Not a word about my hair," she told the other woman with mock severity, which garnered the laugh she'd been looking for. She'd learned long ago that a little lighthearted laughter went a long way to relieving the tension after a potentially dangerous event. She didn't want the team stiffening up and worrying about continuing onward after they'd come this far already.

Satisfied she'd achieved her desired effect, she stalked off behind a few trees to find some privacy while, behind her, Marcos bent to try to help Hugo out of his boots and jeans.

Without water to spare, there was only so much Annja could do to clean herself off but she knew she'd feel better for having made the attempt. Rather than fight with her now-hardening clothing, she chose the easy way out and simply cut her shirt and shorts off with the blade of her knife. She then used a hand towel and some water from her supply to clean some of the grit from her skin and hair, before dressing in a fresh set of clothing.

As she finished, Annja sensed that someone was watching her from the trees behind her.

18

Being watched was a familiar sensation for Annja, not only due to her penchant for dangerous confrontations that tended to breed enemies of a certain type but also because she happened to be the host of an internationally broadcast television show. People liked celebrities and little by little, like it or not, that was what Annja was becoming.

She did not, however, expect to run into any rabid fans out here in the midst of the jungle, so the fact that the watcher was remaining unseen put a little different spin on the situation.

Her first thought was that it might be an animal. Cocos Island had several species large enough to cause such a reaction, but there seemed to be a sense of intent to the feeling that was all too human in nature. She was being watched and it wasn't just idle curiosity from one species to another.

That meant there was a specific purpose behind it.

Annja did nothing to reveal the fact that she was aware of the scrutiny, just continued with what she was doing, but now she was watching the nearest tree line from beneath half-lidded eyes, searching for something that didn't belong. If she could pinpoint where the watcher was hiding...

Annja made a big show out of banging her boots off against a nearby tree and then sat down to pull them on and lace them up. As she did, she caught a glimpse of something moving among the shadows cast by the trees about half a dozen yards ahead of her.

Gotcha!

The figure was definitely bipedal, but it was staying back far enough that it was hard to get a good look at how big it might be.

Had one of the men decided to take an illicit sneak peek or two while she changed? She dismissed the idea. Neither of them seemed the type, never mind the fact that because they would have had to come from the other direction they wouldn't have had time to loop around.

Someone else, then, she thought. *A member of Dr. Knowles's expedition, maybe? One of the missing crew members—if they're even missing, that is—off the Sea Dancer? The individual who left the Supay mask in the Dancer's galley?*

She didn't know.

But she planned to find out.

Annja kept the figure in her peripheral vision as she pretended to dig through her backpack for something she needed. She squatted on the balls of her feet, prepared to push off at a moment's notice, and she could feel the adrenaline flood her system as she readied herself for action. Timing was going to make the difference between success and failure, and she was waiting for that certain feeling when being watched changed slightly as the watcher momentarily looked away, and when it came she intended…

Now!

Annja leaped to her feet and raced directly toward where she thought her mystery watcher was hiding. She kept her gaze focused on that same spot as she ran, not wanting to miss whoever it was if they decided they'd rather get away than face her directly.

It was a good thing she did, too, for the figure bolted the instant he or she realized they'd been seen.

Annja didn't waste any time talking. She just called her sword to hand and gave chase.

Her sudden approach had allowed her to close some of the distance between them and she caught a glimpse of a dark-haired man with deeply tanned skin wearing something colorful around his head as he turned and took to his heels.

Annja had always prided herself on staying in shape, and her daily exercises both with and without the sword had honed her body into a finely tuned piece of machinery, but this guy made her look as if she hadn't run a day in her life. He took off through the trees like a gazelle on speed, slipping beneath branches, leaping over fallen logs and undergrowth, until he disappeared from view before she could get a better look at him.

Knowing there was no way to catch up or even keep pace with him given her current condition, Annja slowed and then turned back the way she had come. She spent a few minutes searching about, trying to find the spot from which the stranger had been watching her, but she couldn't find any evidence that he'd been there at all, not even a footprint or a broken branch.

It was as though he'd been nothing more than a ghost.

At least that would explain how he'd been able to move so quickly, Annja thought wryly.

She released her sword, sending it back into the ether, and glanced in the direction of where she'd left the others, wondering if they had seen anything themselves.

"IT WAS A SETUP."

Those were the words that Marcos greeted her with as she emerged from the trees. In his hands was a backpack, presumably the one Hugo had been running to investigate when he'd been caught in the quicksand.

"Why a setup?" she asked.

In response, he opened the top flap on the backpack and let her look inside.

It was full of nothing but stones.

Someone had filled the pack in order to weigh it down and had then set it where it would be seen.

"I'm telling you it was a setup," Marcos said again. "No question about it. The hat was the lure to catch our attention, and the bag was the bait to make us go after it!"

Annja really couldn't fault his logic. If the backpack had still been full of whatever gear it had originally contained she might have disagreed, but the presence of the stones made the placement of the bag deliberate.

Someone had wanted them to see it. Someone had wanted them to investigate it.

Someone had wanted them to run afoul of the quicksand pit.

Annja had a hunch she'd just seen one of those responsible; she suspected that there were more.

She told the others about the man she'd seen watching her while she'd been tending to her muddy clothes and of how she'd tried to chase him down. Though they hadn't been more than a hundred feet away from one another at any point, the thickness of the jungle foliage had kept the others from getting a glimpse of Annja's mysterious watcher or even knowing that something was happening with her. It was a sobering reminder that they were generally safer if they stayed together in a group.

Marcos was far from pleased. "I knew it!" he said, smashing one big fist into his other hand to emphasize his statement. "Which way did he go? We've got to hunt this guy down."

"No, we don't," Claire said, and the sharp, command-oriented nature of her tone surprised Annja. She wouldn't have thought Claire was capable of it and she was even more surprised when the other woman went on.

"Our priority is to find Knowles," Claire said. "Anything beyond that is secondary."

Find *Knowles?*

That seemed an odd way for Claire to refer to her husband, but Annja put it off as stress and didn't dwell on it. Besides, Claire was right; finding Dr. Knowles and his missing team was their most important goal right now.

"I agree with Claire," Annja said to Marcos. "It makes no sense to go charging off into the jungle searching for a guy we barely caught a glimpse of. Better to continue with our plan, but keep your eyes open as we go."

"This guy tried to kill us and you just want to let him go?"

Annja shook her head. "We don't know that," she insisted. "Hugo wasn't in any danger of dying, not with the rest of us here. He may have simply been lured into the quicksand in an effort to scare us off, get us to leave. And we're not *letting* whoever it was go. We don't have any idea where he is or how to find him, so what's the point of wasting time trying to do so when we have other priorities?"

"Because they're dangerous," Marcos insisted. "Think about it. First, contact with Knowles and his group is lost. Then the crew of the *Sea Dancer* goes missing without a trace. It seems pretty obvious to me that we're next."

But Annja disagreed; she didn't think it was obvious at all. "We don't know what happened to Knowles or to the crew of the *Dancer*. More likely than not they're two separate, isolated events that just seem connected to each other because of their proximity. We can't really be certain until we find the doctor and his team."

"I still don't like it," Marcos said, but he left it at that and didn't argue any further.

"So now what?" Hugo asked.

Claire said, "According to what Richard told me on the phone, he and his team made camp their first night about a half hour north of our present position, close to a small waterfall. No reason we shouldn't, as well."

Doing so had a couple of key advantages, Annja knew. First and foremost, it would allow her and Hugo to wash the rest of the quicksand from their bodies and clothes, which they would both be thankful for. Second, it would give everyone some much-needed rest before pushing on the next morning to the former expedition's last known position.

And it would give me time to check our tail, see if there was anyone hanging about who shouldn't be.

Annja could live with that.

They gathered their gear and resumed their march, heading inland, deeper into the jungle. This time Marcos took point and Annja didn't bother to question his doing so. If it made him feel better being out in front, so be it. She settled into position at the rear of their little formation, happy enough to keep an eye on the trail behind them.

Roughly forty minutes later they emerged from the tree line to find themselves standing on the rocky edge of a large pool of water. On the other side was a sheer cliff face rising up a hundred feet or more, and it was from the center of this edifice that the waterfall Claire had mentioned earlier spouted. Its waters poured over the drop in a thrumming roar and filled the pool in front of them, before racing away down the length of a fast-running river to the east. Two dozen yards away, on a bend in the river, was a stony beach that would serve as their camp for the night.

It had been a long day and all of them were tired from their exertions, so they quickly hiked around the pool and crossed to the other side of the stream to set up camp along the beach. A broken tent spike and a discarded length of rope told them that they weren't the first to camp here, validating Claire's report that her husband's team had done the same before them.

They built a fire pit by bringing some large rocks together in a circle and then set up the tents around the pit, one at each cardinal point of the compass so that all of their doors were facing inward toward the fire.

By the time they finished, the sun had dropped below the tree line, leaving them in heavy shadow. It wouldn't be too long before it was fully dark. Before that happened, Annja wanted to take advantage of the nearby pool and waterfall to wash off the rest of the detritus left over from the quicksand.

Hugo joined her and the two of them took turns standing guard for each other as they washed the grit and grime from their bodies as well as their clothing and boots. When they were done they carried their wet gear back to the fire and laid it out near the flames to get them to dry.

Dinner was a rehydrated stew that Marcos whipped up and Annja had to admit it was pretty decent fare. For camp food, that is. Knowing she needed to replenish the energy she'd burned fighting the pirates and rescuing Hugo, Annja even helped herself to seconds.

The bath had given Annja some time to think about the events thus far. She had originally been under the impression that Dr. Knowles's team had suffered some kind of accident—perhaps a tunnel collapse had buried most of the team members alive or a freak storm had knocked out their communications gear, cutting them off from the mainland—but as her own team encountered increasingly targeted acts of disruption, she was beginning to rethink that hypothesis. When viewed in a different light, all of the strange encounters they'd endured to date had been attempts to keep them from investigating the island or, once there, to keep Annja and her companions from pushing onward.

The pirate attack might have been chance, but then again it might have been deliberately planned to keep them from ever reaching Cocos Island.

The crew of the *Sea Dancer* might have gone off of their own accord or they may have been abducted and their boat deliberately seeded in the *Pride*'s path to serve as a warning to Annja and her team.

Even the stunt with the baseball cap and backpack had seemed more of a warning to Annja than any serious attempt to cause them harm.

That led her to believe that whoever was on the island with them was more interested in getting them to turn away and go back to Costa Rica than in hurting them or worse.

After all, why resort to violence, and the mess it brought with it, if you could scare your rivals into turning away of their own accord?

Rivals. That's it!

They were facing a rival group of treasure hunters; she was suddenly convinced of it. And not just any group of rivals but one that was not afraid to push the envelope a little in trying to get first Knowles's, and now Annja's, team from heading deeper into the jungle after the treasure.

In fact, it wouldn't surprise her to discover that one or more of Knowles's own crew had gone rogue and tried to claim the treasure as their own. They would have known that Richard's wife would come looking for him and would have only needed to plant a watcher in Puntarenas to keep an eye out for her arrival. Once

Claire had come up on their radar, so to speak, they could have easily staged any of the incidents to date.

The only thing that seemed out of place was the recurring use of the Incan death-god motif. Unlike the Greek or Egyptian pantheons, in which gods like Zeus, Aphrodite, Set and Anubis were household names, very few people were familiar with the deities and demigods of the Incans. Even fewer people would know that the grinning, horn-headed god named Supay, the same one they'd encountered twice today, was the Incan version of the devil and was therefore an excellent choice to symbolize the potential danger they were getting into if they continued pushing onward with the expedition.

She pondered that for a few minutes longer and that was all it took for her to come up with a solution. It was a given in archaeological circles that one cannot truly come to know a native culture without studying that culture's religious beliefs. Since Knowles was an expert on South American cultures, it stood to reason that he would have people working for him that were not only familiar with the Incan civilization but also with its pantheon of gods.

To someone like that, Supay was not only an excellent choice, but an inside joke, as well.

Annja wasn't yet ready to share her conclusions with the others, but by the time she called it a night and slipped into her tent to get some sleep, she was feeling confident that she had most of the bigger picture all worked out.

Tomorrow she could put her theory to the test.

19

Annja awoke to a woman's scream.

She threw on her clothes, jammed her feet into her hiking boots and rushed out of the tent to find Hugo trying to console a rather hysterical Claire. The two of them separated as Annja ran over, giving her a chance to see what was behind them, and the sight brought her up short.

The early-morning sun illuminated the symbol that had been painted across the front of Claire's tent with a red substance that looked to be blood. The image was rough, the blood or paint or whatever it was having dripped downward after it had been applied, but it didn't take too much effort to recognize it as a crude drawing of a leering face.

A face with a wide mouth and sharply pointed teeth and horns.

The hair on the back of her neck stood on end and she understood why Claire was so distraught. Whoever had put the symbol there had been less than two feet from where Claire had been sleeping blissfully unaware that danger lurked so close. The realization that the group had quite literally been at their mercy imparted an even greater malevolence to the image.

Some instinct, some long-buried sixth sense, caused Annja to turn and look at the front of her own tent.

A similar image stared evilly back at her.

"It's on mine, as well," Hugo said, and a glance in that direction showed Annja that he was correct.

The implications were staggering.

Turning back to face Hugo, Annja asked, "Is she hurt?"

Hugo opened his mouth to reply but to Annja's surprise it was Claire who answered.

"I'm all right," she said. "Just a bit of a shock."

From her tone Annja could tell that Claire was irritated with her own loss of control, and that was a good sign. She'd be steadier the next time they encountered something unexpected.

And there would be a next time, Annja knew. It was becoming increasingly obvious that someone didn't want them here, and whoever they were, they weren't afraid to show it.

"Where's Marcos?"

The implication of Hugo's question was realized when Annja felt the cold hand of dread squeeze her spine. Marcos's tent stood next to hers, and as she spun around to face it, she saw that the flaps were closed and free of any markings.

The absence of the image that marred all their other tents only deepened her concern.

She stepped over to the entrance to his tent and saw that the flaps were unzipped. She pulled the right one aside and stuck her head inside to take a look.

The tent was empty.

Annja supposed he might have gotten up early and

gone for a walk, maybe try to hunt down something fresh for breakfast, but then she spied that his boots still stood next to each other at the end of his sleeping bag, ready to be pulled on when he awakened that morning.

Who goes for a walk in the jungle in bare feet?

She turned to find the others had joined her and were now looking inside, as well.

Upon seeing the empty tent, Hugo cursed vehemently.

"I knew it!" he said.

"Do you think they have him?"

Annja could only shrug; she didn't even know who "they" were and she said as much.

She stepped away from the tent, into the center of the camp, and turned in a slow circle, surveying the jungle surrounding them. She was looking for some hint, some clue, as to what they were dealing with.

She couldn't imagine one man overpowering Marcos, never mind doing it so quietly that none of them had been disturbed from their sleep. There had to have been at least two, maybe more. With that many people involved, chances were good that they'd left some evidence of their passing behind them, especially if they were dragging an unconscious Marcos between them, but there was nothing. No marks in the dirt. No broken or even bent branches or foliage.

It was just like the afternoon before.

Whoever these people were, they moved like ghosts.

Annja shook off the thought and addressed the others. "Marcos is pretty heavy, so maybe they didn't take him far. He might still be right here somewhere, just out of sight of the camp. Why don't the two of you search in that direction," she said, pointing upstream past the waterfall, "and I'll head this way. If you don't find any sign of him within fifteen minutes, turn back and regroup here."

"We'd better find him," Hugo said, "or somebody's going to pay."

He grabbed the rifle from his tent, and he and Claire headed toward the waterfall and the pool at its base, calling Marcos's name as they went.

Annja waited until they were out of sight and then called her sword to hand and headed off in the other direction. Splitting up at a time like this was a calculated risk; if there was someone out there, still watching them, Annja had just made herself a convenient target. On the other hand, they could cover much more territory if they split up and she, at least, was used to dealing with confrontations with those who had less than her best interests at heart. Putting Hugo and Claire together was a natural combination and created the best set of circumstances that they could hope for in a time like this.

She could hear Hugo's voice carrying on the light breeze, calling for Marcos, but Annja didn't do the same. For one, she didn't want Claire or Hugo to confuse her cries for those of Marcos looking for help, and two, she didn't want to give whoever might be out there any notice that she was on her way.

Whoever they were, they'd messed with her and those under her charge one too many times. Now it was time for payback.

In the end, it was Annja who found him.

She was moving through the trees, looking for signs

that someone had come through this way before her, when she heard the snarl of a large cat.

Jaguar, she thought.

She was about to head in the other direction, intentionally avoiding a confrontation with the local wildlife, when the thought reared up in the forefront of her brain.

Jaguar!

The cat's hunting cry came again and she took off at a run in the direction she thought it had come from, leading with her sword arm as she went.

Seconds later she came upon a small grove of ceiba trees, each one easily eight to twelve feet in diameter, with large, coiling roots that rose in hoops and swirls like the back of a sea serpent.

Annja's gaze was drawn to the base of one tree in particular, where, pacing back and forth in front of the trunk and looking upward, was one of the largest jaguars she'd ever seen.

The cat hadn't seen her yet, so she followed the direction of its gaze with her own, curious what it found so interesting. She gasped when she saw what it was looking at.

Marcos had been strung up against the trunk of the tree several feet in the air, his arms and legs spread-eagled and he was lashed to the tree with ropes made from vines. His head lolled against his chin, unmoving, his eyes were closed and his entire form was so covered in blood that Annja thought he'd been skinned alive when she first laid eyes upon him. She wondered why he hadn't cried out until she saw the gag that had been stuffed in his mouth and tied around at the back of his head to keep it in place.

To Annja, Marcos looked dead.

To the cat, however, he probably looked like an easy dinner, especially with all that blood, and the beast was none too happy about Annja's sudden appearance. It snarled a warning, a keening scream that sent the jungle around them into silence as the other creatures recognized the cry of the predator on the hunt.

Annja was tempted to scream right back at it, but she settled for bringing her sword around in the ready stance and grinning at the feisty feline.

In response, the cat lowered its front half to the ground, its face mere inches above the earth, its eyes locked on hers as its tail twitched back and forth.

"Here, kitty, kitty," Annja taunted, and the fire of battle rose in her heart as the cat charged at the sound of her voice.

20

The jaguar was a beautiful specimen, about one hundred and fifty kilograms of rippling golden-brown muscle covered with a pattern of black rosettes that undulated as it ran. It had yellow eyes and a dark tail that lashed back and forth in anger.

She hated to kill such a glorious creature but she didn't see how she was going to be able to chase it off. It saw her as the interloper in its meal; perhaps even the meal itself now, and it was going to fight to protect the same.

The cat bounded toward her on large padded feet that allowed it to move almost soundlessly, and Annja knew that if she caught a swipe of one of those massive paws across just about anywhere, she was in a host of trouble.

So don't let it connect, her inner voice told her.

Right. Easier said than done.

Then the cat was upon her and she didn't have any time for thought, just action.

The jaguar rushed in, closing to within three feet of Annja before skidding to a stop and rearing up on its hind legs, lashing out with its right paw while roaring at her from close range.

Something in the back of Annja's mind cataloged the

cry—the jaguar was the only cat in the western hemisphere that actually roared like a tiger or lion—but the rest of her was entirely focused on the battle unfurling mere inches away.

As one of the cat's big paws came lashing in, Annja struck out with her sword in turn, cutting a narrow slash across the outside of the cat's paw.

Sorry, kitty, but it's not going to be as easy as all that.

As if it heard her, the jaguar snarled, a harsh, rippling cry, and then lashed out again, once, twice, driving Annja backward, forcing her to keep her sword swinging frantically as she sought to keep those paws off her. The cat was trying to corner her against another tree, where it could kill her and then eat her at its leisure.

Annja twisted and turned, striking out with her sword every opportunity that she had, and before long both of them were bleeding from half a dozen minor wounds but neither side giving any inclination of giving up.

Then it happened.

The cat lashed out with its paw again, but this time the blow connected with the flat of Annja's weapon, ripping it free of her hands and sending it twisting and turning away somewhere into the thick foliage behind her.

If the cat had been capable of smiling, there was no doubt in Annja's mind that it would have in that moment.

Its yellow eyes gleamed wickedly as it let loose a final roar and charged.

Annja turned and ran directly at the tree behind her,

praying she'd be fast enough. The cat closed half the distance in a single bound.

Annja used the first of the ceiba roots that she came to as a springboard, pushing off with her left foot and bouncing to the next on her right, then jumping off with that one to bring her into contact with the trunk of the tree itself.

No sooner had her feet landed against the trunk of the ceiba tree than Annja threw herself backward in a Hail Mary move, flipping end over end as she sailed between the jaguar's paws even as it reared up, trying to catch her. She felt a claw tear down the outside of her calf, but she dismissed it, concentrating on her landing, knowing she was only going to get one chance.

She arced over the jaguar's head, hit the ground on her outstretched hands and tucked into a roll to bring her back around facing the cat. As she rolled upright she called her sword, opening her hand and feeling it slap into her palm with reassuring heft.

The cat had already shifted about, following her dive, and it leaped toward her with a stunning force.

Annja knelt there, sword thrust forward, and watched the big cat plunge toward its death, praying it wouldn't maul her too much in the process.

But the jaguar wasn't ready to die quite yet.

It had been wounded by the sword once already and recognized it as a threat, so as it dropped toward her the big cat twisted in midleap, pulling the majority of its body out of the path of the blade.

Instead of impaling the cat through the center of its chest, as Annja had planned, the sword took it through the shoulder instead. The cat's downward momentum forced its body down the length of the blade and it screamed in pain even as Annja went over backward with it atop her, using her feet to buck the beast up and over her head. She heaved it away from her, releasing her sword back into the otherwhere at the same time to avoid amputating the cat's leg in the process.

Annja rolled over and scrambled to her feet, snatching her sword back from the otherwhere in order to defend herself as the cat hit the ground and landed on its feet.

It turned to face her and for a moment Annja thought it was going to charge a second time, but at the flash of the sword in her hand, the cat apparently decided that discretion was the better part of valor.

It roared one last time and then slunk away into the trees, favoring its injured shoulder.

Annja paused, sword in hand, making sure it wasn't going to change its mind and come charging back. When it didn't, she climbed wearily to her feet and returned to Marcos.

Only to find him thrashing in his bonds, his arms and legs kicking weakly while odd choking noises came out of his mouth from behind the gag.

The sound galvanized Annja into action.

She rushed forward to the base of the tree, staring up at Marcos hanging there several feet above her head. It only took a few seconds for her to realize that the ropes holding him to the tree had been cleverly tied to become their own sort of prison and punishment rolled into one. If Marcos struggled, the ropes tied around his neck tightened, making it more difficult to breathe. The more difficult it became to breathe, the more Marcos struggled. It was devious and cruel but extremely effective, and Annja was amazed that the man had managed to hold out this long.

"Hang on, Marcos!" she called up to him. Standing on the highest root, she could only come up to eye level with his boots, but it did put her into striking range of the ropes if she used her sword.

She reared back and was about to call the sword to slash through the bindings nearest to her when something stopped her. She followed the ropes with her eyes, letting her gaze travel over the various lines and knots. That was when she recognized the problem.

If she cut the lower ropes, all of Marcos's weight would sag against the ropes tied about his neck, finishing the job they'd already started and strangling him to death. She'd have to climb higher and cut the upper ropes first, freeing his neck and eliminating the threat. At that point she could cut through the rest of the ropes once they had figured out how to support Marcos's big frame.

At this point the sword was just going to be a hindrance, so she sent it away with a thought. She was leaving herself vulnerable if their enemies were still around, but that was a chance she was going to have to take. She couldn't make it up the tree while holding the sword; she needed both hands for the climb.

She checked to be sure her knife was in its proper place on the sheath on her belt—she was going to need it in just a few minutes to cut Marcos loose—and then grabbed the trunk in front of her and started to climb.

It was slow going; the bark was slick with humidity and there weren't that many hand- or footholds to make it easy. Only her rock-climbing experience, particularly the skill of finding and sticking to minute holds, kept her from slipping right back down the trunk to where she started. Hand over hand, step after step, she worked her way upward.

She was almost into position to the side of Marcos when she heard Hugo calling her name from nearby.

"Over here!" she cried, and a few moments later Claire and Hugo rushed into the clearing.

"Quick! Support his legs!" Annja directed them. "We need to get the pressure off the ropes before they choke him to death!"

They jumped to do so, clambering up onto the roots just as Annja had before them in order to get high enough to reach Marcos's legs. While Claire steadied him, Hugo put his back to the tree trunk and tried to guide Marcos's feet onto his shoulders.

While the other two were getting into position, Annja was in the tree next to Marcos, thinking of a method to get him back down to the ground alive.

Unfortunately, she wasn't succeeding.

Without any other options available to her, Annja did the only thing she could.

She used her knife to slash through the ropes and watched Marcos tumble forward, landing on the ground in a heap in front of Hugo.

21

It was a good thing Marcos was as tough as an ox. Otherwise, the ordeal might have caused him permanent harm. As it was, he'd be talking in a rattling hiss until his vocal chords recovered and be sporting so many bruises that his body looked as if it had been covered in a quilt dyed black and blue.

After rinsing off all the blood and then assessing Marcos's injuries and overall condition, Claire made the decision to remain there in the camp by the waterfall for an extra day to give Marcos time to rest and recover. Annja didn't think it was a smart move—as long as the enemy knew their position, they were sitting ducks—but Claire would not be dissuaded. The three of them took turns standing watch, rifle in hand.

Marcos regained consciousness later that morning. He'd come through his experience surprisingly unscathed. A bit of rest and he'd be ready to travel again soon. Annja left him alone to recover for most of the day, but as evening rolled around she slipped inside his tent and asked him if he could remember anything about what had happened.

"Not much," he told her, his voice a hoary rasp.

"Flashes of this and that. I don't think it will be much help."

Annja smiled, trying to be encouraging. "Tell me, anyway. Sometimes two seemingly unrelated pieces of information combine to give you the answers you're looking for almost before you realize it."

He shrugged and did what she asked.

"I woke up when somebody slapped a sharp-smelling rag over my nose and mouth. Without thinking about it I sucked in some air to yell, which sent whatever they'd soaked the rag with down into my lungs. I started to get dizzy immediately, which I'm sure was the point. I had the sense that there were two, maybe three, guys in the tent with me, holding me down, and then everything went dark."

Annja wasn't surprised. She'd assumed that they'd drugged him in some fashion; otherwise, he would have alerted the rest of them.

"When I came to, I was hanging in that tree with those ropes around my neck. They slit the neck of a pig and directed the stream of blood pulsing out of it so that it splashed all over my face and chest. They laughed when I struggled and tried to get away, because every move I made forced the noose tighter about my neck." Marcos shuddered at the memory.

"Did they say anything to you?" Annja asked.

"Not to me, but they did talk among themselves."

That caught Annja's attention. "Did you understand anything they said?"

He shook his head. "Some of it sounded kind of familiar, but most of it was just gibberish."

Annja was disappointed. She'd been hoping Marcos

would confirm her suspicions that it was a rival team trying to drive them off, but he hadn't seen or heard enough for his information to be of much use to her.

"Any idea who they were?" Marcos asked.

"They were long gone by the time we found you. You can rest easy, though. We'll be posting a guard and standing watch all night. If they come back, we'll be ready for them."

She turned toward the door, intending to leave him to his rest, when he said, "I don't know what it means, but they said one word several times."

Annja looked back at him. "And that was?"

"*Uthurunku.* Whatever that is."

Annja frowned. "Are you sure? Just like that— *uthurunku?*"

Marcos nodded. "Is it important?"

"I don't know," she replied, carefully keeping her expression neutral. "But at least it gives us a starting point."

She flashed another smile and then slipped out the door.

Uthurunku.

She knew that word.

Her fascination with archaeology had taken Annja to a lot of places in the world, many of which were the kinds of places that were off the beaten track. Finding someone who spoke English in those areas was often difficult and she'd gotten in the habit of learning a smattering of phrases in the local language while working a dig site. Usually they were simple sayings designed to help her communicate with the locals—*hello, goodbye, my name is Annja,* that kind of thing. Sometimes they were warnings about dangers lurking nearby. Being fluent in several different languages was certainly useful when amid the culture and etiquette of the big cities, but when you were squatting to have dinner with the Bushmen of the Kalahari or fashioning a mud mask with the Asaro peoples of Papua New Guinea, it was the little phrases that got you by.

Annja had been in Peru, working a dig at Ingapirca, when she'd first heard the word *uthurunku*. Several of the locals had been hired to help clear back some vegetation at the edge of the forest and Annja had gone with them. They'd mimed the image of a stalking cat and had repeated the word several times.

Uthurunku meant "jaguar" in Quechua, the language of the indigenous peoples of the Andes region of South America. Unlike other indigenous languages, it was still spoken by more than eight million people across the countries of Bolivia, Peru, Ecuador, Colombia and Argentina.

Quechua was also the language of the Inca.

First the representations of the death god and now this.

What on earth was going on?

"Did you learn anything?"

Annja spun around, startled by Claire's sudden presence. She'd been so wrapped up in her thoughts that she hadn't heard the other woman approach.

"No, not really," Annja lied, shaking her head. "They drugged him while he was half-asleep, so he really didn't see anything that could help us."

Claire glanced at the darkness beginning to gather amid the trees surrounding them and then back at

Annja. She shook her head. "I'm worried, Annja. What if Richard ran into the very same people? He couldn't possibly survive what Marcos just went through."

"All the more reason to press on as soon as we can," Annja told her. "Marcos is doing well. I'm sure he'll be able to travel in the morning. How far are we from our destination?"

"Half a day's hike, maybe a little more."

"Then we should have some answers by midday tomorrow. Hang in there, Claire. We'll know soon enough. I'm sure he's all right."

But she wasn't sure, not really, and as she walked away she wondered just what they had gotten themselves into. The treasure was worth millions and that kind of wealth attracted more than its fair share of unscrupulous people who would stop at nothing to possess it for themselves.

Given the events of that morning, Annja thought the chances of finding Dr. Knowles alive and well were swiftly dwindling. Marcos's captors had clearly intended for him to perish at the hands of the jaguar they'd lured to his side with the fresh blood from that wild pig, and it wasn't such a stretch to think that they would have been equally ruthless in dealing with Knowles.

She hoped there was a simple explanation for why Knowles had lost contact with his wife, she really did, but after today, she wasn't going to put money on it.

THANKFULLY, THE NIGHT PASSED without incident and by midmorning Marcos announced that he felt fit enough to travel. They quickly broke camp, packed their gear and then pulled out the map in order to check their position relative to that of their destination.

When asked about the details of their destination, Claire pulled out a piece of paper and handed it to Annja. The paper was an email, sent by Dr. Knowles, noting the discovery of an "iron-banded sea chest" inside a "narrow cave that showed signs of previous excavation." The email gave GPS coordinates for the specific location and noted that the team was planning to begin excavating the rear of the cave the morning after the email was sent.

Annja memorized the coordinates and was about to hand the email back to Claire when the header caught her attention. She let her gaze flick over it and saw that the email had not been sent to Claire, but rather to a Matt Davis at the Science Channel. For a moment she was confused—*Who is Matt Davis? Why wasn't the email sent to Claire?*—but then realized that the Science Channel, a cable television channel about twice the size of her own, had probably financed Knowles's expedition. Knowles's email was probably just one of the many progress updates required by such an agreement. Heaven knew she'd made enough of them herself over the years.

She made note of the name.

If someone had leaked information about Knowles's expedition, then Davis was as much a possible source for that as anyone else at this point. There was nothing she could do about it right now, but she had every intention of tracking down that leak when all was said and done.

Satisfied that they were literally on the right track,

Annja led the way into the jungle once more. Gone was the casual atmosphere that had governed their first day of travel. Now all of them were constantly checking the jungle around them, knowing their enemies were out there, somewhere, and not wanting to be surprised a second time.

Annja concentrated on getting the group where they needed to go with a minimum of delay.

Their course took them out of the lowland jungle and into an area of slightly higher elevation away from the coast as they began to make their way into the foothills leading to Mount Yglesias on the far side of the island.

Several times during the morning's journey they came to places where the trail split off in different directions and each time Annja found Knowles's trademark *K* carved into a nearby tree or scratched on a rock. Annja knew their enemies might have noticed the markings and might have gone so far as to alter them in an attempt to throw them off the trail, so she made a point of checking each one against the GPS signal to ensure that they were always accurate.

Better safe than sorry.

They took a short break to replenish the fluids they were losing in the high humidity and then pushed on. The sooner they reached their destination, the sooner their questions would be answered.

Or so they thought.

Reality, however, had another surprise in store for them.

Knowles and his team had made camp just south of a long, winding ridgeline of dark rock that rose out of the jungle like the blade of a knife, neatly bisecting the island in two. They had cut a clearing out of the undergrowth and erected their tents in three orderly rows with wide footpaths between and a communal mess tent at the far end.

Annja was surprised. Most expedition camps were disorderly affairs, with tents erected hither and yon for no particular reason at all. It was almost as if, in reaction to the necessary order and precision of their daily work, the archaeologists needed an outlet for the chaotic side of their souls and a haphazard camp was one way of allowing for that.

But not this camp. No, this one was laid out with almost military precision.

It was also completely deserted. They searched the camp, top to bottom, and didn't find a single soul. There was an empty feeling in the air, like a circus after it closed for the night and all the marks had gone home and the lights had gone dark. It was beyond empty, if that made any kind of sense, and Annja knew that her fears had been right—something bad had happened here.

"How many people did you say your husband had with him?" she asked as they walked between the rows of silent tents, peering into their interiors and wondering what had happened to them all.

"Fifteen," Claire replied. "Nine scientists and grad students plus six porters to help carry the gear and anything they recovered from the dig."

Fifteen people.

Vanished.

22

Cave of the Unknown
Isla del Coco

They had reached their destination and were no closer to finding the answers they needed than they'd been days before back in Puntarenas. Annja found that totally unacceptable.

"All right, let's spread out and find the dig site. Perhaps we'll get some answers there," she said, and the four of them got to work.

It didn't take long.

The cave mentioned in the email, the one where Knowles had discovered the seaman's chest, turned out to be less than a hundred yards away at the foot of the ridge. The entrance was low to the ground and very narrow, more a fissure in the rock than an actual tunnel opening. If they had come this way several days ago, they probably would have walked right past; it wasn't immediately obvious that the opening led anywhere. But given the amount of effort Knowles and his crew had spent pulling back the vegetation surrounding the entrance, it was clear that there was something worth exploring here.

Annja slipped off her pack and dug around inside until she found her headlamp. She slipped it on, tightening the Velcro strap to keep it from sliding around on her forehead, and then triggered the LED light to test it. Satisfied, she crouched down and peered inside the opening.

The entrance was narrow, yes, but it grew into a slightly wider tunnel about three feet past the entrance, and she could see the mouth of what she took to be a small cavern roughly six feet after that.

It would be a tight squeeze at first, but then she should be free and clear.

Not any worse than some of the other things you've done on a dig in the past.

She turned to Claire and the others and said, "I'm going in to have a quick look around. If there's anything worth seeing, I'll whistle and that will be your signal to come in after me."

"All of us?"

Annja nodded. "Safety in numbers and all that."

The truth of the matter was that one guard wasn't going to do all that much good against the kind of thing that could make an entire camp full of people disappear, so why leave someone alone and vulnerable? Better to have the entire team together in the same place to make a concerted effort to deal with any threats that might arise.

"When it comes to this kind of stuff, you're the boss," Claire said.

Annja gave her a grin and then turned, took a deep breath and slid into the cave mouth on her belly. Her headlamp illuminated the way ahead in a wide arc that made it easy to see where she was headed. For the first few moments she was very aware of the nearness of the rock around her, pressing against her stomach and back, but she did what she could to put it out of her mind and continue forward, one foot at a time.

After the first few feet, the tunnel opened up enough to allow her to get up off her belly and move along in a crouch, but it wasn't until she reached the main cavern ahead of her that she could actually stand upright.

Her light spilled out ahead of her, illuminating the cavern. It was bigger than she'd expected and longer than it was wide. If she had to guess she'd put it in the neighborhood of fifty by seventy-five feet, with the ceiling at least twenty feet above her head.

The rear wall of the cavern had partially collapsed at some point in the past, and it was around and amid the rockfall from that collapse that Dr. Knowles had focused his excavation. The area in front of the wall had been sectioned off into a grid with ropes and stakes, allowing the archaeologists to properly record the original location and position of any artifacts that they pulled from the earth.

To the left of the grid and running parallel to the side wall of the cavern stood several wood-framed sifters, used to sift for smaller artifacts through the earth brought up during the excavation. Several temporary tables, made from semirigid pieces of plastic unfurled across packing crates and bolted down at the corners, stood beside the shifters and held half a dozen artifact boxes.

Inside the cavern, the heavy, cloying scent of the jungle gave way to the dusty smell of rock and dirt.

It was quiet, too; all that rock blocked the very present noise of the jungle, reinforcing the sense that she'd just stepped inside a long-sealed tomb. Annja hoped it wasn't a literal tomb and also that she wouldn't find the bodies of the missing archaeologists stacked in the corner somewhere by persons unknown.

She stood in the cavern entrance for another moment or two and then decided that nothing was going to come charging out of the cave at her. Satisfied, she crossed the floor of the cave to reach the excavation proper.

It seemed as if they'd been working hard for some time, given the amount of activity happening. More than half of the grid squares had been excavated, some to a depth of eight feet or more. A glance at the artifact boxes on the table showed a small but growing collection of items unearthed from the dig—from musket balls to brass hinges and even a few gold coins. A partially reassembled sea chest stood on a table off to the side, and Annja wondered if that was the one Knowles had emailed about.

A cool breeze slipped across her face in a gentle caress, catching her attention. She turned, looking for the source. She was too far from the entrance she'd come through for that to be the cause....

The tunnel mouth was to the side of the rockfall, behind a freestanding shelf that blocked a direct view of it. It was wider than the one she'd entered through; she would have no trouble standing upright in it.

It extended past the reach of her light.

Curiosity beckoned.

She hesitated, considered giving the signal and having the others join her, but she was caught up in the thrill of discovery and decided that making certain the passageway was secure before bringing in the others was the more prudent thing to do.

A closer look showed her that the original tunnel had been blocked by the same rockfall that Knowles's team had been excavating; the current opening was considerably smaller than the width of the passage just beyond it. Marks in the earth around the opening showed where the others had widened it, creating a hole wide enough for a person to slip through, and that was precisely what Annja did at that point.

Once on the other side, she adjusted her headlamp, then called her sword to hand.

She made her way along the tunnel, cautious of the uneven floor beneath her feet, knowing help was a long way off if she unexpectedly injured herself. She kept one hand on the wall to her left and held her sword out before her with the other, ready to take on anything that came out of the dark at her. She trusted her instincts, and the blade, to get her out of trouble if things got too hairy.

The passage ran straight ahead at first and then turned into a series of switchbacks that had Annja cautiously peering around each corner before continuing forward, convinced each time that some danger lurked just beyond. Just as she was starting to relax, she rounded another turn and found herself outside the tunnel complex, staring at the jungle no more than three feet in front of her.

The tunnel had apparently taken her completely beneath the ridgeline and out the opposite side!

She glanced around, curious if any of Knowles's people had come this way, when she saw something through the trees. It looked man-made, but she couldn't be certain without getting a better view, so that was what she decided to do.

She pushed through the waist-high undergrowth and ducked beneath a few branches before emerging into a small clearing.

In the middle of the clearing was a graveyard.

Annja stood and stared, her mind having trouble reconciling the mounds of earth with their wooden and stone crosses with the knowledge that she was hundreds of miles from any known civilization.

Then it hit her.

Had she found the missing archaeologists?

23

Annja moved forward, each step seeming to take forever as her gaze roamed over the graves before her and she mentally cataloged the details as they jumped out at her.

The crosses made from weathered planks.

The lichen-covered stones that carefully surrounded each mound.

The overgrowth of jungle grasses over each grave.

These are not recent, not by a long shot.

She stood over the nearest grave marker and stared down at it, then bent and ran her fingers along the faint grooves in the wood where something had once been written. It was faded by long exposure to the harsh tropical climate, but the word seemed to be *Ellis*.

An Englishman, then, she thought.

She quickly counted and discovered that there were nine graves in all. Each of them was in the same basic state of disrepair due to age and weather. Annja had the gut feeling that whoever had buried these men had done so at the same time; the graves were the result of a tragedy, rather than natural causes, then. She certainly couldn't prove it, but it felt right to her.

Feels right? Very scientific, Annja.

She was intrigued by the puzzle and wanted to stay to see what else she could learn, but she knew she'd been gone long enough. The others were no doubt growing concerned and she acknowledged it was time to let them know what she'd found.

Annja retraced her steps through the tunnel and back into the main cavern. It only took a few minutes for the others to join her after she gave the signal. She'd been right; they'd been getting antsy and were debating whether or not to come in after her when she'd returned.

She led them into the cavern and waited while they examined the same things she had, then brought them down the passageway and out to the clearing beyond. Annja warned Claire ahead of time, not wanting her to have a similar reaction as the one she'd experienced. The four of them stood before the graves, staring at them in fascination.

"Who do you think they were?" Marcos asked at last.

"Hard to say. We're certainly not the first to explore the island," Annja said, "but I don't remember hearing about any of the earlier expeditions losing this many people."

"Maybe they were pirates," Claire suggested, "and their leader killed them to keep the location of the treasure they'd just buried a secret from everyone else."

Marcos frowned, then shook his head. "Burying them so close to the treasure is a bit of a—excuse the expression—dead giveaway, don't you think?"

Before Claire could answer, he said, "Besides, why would they go through the trouble of digging nine extra graves if they'd just dug a hole big enough to bury the treasure in? Seems it would be easier to just bury it all together at that point."

Ever the archaeologist, Annja wondered what they would find if they excavated one of the graves. Contrary to the old saying, in the hands of a competent archaeologist, dead men did tell tales and often rather intricate ones at that.

"Maybe they're from that boat."

Hugo's voice startled her out of her own internal speculations.

Boat?

Annja looked in the direction in which he was pointing but all she saw was jungle.

What boat? What is he talking about?

She stared, trying to see through the tangled mass of jungle greenery, looking for what he was referring to, but she still wasn't getting it. Beside her Claire gasped…and then Annja saw it.

A woman's face, gazing out at her from the foliage.

Her hair was thick and piled atop her head in an elegant coiffure, while her eyes were open wide and gazing outward toward the horizon. A large crack split her brow just above her left ear, giving her a strange, lopsided appearance.

The moment Annja recognized it for what it was— the figurehead on the front of a sailing ship—she saw the rest of the boat looming there amid the trees as easily as if someone had just lit up the entire structure with blinking neon lights. The bowsprit, covered with vines, jutting out over the figurehead as if pointing back in their direction.

The round curvature of the bow.

The dark, gaping holes of the gun ports.

A sailing ship was the last thing she'd expected to see in the middle of the jungle, so her gaze had glanced right over it previously without seeing it for what it was. Now that she knew it was there, it was impossible to ignore.

What was a sailing ship doing in the middle of the jungle, miles from shore?

And how had it gotten here in the first place?

It was too big a mystery to resist.

Annja strode forward, intent on taking a closer look at the ship and getting some answers to the hundreds of questions now whirling about inside her head. She barely noticed the others following her.

She walked right up to the ship and put out a hand to touch it, subconsciously assuring herself that it was real, that there was indeed a sailing ship resting upright between several palm trees as though cradled in their grasp.

This close, the wreck resolved itself into a truly massive vessel. At least three, possibly four, decks high, it rose nearly fifty feet above her head and was probably close to two hundred feet in length. The jungle had wrapped it in its embrace, and vegetation now grew over it in a riot of green leaves and colored flowers, but even so it was easily recognizable for what it was.

A British man-of-war.

Annja felt a wave of excitement sweep over her as she stared up at the surprisingly well-preserved vessel. Pieces of information were starting to click together in the back of her mind, and one suspicion in particular just wouldn't let her go. To see if she was right, she grabbed Hugo and dragged him around to the stern of the ship. She pulled out the machete she carried in her pack and had Hugo help her up into the branches of a nearby tree. From there she climbed higher until she reached the windows looking into the captain's wardroom at the rear of the ship. Just above the windows was a flat stretch of hull on which the ship's name was usually fashioned. Right now, that area was more than half-covered with leaves and other green debris.

Annja began to cut and chop away at the vegetation covering the nameplate, until it didn't take long to reveal the name that was painted across the stern in foothigh letters that were still surprisingly readable after all this time.

HMS *Reliant*.

All Annja could do was stand there and stare, for she couldn't quite believe what she was seeing.

Her Majesty's *Reliant* was the British man-of-war that had defeated the *Mary Dear* and taken her captain and crew into custody. *Reliant*'s captain, Russell Jeffries, hung the entire crew of the *Mary Dear* for murder and piracy on the high seas, sparing only the lives of Captain Thompson and his first mate. Some said that Jeffries did so only in exchange for the location of the Treasure of Lima, but that was all conjecture because the *Reliant* had vanished from history shortly after that.

It seemed she was back for an encore.

A shout broke into her thoughts. "Over here! I've found a way in!"

Annja followed the sound of Marcos's voice to find him standing near a large hole in the hull on the starboard side of the wreckage. Seeing the damage it was immediately clear that the ship would never be sea-worthy again without spending several months in dry dock, but that hadn't stopped someone from trying to seal off the entrance by nailing loose planks over the opening. To Annja it seemed more as if they were try-ing to keep out the local wildlife than make any real attempt at repair, but either way, it still gave them an important piece of information.

At least one person had lived through the wreck.

Lived and cared enough to try to keep themselves and anyone who was with them safe afterward.

As Annja and the others looked on, Marcos stepped forward and kicked with a booted foot at one of the lower planks. With a squeal of nails and the sound of splintering wood, the plank came free.

Marcos looked back, grinned and set upon the bar-rier with a vengeance. Less than five minutes later the way into the wreckage was clear.

The darkness beyond seemed to beckon to them.

Annja reached up and activated her headlamp, checked to be certain the others were doing the same and then led the way inside the ship.

24

Annja had once been a guest aboard a full-scale work-ing replica of Admiral Nelson's flagship, the *Temeraire,* and had been given a rather extensive tour by a good-looking British sailor who was determined to show her every nook and cranny of the place. As she stepped in-side the *Reliant,* she was suddenly grateful she'd agreed to take the man's tour.

Her light cut the darkness ahead of her and she could see that they'd entered the hold. Rotting piles of cloth, mostly likely spare sails, were stacked next to a dozen or more sealed barrels. The barrels were roped together and tied to the bulkhead to keep them from moving in heavy weather. Next to those were piles of spare rigging and hawser ropes, equally secured. A jumbled mass of additional supplies rested against the rear wall of the hold. To Annja it looked as if someone had made an at-tempt to clean up what would have been a terrible mess after the ship arrived here and, finally seeing the use-lessness of it all, had simply shoved it to one side to be picked over at leisure.

"Over there," Claire said, pointing to a ladder extending down into the hold from the deck above.

They were halfway across the hold when something screamed and came charging at them from the darkness on the far side of the room.

Marcos was closest to whatever it was and it charged right at him. Annja had a glimpse of something heavy and low to the ground racing forward toward him and then Marcos's gun spoke, the sound echoing in the confined space. The thing staggered, then slowed, giving Marcos time to fire again before it crashed into him, driving him to the ground beneath its weight.

Annja didn't want to draw her sword in front of so many witnesses, so she drew her knife instead and leaped to his side, ready to give whatever help was needed. Peripherally she was aware of Hugo and Claire doing the same.

Their lights fell upon the carcass of the wild pig that was stretched out atop Marcos's frame, pinning his gun arm to the floor, and then on his disgusted expression as his own lamp illuminated the pig's snout just inches from his face.

"Get this hairy thing off me!" he hollered, pushing at it with his free hand.

Laughing, Hugo said, "That hairy thing is dinner, amigo, so stop insulting it," but bent to help him just the same.

Once Marcos was back on his feet, it was quickly decided that the pig's carcass was going to attract other animals and therefore couldn't be left inside the hold. The solution was for the two men to drag it outside and then hang it in a tree. Only when they were finished did they resume their search of the *Reliant*.

The room above the hold was small and contained a fair bit of lumber, now warped and molded from years in the humid weather, suggesting that it was probably the carpenter's storeroom. They passed quickly through it into several other storerooms, all in the same dilapidated state, before finding a stairwell leading upward.

Their eventual goal was the captain's wardroom, which, if Annja recalled her tour of the *Temeraire* properly, would be on the upper gun deck toward the stern of the ship. To get there they would have to climb up several decks and then head aft. The next set of stairs took them up to what Annja recognized as the lower gun deck, the light coming in from the gun ports throughout the room making it easier to see. The cannons, of course, were a dead giveaway. She counted twelve cannons still in their respective gun ports, the wheels of their support cradles chocked in place to keep them from moving unexpectedly. Several more cannons were lying haphazardly about the deck; thankfully, the ship was fairly level and the heavy iron wouldn't be rolling anywhere soon.

Hammocks had been strung across the port side of the deck between the beams of the ship. As Annja's light swept across the hammocks, she thought she saw something glinting from within the folds of the one closest to her.

She moved closer.

"Annja?"

Claire's voice.

Annja held up a hand in a "hang on a sec" gesture.

Closer now, she could see that the canvas of the hammock was weighted down by something inside it.

"Did you find something?"

Annja reached the hammock and looked inside.

The yellowed skeleton of one of the *Reliant*'s crew members lay nestled in the fabric, its empty eyes staring and its mouth locked forever open in a silent scream.

Annja must have started in surprise, for Claire gave a yell and the others came rushing over.

"I'm fine, I'm fine," Annja said. "Just wasn't expecting to find we had company."

She bent over to take a closer look. She saw that the skeleton still wore the tattered remains of a sailor's shirt and breeches, but what was more interesting was the fact that he had been secured in the hammock with leather straps and buckles. They were loose now, of course, but given how his arms were lying parallel to the rest of his skeleton, it was safe to assume that the straps had been used to immobilize him. Whether he'd been alive or not at the time was another issue entirely.

"Here's another one," Marcos called from a hammock a few feet away.

"And another," Claire echoed.

In the end, they found ten men in all. Each and every one of them had been strapped into their hammocks, and that, more than anything else, made Annja uneasy. Clearly they hadn't done that to themselves; if they had, they would have left their hands free. No, these men had been bound by a third party.

"Maybe they mutinied over the treasure," Claire said.

Annja didn't think so. Mutineers were usually dealt

with quickly. If they weren't hanged, they were usually locked in leg irons and left on deck.

These men had been held down with belts.

Not the most secure material out there.

"Maybe they were seasick," said Hugo.

Everyone laughed but Annja.

Maybe they were sick....

Annja's mind was racing as she saw Marcos reaching out to take the ring off the finger of one of the skeletons.

Fear seized her throat, threatened to swallow her words when she needed them the most.

"Don't touch them!" she forced out around the lump forming there, and breathed a sigh of relief as Marcos snatched his hand back.

"Come on, woman!" Marcos exclaimed. "Don't scare me like that!" But he stepped away from the hammock just the same.

"Annja might be right. They were probably sick and the ship's doctor strapped them in to keep them from infecting everyone else."

The others began to back away from the hammocks.

"If they were sick, I doubt any pathogens would have lasted this long, but better safe than sorry. I think we should move on, anyway."

No one argued with her.

In fact, they all decided that it was time to see who could get up the stairs the fastest.

With a final glance at the mystery she was leaving behind, Annja followed.

The next set of stairs took them up another deck, emerging into a passageway outside several cabins. Annja knew that none of them were the captain's—

that would be up at least one more deck—but that didn't stop the others from investigating.

Inside each cabin was a small table and chair, a dresser with several drawers and a hanging cot that resembled a box with bedding in it.

"Funny-looking bed," Marcos said, giving the first one they came to a little push to set it swinging back and forth. "Looks like a coffin."

"That's because it is one," Annja told him. "The officer would be buried in it if he died at sea."

Marcos didn't touch any more hanging cots after that.

Marcos, Claire and Hugo went through several of the officers' cabins but emerged each time disappointed. To their eyes, there wasn't much of value to be found— a few personal items made of gold or silver that might fetch a few dollars if presented to the right buyer—but Annja knew better. The ship had vanished into history and had been presumed lost with all hands on board. Even a crew member's simple shirt would fetch a fair price at auction as a result, and there were several to be had among the cabins, including what looked to be a full-dress uniform for a royal marine.

Annja didn't say anything, however. The material here belonged in a museum and not in some private collection somewhere. She'd inform the British government of the ship's location when they got back.

After they discovered what happened to Dr. Knowles.

It seemed strange to Annja that Claire hadn't mentioned her husband's disappearance since arriving at the camp, but then again Annja hadn't been dealing with the stress for weeks the way Claire had. Perhaps just being near the archaeologists' camp had settled her down and then the subsequent discovery of the *Reliant* had simply kept her occupied.

But still…

She was about to say something to Claire when Hugo opened the door ahead of them and found the stairs they'd been looking for, the ones leading to the deck above. He gestured for Annja to go first and she took advantage of doing so, climbing the steps to the doorway at the top.

Opening the door, Annja found herself on the upper gun deck, the middle portion of which, where she now stood, was open to the sky above. She found the sunlight exceptionally bright after the darkened interior they'd just passed through.

Annja glanced along the length of the ship, forward toward the bow. It seemed Mother Nature didn't like her territory being invaded. The upper deck was practically drowning beneath a sea of vines and creepers, making it appear like a carpet of green had taken over the vessel. Here and there objects thrust skyward out of the covering—the truncated shaft of a mast, the blunt end of a cannon, even the vent from the Brodie stove down in the galley below.

Looking aft, Annja could see the rounded shape of the ship's wheel and then, past that, the door to the captain's wardroom tucked away beneath the poop deck.

Like a missile following a homing beacon, Annja headed directly for that door, knowing that the room she was actually looking for, the captain's personal cabin, lay to one side or the other of the wardroom.

All it took was a few steps into the wardroom for

Annja to know that she'd just entered senior-officer country. Light streamed in from the row of windows at the back of the room, which was also the stern of the boat itself; Annja's and Hugo's efforts to clear the name-plate had also cleared some of the vegetation growing over the windows. The room was large and its space was dominated by a rectangular table carved of dark teakwood, surrounded by eight chairs of the same. Table settings in both silver and porcelain stood in glass cases along one wall. A chart case occupied another.

For all the splendor, Annja barely noticed. Her attention was drawn almost immediately to the doors on either side of the room. One of the doors on the starboard side seemed to be situated a bit off to the side from the others, so she crossed the room and tried that one first.

The door was locked.

Annja smiled. Every other door they'd encountered on this ship so far had been unlocked, with the exception of this one. Her confidence that she had chosen the right one went up a notch.

She glanced behind her, saw that the others still hadn't joined her and decided to take a chance. She called her sword to hand and inserted the blade between the door and the jamb, parallel to the keyhole. When she was satisfied with its position, she gave the blade a good shove, putting considerable pressure on the lock in the process.

The door popped open with a snap.

"Annja?"

A thought sent the sword back easily into the otherwhere, and she turned just as Claire stepped into the doorway of the wardroom.

"Here," Annja called, drawing the other woman's attention. Of course, if worse came to worst, she could claim to have picked up the weapon from the wardroom table. This was a British warship, after all, and swords were fairly common shipboard weapons.

"Find anything interesting?" Claire asked as their other two companions came up behind her.

Annja gestured at the now-open door in front of her. "Captain's cabin. Perhaps now we'll get some answers."

25

Annja stepped into the cabin and was followed by the others. Her gaze swept across the space, taking it in. It was far more luxurious than even the officers' cabins they'd examined below. A large poster bed stood to one side. Next to that was a hand-carved wooden wardrobe, its slightly open doors revealing several of the captain's uniforms hanging inside. A table with two chairs stood in the far corner, for use when the captain wished to dine alone or with a single guest in the privacy of his quarters. Two large windows, one of which had been broken at some point in the past, allowed a fair bit of light into the room.

But it was the presence of a writing desk and the item atop the desk that caught Annja's attention.

She crossed the room and looked down at the leather-bound journal resting there, knowing instinctively that it was the ship's logbook. The page to which it was open had been damaged by weather, most likely that coming in from the broken window nearby, but a quick check showed that other pages were still intact and legible.

Here, in this book, might be the answers they were seeking, Annja realized.

She looked up at the others. "The ship's log might give us some clue as to where to go next, but it'll take some time to look through it."

Marcos scoffed. "Do you really think a book that's been sitting on that table rotting for the past two hundred years is going to help us find Dr. Knowles?"

Annja nodded. "I do."

"Clearly the heat's been getting to you, then," Marcos retorted.

"I don't know, Marcos," Claire said, stepping in. "Maybe Annja's right. It appears that some of the crew survived. Maybe there was something they saw or experienced that might have some bearing on what happened to Dr. Knowles and his team."

She looked at Annja. "See what you can find. Since we don't know where we're headed after this, we might as well camp here for the night and come up with a working plan for tomorrow."

Claire faced the group. "Tents first and then we'll see about dressing that pig," she told them, then hustled them out of the cabin.

Thankful that Claire had seen things her way, Annja settled into a nearby chair and began to read.

She started with the earlier pages in the journal, which were largely intact. Captain Jeffries had a fine, spidery script that made it easy to read, as well.

The journal told the whole sorry tale.

Captain Jeffries had sighted the *Mary Dear* off the coast of Panama and had given chase, eventually engaging in a running gun battle that ended only when

Jeffries utilized the marines he had at his disposal to board the other vessel and take her by force. The charges against Thompson had been simple, straightforward and beyond much doubt. A trial presided over by Jeffries found Thompson and his crew guilty of murder and piracy. The crew members were hung from the mizzenmast in sets of three, until only Thompson and his first mate were left.

Thompson pleaded for Jeffries to spare his life, one captain to another, and the British commander had agreed to do so, provided Thompson led them to the location where he'd buried the treasure.

With little choice before him, Thompson agreed.

Annja had assumed all of that; the story as outlined by Captain Jeffries was the same as that which had come down through history.

She flipped ahead, seeking something more relevant. She found it several pages later.

October 2
I am astounded that I am alive to write this, for the events of the past forty-eight hours have been a nightmare unlike any I have ever experienced. Only by the Lord's grace and blessing did we make it through at all, though the cost has been considerable.

The morning of September 30 dawned calm and clear. Having retrieved the treasure from Cocos Island the night before, we rendezvoused with the *Mary Dear* off the leeward side of the island and spent most of the morning transferring half of the treasure to her holds. I told Lieutenant

Johann that it was to protect the Crown's invest-
ment should one of our ships run into difficulty
on the return voyage; at the time I had no idea just
how prophetic I was being.

When the loading was finished, a full comple-
ment of crew members, along with dispatches I'd
prepared for the admiralty, were sent over to the
other ship with orders for Johann to make for Bris-
tol at the best possible speed. His was the lighter,
faster ship and I expected him to arrive at least
three days before I would.

We saw them off with a six-gun salute and then
returned to work repairing the last of the damage
Reliant had sustained during her confrontation
with the *Mary Dear* when she was under Captain
Thompson's command.

The storm began about midway through the afternoon watch and grew worse by the hour. The
nearness of the island began to make me nervous,
and as the swells increased in size, so, too, did my
anxiety. As the first dogwatch dawned, I had the
men haul anchor and pointed the *Reliant* toward
the open ocean.

Better to ride out the storm in deep water than
get battered about on the reef, I thought.

No sooner had we turned for open water than
I heard the lookout in the main-mast crow's nest
give a shout. He was hard to see in the rain, but
after a moment I realized that he was pointing
frantically toward the horizon. I dug out my spy-
glass and stared hard into the night, searching for
whatever it was that had gotten him so worked

up. Lightning flashed and what I saw in its light has been carved indelibly onto the inside of my eyelids for all time.

The largest wave I have ever seen filled the horizon and was looming down upon us.

We had one chance and I took it. There was no time to turn about for we'd be caught halfway through the maneuver and swamped by the force of the wave. Same held true for trying to outrun it. The *Reliant* was a 2100-ton vessel without the treasure aboard her. She could lumber about like a behemoth but that was about it. No way did she have the guts to outrun it.

Our only chance was to climb straight up it.

There was no time to furl the sails, so I gave the order to have them cut away. We had more in the hold, so replacing them wouldn't be difficult. The crew jumped to carry out the order without hesitation—they were good men and had been trained well—but even so, by the time the last rope had been severed, the wave had gained on us considerably.

The helmsmen and his crew had just enough time to carry out my orders to bring the boat about, aiming the bow right for the heart of the oncoming wave, before the wave reached our location.

It towered above us, a veritable wall of water that had to be at least a thousand feet high. Up, up, up the face of the wave we went until we were all but vertical on the face of it. At that moment the lowest part of the wave struck the reefs surrounding Cocos and the wave crested, smashing down upon us and sending us flipping away from it like a cork from a bottle lost on the high seas.

Somewhere in the midst of all the bouncing and battering I lost consciousness.

I awoke to the silence of the dead.

The rogue wave carried us several miles inland before depositing us like so much rejected flotsam in the middle of a stretch of decimated jungle. We are sitting more or less upright, the hull wedged between what is left of a dozen trees. A ten-foot hole on the aft section of the port-side hull will need to be repaired before we can even think about being seaworthy again, but I am not in a rush to assign a detail to repair it. It seems futile; there is no way to get the ship back to the coast even if we could fix the damage to the hull.

The loss of life in the storm was significant. Of all the souls that were aboard the *Reliant* when we bid goodbye to the *Mary Dear,* only forty-five remain. Of those forty-five, only eleven, counting myself, are actually fit for duty. The damage to our company is staggering and the men wander about like punch-drunk fighters, waiting for the next blow to fall....

That's one question answered, Annja thought. They had all been wondering how the *Reliant* had ended up in the middle of the jungle and now they knew. The tsunami that had brought the ship here certainly must have been an impressive sight, if Captain Jeffries's guess regarding its size was correct. It might not be the largest on record—that belonged to a 1,720 foot wave in Lituya Bay, Alaska—but it was astounding just the same. Annja had been through a tsunami herself, albeit a much smaller one, and knew the devastation it could bring. She had no trouble believing that the crew of the *Reliant* had encountered something so big that their only choice had been to buckle down the hatches and ride it out.

She started reading ahead in the journal, only to discover a few pages later that it hadn't taken long for that "next blow," as Jeffries had called it, to fall on the crew of the *Reliant*. The beginning of the entry was washed out, but she was still able to understand the gist of it.

The natives returned during the night and this time they were not content to just observe. The men of the watch were slain instantly with arrows through the eyes. The brigands then scaled the hull of the ship and entered the lower gun deck through the open sally ports. Four additional men died before the noise woke the others. The general melee that followed was swift and bloody.

In the end, we were able to repulse the attackers with the judicious use of the ship's firearms but it was close just the same. If they come back with a larger party, we are going to be in trouble. I needed all hands on deck. I informed Mr. Thompson that, given our present circumstances, I was granting him a temporary pardon and releasing him from confinement, provided that I had his word as an officer and gentleman that he would not seek to act against myself or my crew in any fashion.

Thompson agreed.

Additional guards were posted and several of the cannons were moved into the sally ports and primed for use. If the natives returned, it was my intention to blow them out of the jungle before they could attempt to storm the ship a second time.

I needn't have worried. The natives weren't coming back. They had already beaten us; we just didn't know it yet.

Eighteen men had sustained serious injury in the attack, so we converted one side of the lower gun deck to an infirmary to allow the ship's doctor to treat them all in one location. Thankfully, the need for amputations and other major surgical procedures was limited as the natives didn't have firearms or cannons to cause injuries deserving of such treatment.

Three hours after the doctor had finished treating all of their wounds, the first of the injured men grew sick. By dawn the next day, all of the injured men had come down with the same illness. Concerned, I had the lower gun deck declared off-limits to the rest of the crew and restricted access to the doctor and his staff only. It didn't do any good.

Less than forty-eight hours later, the first of the uninjured men became sick.

After that, it was just a matter of time.

There were several pages after that point that were illegible due to weather damage, the pages having stuck together and, on those that weren't, the ink so faded and overgrown with mold that Annja couldn't even tell where one sentence began and another ended.

Then, on October 18, an entry with just a single sentence.

Thompson has fled.

The last entry in the log was written on the very next day, October 19, and within its stark phrases Annja found the answer she was seeking. She knew what had happened to Dr. Knowles and, more importantly, what to do to get him back.

She closed the journal and, taking it with her, went to find the others.

26

The day had grown late while Annja read and reread the captain's journal. By the time she stepped out of the wardroom and onto the upper gun deck, she discovered that the sun had all but set.

The smell of cooked meat wafted up over the side of the ship, causing Annja's stomach to grumble; her body had already grown tired of rehydrated rations, it seemed. She walked to the edge and found her three companions sitting around a large fire, the carcass of the boar they'd killed earlier roasting within the flames. Their voices drifted up to her, but she couldn't make sense of what they were talking about from the few isolated words that reached her.

She turned and made her way back down through the ship to exit exactly as they had entered.

Marcos saw her first.

"Well? Did you find all of the answers we need?"

Annja kept her face even but inside she was frowning. Marcos seemed to be getting more belligerent the farther away from civilization they got. She needed to watch him a bit more carefully, she decided.

To the others, she said, "As a matter of fact, yes. I

think I know what happened to Dr. Knowles and his team."

"Really?" Claire said, her voice full of surprise and excitement.

Annja accepted a plate of food from Hugo and sat down at the fire with the rest of them. She tore off a piece of meat and began to eat while telling her story.

"According to the logbook, Thompson revealed the location of the treasure to Captain Jeffries of the *Reliant* in exchange for his life. Jeffries promptly ordered the treasure dug up again and put half aboard the *Mary Dear* and half aboard the *Reliant*. The *Mary Dear* left for England while the *Reliant* remained to finish up a few repairs."

She paused to gulp down a few more bites; the food was terrific.

"Before the *Reliant* could leave the area, however, she was caught in a massive storm. In the midst of the storm, the *Reliant* was struck by a tsunami of incredible size that carried the ship halfway across the island to where you see it now.

"Here's where it gets interesting. Most of the crew was lost in the storm, but Captain Jeffries managed to get the others organized and working as a team. They buried their dead—" Annja pointed over her shoulder at the graveyard several yards behind her "—and buried the treasure in the cave."

"Wait a minute," Marcos said. "If they were all marooned here, how did word of the treasure's location get out? How did Dr. Knowles know to look along the ridge instead of down by the coast, where it would have made sense for the pirates to bury it?"

Claire beat her to the answer. "Thompson escaped."

Annja nodded. "Jeffries refused to keep him locked up, said they needed every spare hand they could get. Thompson bided his time and then hightailed it out of camp one night when Jeffries wasn't paying attention. Somehow, someway, he made it off the island."

"So Keating wasn't lying—the directions he'd been given to the treasure had actually come from Thompson, just as he claimed!" Claire exclaimed.

"Your husband must have recognized the truth, as they brought him to this place, as well."

"So what?" Marcos said, his irritation plain. "All that ancient history doesn't do a thing to tell us what happened to Knowles. Or the treasure."

Annja didn't agree. "On the contrary, I think it does. Listen to this."

She opened up the logbook and, with the help of the light from the fire, read out loud Jeffries's comments about the attack by the natives.

"Like I said before. So what?"

Annja ignored Marcos, focusing her attention on Claire, for it would be up to Claire where the team went next.

"No one knew there were natives on the island in 1821. In fact, this logbook is the only mention of them that I've ever come across. More than two dozen expeditions have been to this place, looking for the gold, and not a single one of them have encountered them?"

"Because they're all dead! It was hundreds of years ago."

Annja's gaze never left Claire's face. "We know at least one of them who is not. And where there is one, there are probably a lot more."

"Do you believe that?" Claire asked. "That it was an actual native and not someone trying to horn in on the treasure? Perhaps even one of Richard's men?"

"I do. Listen to this.... 'The morning brings with it a shocking revelation,'" Annja quoted, reading the final entry from the logbook aloud. "'The last of my crew disappeared in the night. Eighteen healthy men vanished without a trace.'

"'At first I thought they had decided en masse to reject my leadership. That they had headed for the coast despite my fears that the island would be struck by a secondary wave. But when I checked on the men in the infirmary, I discovered that they had, to a man, been murdered in their beds. Standing in the midst of their lifeless bodies was another of those monkey-faced idols we'd discovered before.'

"'The natives had returned and, for whatever reason, had slain the sick and taken the healthy men of my crew with them when they'd left.'"

Annja glanced up from the logbook and knew from the expression on Claire's face that she'd put two and two together.

But Annja wasn't finished reading. Not yet.

She went on. "'Knowing I couldn't live with myself if I left my crew at the mercy of the natives,'" she read, "'I've decided to go after them. I have several days of food and plenty of water, so when I am done writing this, I will set out in pursuit. I will leave the logbook behind so that there will be a record if I fail in my task. I will also mark the trail in my wake in the rare case that someone finds this logbook and attempts to come after me.'

"'Written this twenty-third day of October, in the year of our Lord Eighteen Twenty-One.'

"'Captain Martin Jeffries.'"

Even Marcos understood the similarities now. Two hundred years, give or take a decade or two, separated them from Captain Jeffries and his crew, but what they had experienced was almost identical to that of the British commander.

"Are you suggesting that not only Dr. Knowles and his team but also the crew of the *Sea Dancer* were taken captive by these so-called natives?" Claire asked.

Annja nodded, her gaze locked with that of Claire. "I am."

"And what are you proposing we do about it?"

"I would think that would be obvious," Annja said with a smile. "Go after them, of course."

From the look on Marcos's face, he agreed with her for a change.

It wasn't long before they decided to investigate the area around the ship for the marker Captain Jeffries claimed to have left. If they found it, they would continue in that direction. If they did not, they would discuss the issue a bit further and, hopefully, come to some consensus as to the direction they should take.

With their plan made, the group finished their meal and then settled in for the night, with each of them taking a turn at watch.

Sunrise could not come soon enough for Annja.

ANNJA WAS CLIMBING high in the rigging of a sailing ship, the rain lashing against her face as she moved upward with every step. She kept her attention on the ropes in front of her, knowing one slip would mean a long fall either onto the deck or into the sea, neither of which would be good for her.

She could hear the captain shouting out orders below, but she had a hard time understanding them over the crack of the thunder overhead and the howl of the wind in her ears. It didn't matter, really; she knew the orders weren't for her. She had a job already—cutting down the sail on the main mast—and that took precedence over everything else for one simple reason. If the sail stayed up, they were all dead, anyway.

She planted her feet, gripped the shrouds tightly and turned her head to look out toward the vast ocean. A flash of lightning lit the sky, and for a second, she saw it silhouetted there against the darkness.

The wave that was coming to consume them alive.

Fear raced down her spine and for a moment she was frozen there, knife between her teeth, fingers clenched around the shroud lines like a corpse trapped in rigor, and it was only the realization that she would become exactly that—a corpse—if she didn't get moving that sent her clambering upward again.

Reaching her destination, she wrapped her hand tightly about the lines, then used the other to take the knife from her mouth and begin sawing through the thick ropes that held the sail to the crossbeam of the mast. The cold rain wasn't making it easy; her fingers were having a hard time holding on to the knife.

A frantic glance over her shoulder.

The wave was not only closer, but larger, as well.

She began to saw faster....

The scene shifted. The wave was left behind and she

found herself in the dimness of the lower gun deck, cut-lass in hand as she fought in the half-light against an unknown assailant.

It was the cutlass that clued her in that she was dreaming. There was only one sword she would will-ingly choose to fight with, and a cutlass certainly wasn't it. She tried to get herself to wake up, but either her subconscious wasn't listening or there was something it wanted her to see, for it completely ignored her com-mands and the dream continued around her, unabated. Unable to stop it, Annja simply went with the flow.

The lanterns had been extinguished earlier, and without them it was hard to see exactly who they were fighting against. What little moonlight there was showed Annja glimpses of men in tunics, carrying shields and spears. They shouted in an unfamiliar language as they charged the line of half-awake sailors....

Another scene shift and this time she found herself standing outside the hull of the Reliant *in a light tropi-cal rain, gazing back at the wreckage with a mixture of sorrow and determination. She had the sense she wouldn't see the old girl again and that saddened her; the* Reliant *had been her command for the past several years and the two of them had taken care of each other for all that time. She was a sturdy ship and it wasn't fair that she should end her days marooned in the middle of the jungle on an ignored island like this one, but there was little that could be done about it.*

Filled with the sense of abandoning an old friend, she stared out into the jungle, wondering if they were out there, watching, even now. She suspected that they were. Believed, in fact, that they'd been under con-

tinuous observation ever since the storm had dumped them in this place.

So be it.

She cast about looking for the ideal spot to affix her mark. Several rocks jutted out of the jungle floor nearby and from this perspective they reminded her of a giant python. She stepped over to the first stone, the head of the snake, so to speak, and, taking out her knife, carved an arrow pointing north onto the surface of the stone. Beneath it she carved the date—1/25.

Satisfied that she'd done what she could to direct anyone who might come after her, she set off into the jungle.

From the bushes, several pairs of eyes watched her go....

ANNJA AWOKE WITH A START. Her heart was racing and her body was covered with a sheen of sweat, as if she'd just run a mile through the rain.

It was early morning, the sunlight just beginning to filter through the trees. Mists of steam rose from the jungle floor as the heat began to bake away the moisture from the night before. A glance showed Claire and Hugo still in their sleeping bags. For a moment she couldn't find Marcos, but then spotted him sitting against the hull of the *Reliant*, looking outward into the trees around him; he'd had the night's final watch. He nodded in her direction but didn't make any move to get up, for which Annja was grateful. She didn't want to make small talk and take the chance of forgetting some of the details from her dream. She had this crazy idea…

Annja slipped out of her sleeping bag, pulled on her

boots and walked around to the other side of the *Reliant*.
In her dream she'd been standing with the wreckage of
the ship to her left and slightly behind her, so she put
herself in a similar position and then began searching
for the snakelike rock formation.

It took a few minutes. The rocks had sunk deeper
into the earth and were hidden in part by an overgrown
patch of ferns, but after some searching she found them.
Once she'd located them, she moved to the stone that
served as the snake's head and began examining its
surface, looking for the mark. The fact that the stones
themselves were here at all had buoyed her confidence
that she wasn't totally crazy for thinking there was even
a speck of truth to her dream. Now all she had to do
was find the arrow....

But it wasn't there. She searched the top of the rock,
even scraping away the lichen that had grown there,
looking for it to no avail.

You imagined it, her inner voice told her. *You saw
the rock from the deck of the ship and your subconscious just added it to your dream. There's no mark.
There never was.*

She wasn't yet convinced of that. She had that gut
feeling that it should be here. But where?

She stepped back and stared at the rock for a long
minute, trying to see if it was the right one. It looked
right, but then again they all pretty much looked the
same. Perhaps there was another stone in front of this
one that was still concealed by the underbrush.

A quick check assured her there wasn't.

Annja was about to give up in frustration when she
turned back to face the stone she'd previously searched

and finally saw it. About halfway down the side of the stone, partially covered in green lichen, was an indentation in the stone that was too straight to be natural.

"Got you!" she crowed as she stepped forward and brushed at it with her hand.

There, plain as day, was the arrow Captain Jeffries had carved into the face of the rock in her dream!

27

After hearing about Annja's dream and seeing the mark, the others didn't need too much convincing that where the arrow was pointing was the direction they should head. They weren't entirely comfortable with it, and several times during the morning's march Annja would catch Marcos or Hugo looking at her with an odd expression on their face, but no one suggested that they change their course.

For the first time since arriving on the island, it rained for longer than a brief shower. In fact, Mother Nature seemed to be trying to make up for her lack of precipitation over the preceding days. It didn't just rain, it poured, hammering down on them like some judgment from above.

Now, more than ever, both Claire and Annja believed time was of the essence, so there wasn't any talk of waiting for it to pass, as they normally would have. Instead, they pulled on plastic ponchos and continued on their way, moving a bit slower and more carefully.

Their path took them northward, into the slowly rising foothills surrounding Mount Yglorias, the island's highest peak. They'd been walking for about forty five minutes when Hugo shouted, "Look!" and pointed to a large boulder off to one side of the trail.

An arrow had been scratched into its surface, pointing northward.

Jeffries.

But even more surprising was the much newer mark scratched beneath it.

A capital letter K.

Jeffries wasn't the only one who'd come this way. Dr. Knowles had, as well.

The sight of the marker gave them all hope, especially Annja. She had been half-convinced that Knowles and his team had been slaughtered outright, just as the sick among Captain Jeffries's crew had been killed. As the incident with Marcos and the jaguar had shown, it wasn't all that difficult to dispose of bodily remains out here in the middle of the jungle. In fact, it was far too easy.

Now, however, they had some evidence, no matter how slim, that Knowles was alive.

She studied the symbol for a few minutes, trying to piece together the puzzle before her. Unlike Knowles's earlier markers, this one looked as if it had been done by the shaky hand of a kindergarten student. The *K* was lopsided, uneven and partially on its side. *What could he have been doing to cause him to get so sloppy?*

Finally she thought she had it worked out.

She imagined Knowles and his crew being taken captive. Hands tied behind their backs with crude rope made from local materials. Being marched north from the excavation site as captives of the natives. When they'd reached this point, the group had taken a break. Knowles's keen eye had spotted the earlier marker and, after casually strolling over to lean against the same rock, had used something sharp to carve his *K* into the stone, all the while keeping his hands behind his back and out of sight.

Seemed reasonable to her.

Her respect for Knowles went up a notch and she still had yet to meet the man.

They got back under way, this time trying to keep their eyes on both the trail and the surrounding terrain so they wouldn't miss any potential markers. If he'd managed to do it once, Knowles had probably found a way to do it again, Annja suspected. The trick was going to be finding the markers amid all the rain.

And unfortunately for them, the rain showed no signs of stopping. If anything, it grew worse. The wind whipped it into the open hoods of their ponchos, until water had drenched their hair and seemed to be running in a continual stream down their backs. Annja felt like a drowned rat and she knew the others must be feeling the same.

With all the water pouring down the slope in front of them, gradual as it was, the footing beneath their feet began to grow less and less reliable. Several times Annja or one of the others had to catch themselves on a nearby bush or branch to keep from having their feet swept out from under them.

When the rain showed no signs of stopping, Annja pulled Claire aside.

"This is getting too dangerous," she told her. "If one

of us slips and breaks a leg or, worse yet, gets swept away by the storm, the entire expedition will be in serious trouble. We need to stop moving and find some shelter."

But Claire wouldn't have it. She had grown more eager to press on since they'd found the marker from Dr. Knowles and had no intention of stopping because they were getting wet.

They hadn't gone another fifteen minutes, however, before Annja heard a steady rumbling in the air. She'd heard it before, she knew she had, but it was hard to place given the loud, thundering rain around them.

Rain...

Annja suddenly understood what was coming toward them, and perhaps more importantly, she understood just how little time they had at their disposal.

"Find the nearest tree and secure yourself to it! Move!" she shouted.

She didn't wait to see if the others followed suit but raced over to the closest ceiba tree she could find and anchored herself to it with an extra few feet of rope and a pair of carabiners to lock the rope in place.

Perhaps it was because of Annja's urgency, or perhaps they simply understood the threat headed toward them was like a runaway freight train—whatever the reason, it didn't really matter. What mattered was that they jumped to follow suit, working frantically as the sound grew louder around them and the ground beneath their feet began to shake.

Annja had just finished securing herself to a tree and was trying to see how the others were doing when the wave of water they'd been hearing headed down the mountainside. Suddenly it broke through the tree line above and rushed toward them with a vengeance.

The wave hit, breaking against the tree trunk in front of Annja with savage force, and she knew if she'd been caught in the open there was no way she would have survived. As it was, she could barely hold on to the tree trunk as the water cascaded around her and swept past on its way down the hill.

A glance showed her both Marcos and Hugo hugging trees similar to the one Annja herself was secured to, but when she sought out Claire, she couldn't see her anywhere. Annja glanced frantically about, thinking perhaps Claire had fallen back behind them.

A scream to her right caught Annja's attention over the thunder of the water and she glanced in time to see Claire lose her footing.

"Grab my hand, Claire!" Annja shouted, thrusting out an arm as the other woman came flying toward her.

Their fingers brushed, their hands caught, slipped... and then held.

Unfortunately, that left Claire on her back in the path of the water, bouncing around under the flow and struggling just to find enough air to breathe.

Annja had a death lock on the woman's wrist, refusing to let go, and afterward knew that doing so had saved Claire's life.

Thankfully, the muddy slide of water could only last so long, and just a few moments after it started, the deluge began to abate and finally ended.

When she was sure it had passed, Annja released Claire's hand, letting the woman fall, coughing, into the mud while she untied herself. Marcos and Hugo were busy doing the same. The three of them then gathered around Claire.

Their leader was bruised, battered, but Annja's quick action had kept her from being swept away. For that, they were all thankful.

As if to torment them, the rain began to slow shortly after the flash flood and half an hour later stopped entirely. The clouds parted, letting the sun out to begin baking everything dry in the endless cycle of the tropical rain forest. By the time they stopped for lunch, the world around them was steamy with evaporating rainfall.

They had a cold meal of previously cooked boar meat, which, in Annja's opinion, wasn't anywhere near as tasty the second time around. What had been mouthwatering the night before had become tougher than shoe leather and about as flavorful. Still, they needed the protein for the hike ahead and she made sure to down her portion without complaint.

The afternoon brought them into the highlands proper. Rocky ridgelines and miniature canyons began to pop up here and there amid the jungle vegetation, reminding Annja of pictures she'd seen of the South Pacific islands during the Second World War. The jungle rose over and covered everything, it seemed, even knifelike ridgelines that would have made a billy goat nervous.

A fork appeared in the trail early that afternoon, which gave the group a reason to rest for a few minutes as they debated the alternatives. The left-hand path seemed to be less steep, sloping downward slightly as it headed into a valley between two ridgelines. The right-

hand path, on the other hand, appeared to be more strenuous, taking them higher into more rugged country.

"Check for a marker," Annja told them, and they
spread out to do so. Fifteen minutes later, however,
they had to admit that if there had ever been a marker
here, it was gone now.

"What do you think?" Claire asked Annja as she
stood eyeing the two alternatives.

Annja wasn't sure. Her feet were telling her to take
the less strenuous path to the left, but her heart was
saying to stay with the more difficult path to the right.

She stepped away from the others, closed her eyes
and tried to listen to what her senses were telling her.
Left or right? Valley or ridgelines?

She couldn't explain it, but when she opened her eyes
a moment later, she knew they had to continue to the
right. She felt drawn in that direction, as if there was
something waiting just for her around the next corner.
She couldn't leave this place without investigating for
herself.

"That way," she said, pointing.

There was a collective groan from the others, for
she'd chosen the harder path, but she'd been right in all
of her other decisions for the group and so they had little ground to argue. A few swigs of water to keep them
hydrated and they continued on.

Almost immediately they encountered a series of
switchbacks, taking them higher into the hills and
deeper into the jungle at the same time. There had
been no further sign that either Captain Jeffries or Dr.
Knowles had taken this route, and Annja was just starting to second-guess her choice of direction when they

rounded a final corner and stopped, gaping at the sight before them.

There, rising out of the dense jungle, was a completely intact Incan pyramid.

28

Pyramid of the Stars
Cocos Island

Annja couldn't believe it. She stood and stared at the structure covered in foliage, drinking in the sight.

The pyramid was about one hundred feet in height and seemed to be in near-perfect condition. It had been built in the traditional Incan style, with large blocks of stone carved so perfectly that they didn't need mortar to hold them together. Each of its four sides was bisected with a raised staircase that rose directly to an opening on each of the four sides of the temple structure on top. Even from this distance, Annja could see several carved pillars in the doorways of the temple, the colorful pigments that had once decorated so many other Incan monuments still visible on this one.

Without prompting, Marcos left the path they'd been following and headed for the pyramid, using his machete to cut a path through the undergrowth. At the rate he was going, it would only take him a few minutes to reach the base of the structure.

Eagerly, Annja followed.

As they drew closer, they could see that the pyramid

rested on a small shelflike plateau that jutted out from the side of the mountain. Vegetation grew over much of the structure, though to Annja's trained eye it didn't have the haphazardness of wild growth but seemed to follow specific lines and contours. She tried to imagine what it would look like when viewed from above and realized that the structure would probably be nearly invisible from the air, so cloaked was it in a sea of green.

A sudden thought occurred to her.

Was the structure still being used?

She hurried forward, eager to find out.

They made it to the base of the pyramid without incident and started up the stairs toward the temple on top. They hadn't gone far before Annja slowed, then stopped. She turned and looked out over the jungle around them, searching for...she wasn't sure what, actually.

She didn't see anyone lurking in the trees or hiding along the rocks of the ridge. On the contrary, it looked as if they were the only human beings to have come this way in centuries. And yet the feeling remained.

That feeling of being watched.

"Everything okay?" Hugo asked, and Annja noticed him standing close, his gun in hand, his gaze fixed on the jungle, as well.

She hesitated, her eyes still scanning the trees around them, but eventually she said, "Yeah. It was nothing, I guess. Just nerves."

"Happens to the best of us," Hugo said, but he didn't look any more confident than Annja felt.

The two of them had just turned to continue up the

stairwell when a scream split the afternoon air, startling them both.

It was shockingly loud and it hit them at a visceral level, making their guts tighten and their skin crawl. Hugo spun around so quickly that his foot slipped off the step. If Annja hadn't reached out with lightning-quick reflexes and caught him, he would have fallen.

"Easy there," she told him, helping him back to his feet and then continuing with him up the next several steps until they reached the others.

"What the heck was that?" Marcos wanted to know, his gaze still on the jungle below and beside them.

Before Annja could answer, it came again—a howling scream that sounded as if something had just been shoved into a buzz saw. Almost as one, the four of them dropped down, instinctively trying to make themselves as small a target as possible.

That time, however, after a moment's reflection, Annja recognized the sound and laughed in relief when she did.

She stood up. "It's okay," she said to them. "It's okay. It's a jaguar."

Hugo disagreed. "That was no cat, Annja."

The absolute conviction in his voice made Annja want to argue, but she knew it would be the wrong thing to do then. Instead, she put her hand on his arm, trying to get him to lower his gun and calm down.

"Have you ever heard a jaguar scream, Hugo?"

"No."

"Then how do you know that wasn't a jaguar?"

He glanced at her, doubt settling into his features. Annja was about to say something soothing when movement below them caught her eye and instead she pointed over his shoulder.

"See? What did I tell you?"

A large cat, most likely the one who had just been making the cries they'd heard, wandered out of the undergrowth and stared up at them from the edge of the brush. Unlike the cat she'd faced off against the other day, this one was a rare specimen, its fur a smoky black instead of orange, giving its spots an oddly hypnotic effect if you stared at them too long. Its yellow eyes followed the group, but it made no move to advance, just settled down beneath an overhanging palm frond and watched them with lazy interest.

"Good kitty," Hugo mumbled beneath his breath.

Annja would have laughed if she hadn't noticed Marcos lining up his rifle to take a shot at the big cat.

She leaped up the two steps that separated them and knocked the barrel of the rifle up and away in the split second before Marcos pulled the trigger.

The shot went wide and the sound echoed off the mountainside for several long seconds.

Before Marcos could react to her interference, Annja snatched the rifle out of his hands.

"Are you out of your mind?" she said, avoiding shouting in his face only by the thinnest of margins. "Announce our presence to everyone within half a mile, why don't you?"

Marcos barely heard her. His attention was still on the jaguar, which, oddly enough, hadn't moved an inch. "Give me that gun!" he told her, trying to grab it from her as he did so. "I'm going to take care of that cat...."

"You'll do no such thing," Annja said, and the steel

in her voice got his attention. She watched him take in the fact that she'd changed her hold on the weapon and was standing there before him with one hand near the trigger and the other around the forestock. It was a position that would let her bring the weapon to bear quite easily if she chose to do so.

"That cat isn't bothering you, and you're going to leave it alone even if I have to break your fingers for you to get the message."

Marcos sneered. "You go right ahead and give it a try."

That made Annja smile. "Hold this for me please, Claire," she said, extending the rifle toward the other woman, her gaze never leaving Marcos's own.

The fact that she was so clearly unintimidated by him gave Marcos pause and he glanced at Claire in confusion before taking a step backward.

Annja was about to move in, fully prepared to prove her point and not liking the big guy all that much, anyway, when Claire slipped between them.

"All right, that's enough. Stop acting like children and let's focus on what we are here for. My husband is still missing, remember?"

With a last glance at the jaguar, which still hadn't moved from its spot in the shade, Annja continued up the stone steps toward the temple at the top of the pyramid.

THE TEMPLE WAS GORGEOUS.

It was simple—there was no other adjective that so encompassed the condition of the place to Annja. She'd seen her fair share of ancient ruins and architecture, but she'd never seen a building from an ancient culture the way it was meant to be viewed, with all the vibrancy and color of the time in which it had been settled. This particular structure looked as if it had been built yesterday.

Lining the entire interior of the temple, starting at about ankle height and rising to eye level, was a glorious full-color mural. It showed scenes from Incan mythology, from the creator god Virachoca bringing the world into being and pulling the sun and moon from the waters of Lake Titicaca, to the transformation of a flirtatious woman who was cut in half by jealous lovers into the goddess of health and beauty, Cocomama. Image after image splayed out along the walls, all of them done in exquisite detail, the likes of which Annja had never seen.

The centerpiece of the temple was a twice-life-size statue of the sun god, Inti, the second most powerful god in the entire Incan pantheon, subordinate only to Virachoca himself. Inti was usually represented by a humanoid figure sitting crossed-legged with his hands in his lap. The top half of his head was a vast array of sunbeams, extending outward like an unfurled ladies' hand fan.

That alone should have been enough to keep an archaeologist like Annja in heaven for weeks, but the fact that the entire statue was made from gold sent the treasure-hunter side of her reeling, as well.

The value of such a piece was incalculable.

Marcos gave a low whistle when he saw it, and it did the one thing none of the others thought was possible: it struck him dumb at the site. All he could do for several minutes was stand and stare.

Annja didn't blame him.

As she turned away, intending to look at other parts of the temple, she spotted something on the floor behind the statue. Stepping over to investigate, she found a tan fedora, very similar to the ones that she'd seen Dr. Knowles wearing in pictures taken at his various dig sites. When she bent to pick it up, she discovered a satellite phone underneath it.

"That's Richard's hat!"

Annja stood as Claire rushed over and grabbed both the hat and the phone. Claire immediately tried to turn the satellite phone on, only to discover that the battery was dead. Still, both items were proof that they were still going in the right direction.

They didn't seem like the kind of objects one would simply forget, so Annja guessed that Knowles had left them behind intentionally, just like the marks he'd made along the trail. Dr. Knowles was trying to tell anyone coming after him that he was still alive and kicking.

Or, at least, he had been recently.

"Hey, come take a look at this," Hugo called from the other side of the statue, and the group joined him near the back wall. The mural Annja had been examining continued here, but now it was different. Where the earlier scenes had been images captured from Incan mythology, these pictures chronicled events a bit more recent than that. In the image Marcos was pointing at, there was the unmistakable picture of a sailing ship with three masts that sailed into port and deposited three groups of people on the beach before continuing on their journey. There was little doubt in anyone's mind that they were looking at a picture of the *Reliant*.

Later scenes showed the Incas attacking the ship, leaving the captain for dead and herding the captives into the jungle. What seemed to be a long march followed, with the captives ultimately ending up in what Annja thought appeared remarkably like an Incan city.

They moved "down" the mural a few feet, their eyes widening at the number of ships and expeditions to the island that were cataloged in the images on the walls. The pictures of the ships progressed from sailing vessels to more modern-looking motor yachts, including two that Annja would have sworn were the *Sea Dancer* and the *Neptune's Pride*.

There were several images of Dr. Knowles's expedition, identified by the cave full of treasure drawn nearby. Like the crew from Jeffries's *Reliant,* it seemed that Knowles and his people had been captured and taken to the temple as well, if the images were to be believed.

Now all they needed to do was find this Incan city and they should find Knowles and his team. And if there was one thing that Annja was good at, it was finding things that other people didn't want found. Ancient or modern, it didn't matter—she had the skills and capability to track them down if given enough time.

The very last image in the mural was chilling, though, for it showed an individual who could only be Marcos being taken from his tent in the midst of their camp and strung up in the tree while a jaguar sat patiently at his feet.

Well, we foiled that plan, Annja thought. *Guess they will need to have the artist do some touch-ups by the time we're done.*

She was poring over the images, trying to find some clue as to the whereabouts of the Incan city, when the jaguar outside let out another scream.

This time, however, the cat was answered by another.

Annja knew it was two different beasts; the second call had a deeper timbre than the first.

She would have passed it off as two unfriendly cats hunting the same source of food if it had stopped there.

But it didn't.

The first and second calls were answered by a third.

And then a fourth.

Four jaguars in the same place?

That didn't make any kind of sense at all. Curious, she stepped over to the door they'd entered through and looked down to where the jaguar had been sitting in the shade when they'd entered the pyramid half an hour ago.

The cat was still there.

But a new cat sat at each of the other cardinal points of the compass, guarding the steps down from the pyramid.

The activity was too human to be anything but trained.

Even as she looked on, she saw figures moving through the trees, converging on the pyramid. Most likely brought there by Marcos's rifle shot earlier.

"We've got company!" Annja called.

The others rushed over to join her.

By then the figures had revealed themselves to be a hunting party of about fifteen men. All of them were dressed in lightweight tunics and pants made from local materials and decorated with colorful thread arranged in geometric patterns.

Annja had seen clothes just like these before on the Incan warriors in her dream the other night.

It seems their adversaries had finally chosen to reveal themselves.

Armed warriors and trained hunting cats.

Perfect.

29

Slopes of Mount Yglesias
Cocos Island

Incan warriors. Here, on Cocos Island.

Annja was having trouble wrapping her head around the idea. One side of her was saying, *Yes, of course it's the Inca. Who else did you expect it to be?* while the other half was telling her how ridiculous it was to even think that the men at the foot of the pyramid were members of a civilization that had disappeared in the sixteenth century.

She might still be standing there staring if Hugo hadn't brought his rifle up to his shoulder and aimed it down the slope of the pyramid at the newcomers below. Claire followed suit seconds later. The sudden motion broke her mental paralysis and focused her on the problem at hand.

She reached out and put a hand on Hugo's arm while, below them, the Incan warriors reacted in predictable fashion, bringing their weapons—blowguns, bows and arrows, and long, metal-tipped spears—to bear on the four of them atop the pyramid.

"That might not be a good idea," Annja said to Hugo

gently, not wanting to spook him into accidentally pulling the trigger. She hoped that Claire was listening.

"Why not?" Hugo snarled at her, without taking his gaze away from the warriors below.

Annja kept her voice calm. "Because they'll turn you into a human pincushion full of darts and arrows before you could even get off a second shot. And that's if the cats don't get you first."

As if on cue, the cats had risen to their feet and were leaning forward, lips drawn back from their teeth and their tails twitching behind them as they stared unblinkingly at the threat above. One of them let out a snarling cry that gave no doubt as to its intentions.

"What do you want us to do? Surrender?" Hugo hissed at her, suddenly afraid to raise his voice.

"If you want to live to see tomorrow, then yes. We can't escape if we're dead."

One of the warriors stepped forward and shouted up at them, gesturing at the same time. Annja didn't understand a word, but the gist of it seemed plain enough.

Drop your weapons and come down here.

Sounded like a quick way to get themselves killed, but really, what choice did they have? They were cornered like rats, with nowhere to go. All the warriors had to do was sit there until Annja and her companions were too weak from the lack of food and water to resist, then climb the steps and take them captive, anyway. Annja didn't see the point in going through all of that just to end up at the same place. Better to be seen as cooperating, which might gain them some mercy at a crucial time, than fighting and generating more ill will than they'd apparently already gained.

The warrior repeated himself, this time a bit more sharply.

"He wants us to drop our weapons," Marcos said from where he stood on the other side of Claire.

Annja glanced his way, ready with a quick retort about stating the obvious, when she saw the expression on his face—surprise, wonder, amazement, confusion, all rolled up in one.

"What?" she asked sharply, concerned.

But she needn't have worried.

"The language. I recognize it," Marcos said. "Or at least some of it."

Claire stared at him.

"You do?"

Marcos nodded. "It's Quechua. Or close enough to it that I can get the gist of it."

Quechua was one of the indigenous languages of South America, spoken by nearly eight million people throughout the nations of Bolivia, Ecuador, Columbia, Peru, Chile and Argentina.

It was also the main language of the Incan Empire throughout most of its history.

It all seemed so obvious in hindsight, but then again, that was why they said hindsight was twenty-twenty. Hard not to see the connections when you already knew the answers.

Beside her, Claire said, "Annja's right. Do what she says, Hugo."

Hugo grumbled beneath his breath, but complied.

Annja and Marcos raised their hands over their heads. Claire and Hugo lowered their weapons, slowly put them down on the ground by their feet and then did the same.

The leader of the warriors, the one who Annja decided to privately call Cuzco after the capital city of the Incas, shouted something else up to them and then gestured for them to come down.

Annja didn't need Marcos to translate that one.

"What do we do?" Claire asked.

"Unless you've got a full case of jaguar repellent hiding in your shorts somewhere, I'd do what the man says," Annja said laconically. "Come on, let's get this over with."

Hands in the air, she started down the stairs.

Behind her, the others followed.

She was halfway to the bottom when one of the warriors stepped forward and looped a leather strap—a leash, really—around the neck of the cat at the bottom of the steps. The cat barely noticed, its gaze fixed firmly on Annja as she came down the steps toward it.

Hope he's got a good grip on that leash, she thought and then reassured herself that she wasn't entirely without protection if the cat somehow broke free. She really didn't want to face off against another jaguar, but she'd do so if necessary.

When she reached the bottom, two warriors came over to her, took her by the arms and led her over to stand in front of Cuzco. They pushed her down to her knees, firmly but without any sense of anger or intent to harm that Annja could pick up. Just two guys doing their job. She was surprised a bit at their lack of curiosity. Then again, if their group had recently snatched the crew of the *Sea Dancer* as well as the members of

Dr. Knowles's dig team, they had probably seen more mainlanders in the past few weeks than they hoped or wanted.

Her three companions were forced down to their knees beside her.

"What are they going—"

Claire didn't get a chance to finish her sentence, for the warrior behind her cuffed her across the back of the head to silence her.

Cuzco eyed them all for a long while and then said something in Quechua to Annja.

Annja frowned and, not understanding, glanced at Marcos for some help.

"He's either asking why you're here or where's your lama. I'd go with the former if I were you."

Annja had no idea if any of the warriors understood English, but she gave it a try, anyway.

"We mean you and your people no harm. We are here to find our missing friends."

Cuzco's expression didn't change as Annja spoke; he just kept staring at her.

"Can you say that in Quechua?" she asked Marcos.

He shook his head. "I can barely understand it, never mind speak it."

"Try it in Spanish, then."

Marcos obliged, but Cuzco barely glanced in his direction and clearly didn't understand a word that he was saying. More rapid-fire Quechua followed, all of it seemingly directed at Annja. When the Incan leader was finished, he gestured to the men standing nearby.

Annja felt her arms lifted behind her back and tied together with some kind of rough cord. A glance to the side showed Claire getting her hands tied, too. The men were searched first, the warriors removing knives from both of them and a pistol from Marcos's belt, before they, too, were bound. Hugo started to struggle when they began to loop the cord around his wrists, but quickly subsided when one of the cat handlers walked his cat closer to where Hugo knelt on the ground. Once they were tied, blindfolds were produced and slipped over the captives' heads.

The fact that the Inca had blindfolded them allowed Annja to relax a little. The blindfolds meant the Incans didn't want them seeing something, most likely the route to wherever it was that they were headed, which in turn meant they weren't going to be killed outright for violating the sanctity of the temple. They might still pay that price, but it wasn't going to happen immediately, and that was a good sign.

Annja was pulled to her feet and, at another sharp command from Cuzco, marched forward. The Incan who had tied her hands behind her back became her minder, keeping one hand on her biceps at all times as they walked along. Initially she was worried that they were separating her from her companions, but then she heard a grunt of annoyance from Marcos as he misjudged a step, and she relaxed, confident that they were still together.

The group got under way, moving at a slightly faster pace than Annja and her companions had been traveling earlier. The bottom edge of Annja's blindfold was just loose enough to allow her to see her feet, which kept her stumbling to a minimum, but from the regular exclamations coming from some of the others behind her, she knew they weren't so fortunate. The same view allowed her to see that they were on a trail of some kind, perhaps even the same one they'd been on earlier. It was just wide enough for her and her minder to walk abreast of each other, with relatively little debris to step over along the way.

About an hour into their march, they left the jungle behind. Their steps took on a bit of an echoing quality. The air around them stilled and the light became greatly reduced, leading Annja to believe that they'd entered a cavern or tunnel of some kind. Her captors seemed to calm a bit; the grip her minder had on her arm lightened, as if he were no longer as worried about her making a break for it as he'd been at the start of their journey together.

A considerable time later, her minder brought her to a stop and then let go of her arm. As he hadn't done that since the group had begun walking, Annja was momentarily alarmed, but that subsided when she felt his hands untying the knot of her blindfold. They'd been going for what felt like hours, though she knew time could be deceptive without the usual visual references to mark it. Her eyes had adjusted to the dim light that had been filtering in through the cloth, so it took a moment or two for her eyes to get used to the sudden light. But when they did she couldn't do much more than stare ahead of her in amazement and wonder.

She stood in a massive cavern, the space stretching out before her as far as she could see and the ceiling literally hundreds of feet above her head. The enormity of the cave might have been enough to get her to stop and stare, but it was what was in the cavern that captured her attention and held her mesmerized.

An entire Incan city stretched out before her.

30

Annja stood on a ledge about halfway up the cavern wall, giving her a bird's-eye view of the city laid out in a gridlike pattern below her. Wide streets ran through the city center and gradually gave way to more narrow pathways once one left the main thoroughfares. Buildings rose up in orderly fashion, everything from pyramids and temples to administrative centers and residential space. Areas that could only be parks were scattered here and there throughout the city, their brilliant green competing with a plethora of other colors amid the brightly painted structures. Everywhere she looked was a riot of color, an explosion of exuberance that Annja had always imagined might be the norm for the Incan civilization but until now had never had the opportunity to prove.

Oh, the things they could learn in this place, she thought.

She heard Claire gasp in amazement behind her and knew her companions' blindfolds had been removed, as well.

It suddenly occurred to Annja that despite being entirely underground, the city before her was bathed in the rich light of the afternoon sun. Almost reluctantly, she tore her gaze away from the city streets and looked to the walls of the cavern rising high around it, searching for the source of the light. At first it was hard to see, the light being brighter there than anywhere else in the cavern, but then she saw that an intricate series of mirrors had been put in place along the walls of the cavern. A massive mirror near the roof captured the rays of the sun and then relayed them to the other mirrors throughout the cavern, bathing the entire city in the same level of light. As the sun set outside, so, too, would it set inside. It was an incredible engineering feat for a civilization without modern tools and construction techniques, but Annja knew she shouldn't be surprised. The Incan civilization had invented terrace farming, aqueducts and freeze-dried foods, just to name a few, so a working system of mirrors certainly wasn't beyond their capability.

Her minder reached out and grabbed her arm again, indicating that sightseeing time was over. The group made their way down the cavern wall by means of a long series of switchbacks. At the bottom of the wall, the cat handlers and their charges separated from the group and went in a different direction while Cuzco led the rest of them into the city proper.

The city was truly beautiful. It was built entirely of cut stone and the Incas' reputation for being master stoneworkers was clearly evident in every single building they passed. From homes to schools to official-looking buildings, each and every one of them had been constructed with the same level of care and attention to detail. An intricate system of aqueducts ran throughout the city, carrying water to and from the various buildings as well as the public gardens, which themselves were carefully tended and groomed.

It didn't take them too long to arrive at the massive public square that was set in the city center, and as they approached Annja could see that word of their coming had traveled ahead of them. A huge crowd was waiting there to check them out. Annja guessed there had to be a couple of thousand, at least—all ages and walks of life, it seemed. Annja's captors didn't seem concerned, so Annja tried not to let their presence bother her, either, but if that many people suddenly decided she and her companions were a threat, there wouldn't be much she or any of the rest of them would be able to do to stop them all.

Cuzco marched them right through the crowd and straight toward the pyramid rising in the center of the square. The crowd pressed close for a good look at the newcomers but kept their hands to themselves and made no attempt to impede their forward momentum. Cuzco led them up the stairs—Annja counted two hundred in all—and into the building at the top, which wasn't the temple Annja had been expecting, but rather the king's audience chamber.

That made the man sitting on the raised throne at the back of the room—a throne made entirely of gold, if Annja wasn't mistaken—most likely the Incan king himself.

Guards stood on either side of the throne, protecting the king, and servant girls waved large palm fronds in fanlike motions to keep the king cool. Another servant stood on a small platform to the right of the throne, holding a tray of food and drink at shoulder level so the king could reach it without difficulty.

The king was a sharp-faced middle-aged man wearing a cloak of multicolored feathers around his bare shoulders, a pair of breeches made from some kind of soft and supple cloth, and leather sandals on his feet. He was busy talking with several nobles standing nearby but broke off as Cuzco and his charges approached.

Cuzco and his group stopped a few yards in front of the throne. As Cuzco bowed deeply, the prisoners were forced to their knees before the king. Annja didn't like it, but she knew resisting would only end with her getting hurt, and she didn't see the point in forcing a confrontation. She bowed her head, but didn't avert her eyes.

The king eyed Cuzco up and down and then waved him forward.

Cuzco stepped up to the throne and began talking to the king in a low voice, gesturing several times back in the prisoners' direction, no doubt informing the king of all that had taken place that morning.

Seeing the two of them together made the familial link between them obvious. *Father and son, perhaps? Older and younger cousins?* She couldn't be sure, but there was no doubt that the two men were related.

Cuzco bowed to the king a second time when he was finished explaining and then stepped back.

Annja kept her gaze fixed firmly on the king, ready to leap to her feet and draw her sword if it looked as if things were about to end for them right here and now.

The king bent over the side of his throne and said something in the ear of an elderly man waiting there. The man disappeared into the crowd before returning with an Incan woman in tow.

The newcomer was older than the king by at least twenty years and needed to be helped into the room, but there was nothing wrong with her steely gaze or the strength in her voice as she addressed herself to Annja.

"Why have you come here?" she asked in perfectly passable English.

Annja was so surprised that she couldn't speak. The question of where this Incan woman learned such excellent English bounced around in Annja's head while she struggled to force out an answer.

"We mean no trespass," Annja managed to stammer out. Annja's voice steadied and grew stronger as she continued, "We are searching for our friends who came to the island before us and then vanished."

"So you admit to invading the territory of Inca Amaru Tupac without provocation?"

Annja shook her head. "No, we did not invade Inca Tupac's territory," she said. Knowing the Incan word *inca* meant "king" allowed her to determine the king's name from what the woman had said. Inca Amaru Tupac. King Tupac.

"Inca Tupac did not give you permission to be in his territory, and yet here you are, with weapons in hand. Tell me, sword-bearer, how is this not an invasion?"

The woman had either been listening when Cuzco made his explanations to the king or else had received updates earlier when the group had first encountered the Inca several days ago. The use of the name *sword-*

bearer had Annja concerned; clearly, someone had seen her with her blade, probably more than once.

Annja started to answer but was cut off by Claire.

"You can't be serious!" she said, the indignation clear in her voice. "Since when do four people amount to—"

She didn't get any further.

The king's spokeswoman gestured once with her hand, and the guard behind Claire promptly bunched his fist and struck her in the side of the head, sending her facedown on the stone floor. Since her hands were still tied behind her back, she had no way of stopping herself and barely managed to turn her head to the side before she struck the floor.

Annja winced; Claire was going to be a mass of bruises come morning.

The king said something sharply to the interpreter in his native tongue and she in turn addressed the guard. "If she speaks again, cut out her tongue," she said calmly.

The guard dragged Claire upright. Blood spilled from her nose but she wisely kept her mouth shut and didn't say anything to rile the king, the woman or the guard any further.

Annja didn't miss the look in Claire's eyes, though. *Someone is going to pay for that later.*

The woman turned to face Annja again and calmly waited for an answer as if nothing had happened.

Annja thought quickly. "Invasion requires intent," she said. "We had no intent, as we did not know that you claimed this territory. It was a simple accident, nothing more."

The interpreter considered her words, frowned and

then turned and spoke to the king for several minutes. The king turned his gaze on Annja about midway through the interpreter's explanation, and Annja did her best to look as unthreatening as possible. It was difficult; being meek was never one of Annja's virtues.

The king stared at Annja; she did her best not to fidget. Finally, the king turned to Cuzco, said a few words and then waved his hand in dismissal.

The guards dragged them to their feet as Cuzco walked toward them.

Beside her, Annja heard Hugo whisper, "Are they gonna let us live?" but she didn't have an answer for him and could only shrug.

Cuzco issued a terse set of instructions to the guards and then the group turned about and left the audience chamber, their prisoners once more in tow.

They were directed back down the steps of the pyramid and over to one side, where a wheeled cart that looked like a prison cell on wheels waited for them. Annja smiled in delight when she saw the cart, prompting a remark from Marcos.

"Something about being stuck in a cage funny to you?" he asked with a snarl as the guards forced him inside.

"Not at all," she answered coolly, climbing up into the cart on her own without giving the guards a fight. After all, it hadn't gotten Marcos anywhere. "I was smiling at the fact that they are using wheels. The Inca, or at least those on the mainland, never invented them. A cart like this would have been something like magic to their ancestors!"

It was almost magic to Annja herself. To see an ancient culture brought to life in the twenty-first century, to walk among them like this, was an archaeologist's dream. It didn't matter that she was a prisoner; the opportunity she had here was priceless. She had to force herself to keep her attention on the problem at hand— namely, finding Knowles and getting everyone out of here, with or without the treasure—rather than lose herself in observing the Inca around her.

Once they were all inside the cart and seated on benches that ran along either side, facing inward, the door was secured behind them and the cart got under way. It traveled through the city at a slow pace, allowing them to take in the sights.

Gold was everywhere; the Inca used it to decorate everything, from the walls of the temples scattered about the city to the jewelry worn by many of the people they passed on the street. Annja wondered if the modern Inca thought of gold as the sweat of the sun god, Inti, as their ancestors had; they certainly seemed to attach as much importance to it.

Hugo noticed the abundance of the precious metal as well and wondered aloud where it all came from. As it turned out, they were about to get a firsthand look at the answer to that very question.

31

The gold mine
City of the Sun

It took them nearly half an hour to reach their destination, what appeared to be a mining camp on the outskirts of the city limits near the edge of the cavern wall. Men in little more than loincloths and sandals streamed out of several tunnels carved into the cliff face, carrying baskets full of overburden, or the waste rock left over when digging out a mine. Judging from the size of the pile, it looked as if they had been here for some time.

There were several guards standing around watching the miners, but they didn't seem too focused on what was going on. The miners appeared to be doing their work, and the guards appeared to be leaving them alone. Annja had the sense the guards were there more to give them something to do rather than to be on alert for any miners who would suddenly stop working and make a run for it.

Since their hands were still tied, Annja and the others were helped down out of the cart one at a time. They were pulled into a rough line, with Marcos and Hugo in front, followed by Claire and then Annja. Satisfied that they were under control, Cuzco led them up a winding path that after several minutes brought them to the opening of another tunnel Annja hadn't noticed before. Instead of leading to a mining tunnel, this particular entrance led into an oval-shaped cavern whose interior was lit by the fires burning in several braziers situated around the room.

A series of cave mouths were visible in the cavern wall to Annja's left, their openings covered by doors constructed the same way the jailer's cart had been, with saplings lashed together in a grid to form cell doors. Given the guards standing by several of the doors, Annja assumed they'd reached what passed for the city jail.

Cuzco and their guards marched them deeper into the cavern. As they drew closer, Annja caught a glimpse of several people standing just inside the doors, watching them approach, but then the guards noticed them as well and used the butts of their spears to force them away from the doors, so Annja couldn't see who they might be. Angry chatter erupted in the wake of the guards' actions, however, and while Annja might not be able to understand Quechua, there was no mistaking the language she was hearing. Whoever was in the cells, it was not Dr. Knowles and his team.

They continued deeper into the cavern and suddenly Marcos gave a long, low whistle to catch their attention and then indicated something to their left with a nod of his head. The action earned him a smack but accomplished his purpose; Annja and the rest of them looked in that direction as they moved past.

The first thing she noticed was the life-size statue

of the Virgin Mary and the baby Jesus, cast from solid gold, that stood in the center of the room. Dumped haphazardly around it were several sea chests, some of which had burst open to show their contents. Contents that included gold and silver coins, gemstones, jewelry of all shapes and sizes and more, all of which told Annja what she was looking at.

After more than two hundred years, the Treasure of Lima had at last been found!

In a surprising twist, it was also in the hands of the people who had provided most of it in the first place, the Inca, a situation Annja found rather ironic and amusing.

At the back of the room were two cells that faced each other at a forty-five-degree angle. The cells must have been occupied already, for the guards shouted some orders through the door, most likely telling those inside to move back. Marcos, Hugo and Claire were pushed forward into the first cell, but when Annja moved to join them, a guard took her by the arm and pushed her into the second cell, away from the others.

A tall, wiry, bald-headed man with a grizzled salt-and-pepper beard stepped forward to catch Annja as she stumbled. He steadied her and asked, "Are you all right?"

Annja watched the guards secure the door and walk away. She nodded and stepped back, uncomfortable with being that close to a stranger. She noticed that there were a handful of other people in the cell with them, arrayed in a semicircle behind their leader. She went to thank him and was struck with the recognition of who he was.

"Dr. Knowles?" she asked, a hopeful tone in her voice.

Warily, he replied, "Yes. Do I know you? You look familiar."

"No, but I know you," Annja told him. "In fact, I was hired to find you. My name's Annja Creed."

Now it was Knowles who smiled with unexpected delight. "You're the host of that *Chasing History's Monsters* show. I knew you looked familiar!"

He stuck out his hand and they shook.

"It's a pleasure to meet you. I'm a big fan!"

Annja was surprised. "You are?"

"Oh, yes. Anything that popularizes archaeology and therefore helps to bring in funding when it's time to launch a new expedition somewhere is a very good thing in my book. I could do without some of the supernatural silliness," he said with a wink, "but you do what you have to in order to keep ratings high, I'm sure."

If you only knew.

"Are you and your team all right?"

"Fair enough. They've had us working in the mines, but we're getting proper food and water and so far no one has been subjected to any kind of discipline. They even treated Gregor's fractured wrist." He pointed to a younger man with a splint on his right arm. "You said you were hired to find me?"

Annja could have kicked herself. How could she be so stupid?

"Yes. I'm sorry, I should have said something right away. When you stopped reporting in, your wife put together a small expedition to search for you. We found the camp you'd set up and the cave you'd been excavating, but by the time we—"

"Excuse me," Knowles said a little forcefully as he cut into her comments. "Did you say my wife?"

Annja let her comment trail off, puzzled by his reaction. "Yes. Your wife, Claire."

A cloud seemed to pass over Dr. Knowles's face. He reached out and grabbed her arm, his anger now evident.

"Is this some kind of joke, Miss Creed? Because if it is, I'm not finding it funny."

Annja was nonplussed and wasn't sure what to say. She made no move to pull free, worried about antagonizing him further. She caught his gaze with her own and said carefully, "I'm not joking, Dr. Knowles. I was hired by your wife, Claire, to help find you. She's across the hall, in the opposite cell."

Knowles stiffened. "I don't know who is in that other cell, Miss Creed, but I can assure you it is not my wife. Claire suffered a near-fatal car accident six months ago and has been in a coma ever since due to a traumatic brain injury. Even if she were to regain consciousness, which the doctors tell me isn't likely, she wouldn't have the mental capabilities of a five-year-old."

His voice shook with pain as he said, "I don't know who you've got with you in that other cell, but one thing's for certain—whoever she is, she isn't my wife!"

32

Annja couldn't make heads or tails of what Dr. Knowles was saying. She understood the words, but what they meant was so far outside of what she'd expected him to say that they just weren't coming together with any type of cohesion.

That was when the clapping started.

Slow, measured claps from the cell across the way.

Annja and Dr. Knowles turned at the same time and stared across the space between them to where Claire stood at the door to the other cell, her hands between the bars and clapping together mockingly. Knowles's loud voice had apparently carried that far.

Claire stopped clapping and looked at Knowles with what could only be described as derision. "You always were such a dramatist, Richard."

Knowles stared, his mouth hanging open in surprise.

"That's her," Annja said to him softly, so that Claire wouldn't hear her. "The woman who claims to be your wife." Annja hadn't missed the look of recognition that had crossed Knowles's face a moment ago. "Do you know her?"

"Yes, I know her," he said through gritted teeth.

As if to prove his point, Claire called, "What's the matter, Richard. Didn't expect to see me again so soon?"

Richard grimaced and stepped away from the scene.

"Yes, I know her," he repeated. He sounded as if he was trying to control his temper. "Her name is Claire Dunham and she's my former research assistant." He glanced back at her in disgust before facing Annja again. "I fired her two years ago for pillaging artifacts from my dig and then trying to sell them on the black market. We were in England at the time and she fled the country before Interpol could get ahold of her."

Claire called across to them, "Come now, Richard, you can't still be angry at me. It was just a few trinkets. They didn't sell nearly as well as the treasure I'm going to steal from you this time!"

Annja was furious, both at Claire for deceiving her in the way she had and at herself for not having checked further into Claire's story. She'd let the other woman lead her around by the nose, all because she'd become overwhelmed by her own desire to find the lost treasure. It would have been bad enough to be overwhelmed with treasure fever, but that wasn't what was driving her. No, she'd been a victim of her own ego, and that was especially galling.

"My apologies, Dr. Knowles. She had emails that you sent from the dig site, detailed summaries of what you'd accomplished to date—everything looked legitimate."

Knowles had himself back under control. "It's not your fault, Miss Creed, so please don't blame yourself. She must have hacked my email account," he said. "That's the only way she could have gotten that information, because the only person it was sent to was my representative from the Science Channel, the expedition's sponsor."

He smiled ruefully. "When going after a treasure this big, I've found it best to keep my mouth shut."

All this time Annja had been worried about another group of treasure hunters horning in on their claim and the whole time the enemy was right there with her. How stupid could she be!

Apparently very.

Claire had stopped taunting them and was deep in conversation with her two underlings. Annja didn't trust any of them anymore and vowed to keep an eye on them. She assumed the three of them were discussing how to get out of this mess, as none of them were the type to sit down and accept the status quo without fighting back. If Marcos and Hugo could get their hands on some weapons, Annja had no doubt that they'd shoot first and ask questions later.

Annja also knew that any plan Claire came up with would no doubt not include her or Dr. Knowles and his team. That meant she would need to be ready to act at the same time Claire did or they'd be left behind to deal with the aftermath of Claire's escape, which could be anything from increased security to reprisals against the remaining prisoners.

She had no intention of letting that happen.

A quick examination of the cell door showed her that it was merely tied shut with a thick, vinelike cord. A single blow from her sword would take care of it when the time came. They would still have to face the guards outside, never mind an entire city of people who would easily recognize them as foreigners, but she'd work that out when necessary.

One thing at a time.

Worn-out from their long trek and now satisfied that she could get them out of the cell when she needed to, Annja settled down against a nearby wall and tried to relax. Knowles told her his story—how they'd found the treasure and excavated it, how the Inca had swooped in shortly thereafter and taken them, and the treasure, captive. He introduced her to the other men and women in the cell with them, all of whom were part of his dig team. The rest, he explained, were across the hall in the cell with Claire and her hired men, along with the crew of the *Sea Dancer.*

Annja told him about her own journey—their encounter with the pirates, the discovery of the empty *Sea Dancer,* the trek to the dig site. They spent some time marveling at the Incan civilization they'd discovered and speculated that perhaps the island's designation as a World Heritage site had done more to protect the natives' secret than anything else. It was all conjecture, but Annja hadn't had the time to sit down and talk with a colleague as experienced as he was in some time and she enjoyed herself, despite their surroundings.

The guards came back about three hours later, escorting two cooks who carried a large stew pot between them. At the first sign of them, the prisoners lined up single file to the left of the door, bowls in hand. Unlike those who'd been here for a bit, Annja didn't have a bowl, so Knowles handed her his.

"Go on. Eat. I'll get some when you're finished."

The stew was thick with vegetables and meat, most

likely boar or something similar based on the taste. Annja didn't have utensils and had to scoop it into her mouth with her fingers, but everyone else was eating the same way and so she didn't mind. When she was finished, she handed the bowl to Knowles, who was just in time to get the last dregs in the pot before the guards took it away.

They talked for a bit longer before Knowles suggested they get some sleep. The guards would stay outside the cave and not bother them until morning, but when the sun came up they were expected to start their shift in the mine and they'd need all their strength to make it through the day.

With thoughts of digging for gold dancing through her head, Annja laid down and tried to get some rest.

A NOISE BROUGHT ANNJA out of her sleep.

She laid still for a moment, eyes closed so as not to give herself away, and listened. She didn't hear anything at first and then the sound resumed. It was rhythmic, a back-and-forth sawing sound that was coming from the cell across the hall.

Claire!

Annja quietly rose and waited for her eyes to adjust. The braziers had burned down to little more than hot coals, bathing the cavern in a faint red light. Once she was confident she could see the others sleeping on the floor before her, she made her way through them on catlike feet to the door of the cell, where she crouched down and stared across the hall.

She was able to make out the darker shape of someone standing just inside the door to the other cell. The sound was louder here, and when she focused on it Annja could see something flashing dully in a repetitive pattern near the edge of the cell door.

Someone was sawing through the bindings that were holding the cell door shut.

Where had they gotten the knife?

Annja thought about it for a moment and concluded that it must have been hidden on Claire somewhere. The men had both been frisked when they'd been captured but the Incas had left Annja and Claire alone. Cultural blindness, she guessed; women in Incan society did not carry weapons or hold status as warriors.

The knife finally sliced through the rest of the binding holding the door shut and it gave way with a bit of a twang, like a string on a guitar breaking under pressure.

In the stillness of the cavern, the noise seemed unnaturally loud.

She froze, as did the individual across the way, but no one came.

After a few seconds the door to the other cell creaked open and Claire stepped out into the dimly light cavern. She glanced in Annja's direction but Annja stayed still and Claire looked away.

Annja didn't think she'd been seen. She watched Claire take a few tentative steps out into the center of the cavern, watched her peer down the hall toward the entrance, and then abruptly do an about-face and slip back into her cell, pulling the door shut behind her.

Annja watched all this in surprise, wondering what was going on. She didn't have to wait long to get her answer, as she soon noticed the light getting brighter and heard someone approaching. The sound of sandals on stone grew louder until a guard stepped into view.

As quietly as possible, Annja drew back from the door, her gaze never leaving the Incan warrior just beyond.

The guard stood in the center of the cavern, glancing back and forth between the two cells. Annja watched him raise his torch high over his head in an attempt to cast more light on the situation, to no avail. The darkness of the caves must have defeated him for he gave an audible sigh as he stepped over to the door of the other cell, lowering the torch as he did so to help him better see inside.

The light fell directly on Claire, who was standing just inside the cell door.

"Hi," she said, smiling, and then shoved the door violently forward directly into the guard's unprotected face.

There was a solid thunk as one of the poles making up the door collided directly with the guard's forehead, sending him stumbling backward, arms flailing.

Claire was on him in a flash. The torch rolled free and all Annja could see was a dark-shrouded mass that she knew was the two of them atop each other and then an arm rose and fell, rose and fell, and rose and fell again before going still.

Climbing off the guard, Claire retrieved the torch and came back to look at her handiwork. Even from where she stood behind the edge of the door, Annja saw the dark flow of blood draining out of the stab wounds in the man's neck. If he wasn't dead now, he would be in a matter of moments.

33

The die has been cast, Annja thought.

Blood had been spilled and it was only a matter of time before the Inca demanded blood in turn. Any chance of their being spared without further injury just went out the window, she realized. They needed to get out of here before the guard was discovered or there would be hell to pay.

In her distress Annja must have made some kind of sound because Claire whirled around and stared directly at her cell door. Very slowly Annja crept backward until she bumped into someone about a yard or so behind her. She would have screamed if the other person hadn't clamped a hand over her mouth and indicated with his other hand that they should be quiet. Annja kept absolutely still so as to not garner more attention from Claire.

Deciding that she may have heard something after all, Claire strode to the cell door and shone the torch light inside. Annja saw that the rest of the dig team were all sleeping in the same position, with their feet toward the door, which must have made it difficult for Claire to see who was who. Annja and Dr. Knowles crouched just out of sight. Claire moved back and forth, trying to get a better look, but quickly gave up.

As Annja and Dr. Knowles allowed themselves to breathe again, Claire gestured back toward the cell she emerged from and Hugo and Marcos appeared. Both men had knives in their hands. Hugo disappeared down toward the cavern entrance while Marcos stopped beside the dead guard's body, bent over and wiped the blade of his knife several times on the guard's tunic to clean the blood off it.

Annja's heart raged at the sight; unless he'd cut himself with his own knife, which was highly unlikely, there was only one other way he could have gotten blood all over his blade. She felt Knowles stiffen behind her as he came to the same conclusion. Annja had no doubt that when they got into the cell across the way they'd find all of the other prisoners murdered in their sleep.

She almost drew her sword then and there. When Hugo returned he not only had a pistol in hand, but he also had their packs with him. Annja was surprised; she hadn't known their gear was nearby. Nor that the others had handguns in addition to the rifles they'd been carrying. Seemed she'd missed a lot.

While Hugo stood watch, Claire and Marcos pulled additional handguns and ammunition from inside the packs and then dumped the contents onto the floor of the cave, leaving them with empty packs.

Not that they'd be empty for long.

Using her knife, Claire cut away the ropes of the door to the treasure cave and stepped inside. She moved immediately to one of the sea chests full of gemstones and began shoving handfuls of them into the backpack.

Marcos did the same with one of the chests of gold doubloons. When they were finished, they stepped back into the main cavern and let Hugo fill his backpack while Claire stood watch.

Finally, the three of them were ready to go. But they couldn't do so without having the final word.

Claire sauntered over to the door. "I know you're awake in there," she whispered into the semidarkness, apparently having seen more than Annja realized. "Nine of you went to bed and I only see seven of you sleeping the night away."

Annja stepped out of the darkness and walked to the doorway, her anger hot and fresh.

"Just going to leave us, are you?" she asked, playing the part so the other woman didn't get suspicious.

"You're lucky I don't shoot you all before I go," Claire said with a sneer. "But don't worry, we'll be back with enough mercenaries and packing crates to get the treasure out of here whether they want to give it to us or not."

Annja shook her head. "You won't get away with this," she told Claire. In truth, she hoped they would be able to escape, because that meant that Annja and the rest of them could follow in their wake. But she'd never admit that to Claire.

True to form, Claire laughed. "Watch me."

They were all so caught up in their conversation that none of them saw Cuzco approaching down the hallway until he was right on top of them. He must have stopped by to check on the prisoners, found the guard missing and then moved deeper into the cavern in an attempt to answer why. By the time he realized that the people in front of him were not his guards, it was too late.

He turned to run, but never made it.

Hugo was the first to react. His hand went to his belt; he drew his knife and flipped it through the air before anyone else had recovered from their surprise. The knife embedded itself in Cuzco's calf, driving him to the floor.

Annja noted that he rolled over quickly enough, ready to spring to his feet and defend himself, but Hugo was there with his gun before the other man could rise to his feet and that was that.

"Bring him over here," Claire demanded.

Hugo did so. He also offered a little unsolicited advice in the process. "No witnesses, remember? He's seen our faces—he's got to go."

Claire glared at him. "This isn't my first rodeo," she told him. "I've got it under control. Go finish up with the rest of the gear."

She looked over the prisoner for several minutes, trying to decide what to do with him. In the end, she decided that Hugo was right. Better to just get it over with and not drag it all out.

"Goodbye," Claire said to him, smiling, and started to bring her gun up.

Annja had seen and heard enough. If they killed the king's son, they were all going to be in terrible trouble. She had to stop them.

She asked Dr. Knowles to go check on the others. As soon as his back was turned, she called for her sword and slashed at the bindings holding the door shut. When she stepped out into the main cavern, Marcos spun around to face her, aiming his weapon in her direction. Annja did her best to ignore both it and him.

"You can't shoot him, Claire," Annja told her urgently.

Claire wasn't listening. "Watch me," she said.

The gun still hadn't left the prince's face.

"Don't be an idiot, Claire. That's the king's son. You kill him and they'll hunt you across the planet and to the end of time to settle their blood debt." Annja spoke as rapidly as she could, hoping to get through to Claire before the other woman did something stupid.

Apparently her words had some effect, but not the effect she wanted. Rather than reducing the risk to the prince, she only made it worse.

"He's the royal heir?" Claire laughed. "Oh, that's rich. Seriously rich."

She stalked over to where he stood and pointed her gun at his head from just a foot away. "Killing him before was just a necessity. Now, though, now I'm going to enjoy it."

Annja didn't think Cuzco could understand English, but it didn't take much to understand a gun pointed at your head wasn't a good sign.

Cuzco apparently wasn't going to stand for it. He chose that moment to make a break for it. Surging upward, he knocked Claire's gun out of her hands, sending it spinning across the cavern. He didn't stick around to see what happened, either, but turned heel and headed down the passageway toward the opening.

Annja reacted as well, rushing forward, trying to put herself between Claire and Cuzco to give him time to escape without being shot in the back.

Marcos moved to intercept her and she slashed at him with the sword, cleaving the front of his handgun right off and only narrowly missed taking his hand with it instead.

She took a few more steps forward, her attention focused on Claire and the gun the other woman was scrambling to recover, and didn't see Hugo step out of the open cell on her left. In his hand was a heavy, jewel-encrusted crucifix and he swung it savagely at the side of Annja's head.

The two connected and Annja hit the floor.

Annja knew right away she'd been badly hurt. Her brain was sending signals but her body wasn't listening to them; no matter how hard she tried, she couldn't move an arm or a leg.

Her senses were fading, as well. She could hear Dr. Knowles shouting her name, but his voice sounded very far away. Her vision was blurry, but she could see Cuzco charging hard for the exit and then Hugo stepping forward, his gun hand coming up.

Annja must have screamed.

Cuzco looked back and Annja thought she heard a gunshot.

Darkness claimed her.

34

When Annja came to, she found herself lying on the floor at the back of a room somewhere. A crowd of people stood in front of her, listening as someone begged someone else for something. She couldn't understand the words—her head was spinning and she was having trouble sorting her thoughts—but the voice was familiar. Whoever it was didn't appear to be all that popular, though, if the attitude of the crowd in front of her was any indication. They wanted blood; she could see it in their stance, their body language, even in the angry outbursts that threatened to interrupt the speaker at any moment.

She pushed herself into a sitting position. The room swam before her eyes and then steadied. She couldn't see much over the heads of the crowd but she recognized the outer edges of the golden fan that spread out from the top of the king's throne and realized that she must be in the king's audience chamber.

On the heels of that realization came another. The voice she was hearing was that of Dr. Knowles, and if she was hearing him correctly, he was currently pleading with the king for their lives.

Something to her left caught her attention. She focused and saw a male Incan warrior lying on a mat similar to the one she was on. His arms were crossed over his chest and his eyes were closed.

He looked as if he was sleeping.

Except that his chest was still.

Puzzled, knowing that there was something wrong with her thought processes, that she was not connecting the dots properly or with her usual speed, Annja tried to stand, only to be overcome by a wave of dizziness. She sat back down and waited until the room stopped spinning around her and then slid onto her hands and knees instead.

She crawled toward the sleeping man.

It was less than two yards, but it seemed to take forever.

With each movement forward her thoughts seemed to grow clearer. She started to remember recent events—the initial audience with the king, the move to the gold mine, the confrontation with Claire and the others. Even the blow from Marcos that had rendered her unconscious. By the time she reached the man on the mat before her, her thoughts had returned to their usual order and she knew who she would find lying there.

Cuzco.

She was right. The Incan prince lay unmoving on the mat and she didn't need to touch his cold flesh to know that he was dead. The bullet hole in the center of his forehead confirmed what she already knew.

When his usefulness had run out, Claire, or one of her mercenaries, had killed him.

Suddenly it was too much.

Tears began to pour down her face, crossing her

cheeks to fall wetly on the body in front of her like raindrops from the sky, and great racking sobs burst up from her chest and fell from her lips. She was unable to stop them and could only let it pour out in a flood.

Dimly, in the back of her mind, she told herself, *You've got a concussion. Memory loss. Wildly swinging emotions. No ability to think clearly. All signs of injury due to blunt trauma to the head. Hang in there and you should balance out again.*

Gradually, she became aware that the room around her had grown silent. She could feel the eyes of others staring at her back, but she couldn't seem to take her gaze away from Cuzco's face and that damning bullet hole in the middle of his forehead.

It was her fault, she realized. If she hadn't agreed to lead Claire and the others here, they might never have found it on their own. She was to blame and she loathed herself for it.

EASY, NOW, THAT VOICE in her head warned. *Remember that you've got a concussion...*

Tears slipped down her cheeks.

Someone was kneeling next to her and Annja turned slowly to find the dark-haired interpreter watching her from a foot or so away.

"Why do you weep?"

The question caught Annja by surprise and she answered with the first thing that came to mind.

"Because it is my fault."

The interpreter's face was carefully blank as she said, "What is your fault?"

Annja gestured toward Cuzco's body. "This. His death. Everything."

"Did you pull the—" she struggled with the proper term and, not finding it, was forced to change the sentence "—shoot the weapon that did this?"

Annja shook her head. "No, but I guided them here in the first place. I led them to the island. Without me, they never would have found the dig site. Without me they never would have encountered you. And he would still be alive!"

Annja's voice rose as she continued to talk and she was practically shouting by the time she finished.

The interpreter stared at her and then did something entirely unexpected. She bent over and kissed Cuzco's lips.

In that moment Annja understood.

The interpreter was more than just an interpreter. She was the king's wife, the queen, and the man on the mat in front of her was her son, the king's heir.

And Annja had just admitted to being responsible for his death.

The queen straightened and then without warning viciously slapped Annja across the face.

The blow sent Annja's head to reeling again.

Dimly she heard the queen shouting something across the room, but she was too busy trying to understand what was going on.

"Annja! Are you all right?"

Dr. Knowles was bending over her, his face full of concern. It was his fear more than anything else that brought clarity back to her.

"Yes," she said, weakly at first and then with more strength. "Yes, I'm all right."

Knowles gently helped her to her feet, but when Annja looked up she found that they were surrounded by guards with very angry looks on their faces. She was convinced the guards would have torn her and Richard limb from limb if the king wasn't in the room.

Instead, they forced them to kneel in front of the dais, where the king waited, the queen at his side.

The king glowered at them, then tapped his staff of office three times, bringing silence to the room.

Whatever's next is going to be official, Annja thought, and indeed she was correct.

It was official.

An official death sentence, in fact.

The king spoke and the queen translated. "Since you have admitted your responsibility in the death of my son, Quehuar Tupac, your blood is forfeit in exchange for his own. You shall serve him as a concubine in the afterlife. Sentence to be carried out immediately. I, Inca Tupac, have spoken."

The guards stepped forward, intent on dragging her outside and carrying out the sentence, but Annja had other plans. Her thoughts were back in order and she knew she had only one option available to her, one thing that might allow her to live longer than the next five minutes, and that was a card she was eager to play.

"I demand a blood debt," she called out. And then again, louder this time, "I demand a blood debt!"

For the second time that day the room went silent.

The queen stared at her and said, "She is not one of us. She has no right! Carry out the sentence!"

The guards closed in. Annja was about to call her sword and go down fighting rather than be taken for execution when the king's voice boomed out.

The guards stopped, looked back toward the throne. The king and queen stood there, arguing vehemently. After several tense minutes the queen bowed her head in acquiescence and accepted whatever it was the king had demanded.

"The prisoner will rise and speak," she said, refusing to look at Annja.

Annja didn't care; she'd gotten a chance to speak and that was all she cared about right now. She rose to her feet, shook off the hands of her guards and then stepped forward to face the king.

"The same woman who killed your son killed my people, as well. My life is forfeit to the king to repay the blood debt owed him for his son, but my blood debt is just as valid and must be paid before sentence is carried out. I demand the right to track this killer and return her to justice to satisfy the debt owed to me."

It was a long shot. Annja knew that. It had been some time since she'd done a focused study on Incan customs and religious beliefs. If she was incorrect about any of the elements she'd just strung together, she'd find out soon enough.

At last, the king nodded.

She had won a reprieve for herself, only a temporary one. But that wasn't all the king had to say.

Speaking through the translator once more, the king said, "You know our customs. You respect our laws. You weep for my son as if he were your own. And yet... and yet you do not speak our language and it is on you that this killer is in our midst. I do not understand you. Nor do I trust you."

He paused, considering. "You have four days to track this killer and return her to this place to face justice. If you succeed, your blood debt will have been repaid.

"If you do not succeed, if you fail to return, know that I will slaughter each and every one of the prisoners left in my care, starting with this one."

The interpreter pointed at Dr. Knowles.

He would be the Incas' hostage until Annja returned.

Great. No pressure.

35

Annja knew she had her work cut out for her. A quick check in with Knowles before they led him away let her know that she'd been unconscious for a good three hours, maybe longer. Claire and her murderous bodyguards had that much of a lead. Never mind that they weren't traveling with a concussed head to slow them down.

Thankfully, the Inca had one more trick up their sleeves. When she had assembled a pack full of food and water and prepared herself for the journey, two Incan warriors showed up, accompanied by the queen.

"Will they return to their boat?" she asked.

Annja thought so and said as much.

"If you can beat them to the boat will you be able to stop them?"

"Without a doubt," Annja replied.

The queen considered this and then said something to the two men with her in their own tongue. After they replied, the queen said, "These two men will escort you on a path through the mountain. It should cut your travel time in half, if you keep up with the pace they set. Do so and you should beat them to your destination."

Annja liked the sound of that but something didn't seem right. "Why are you helping me?" she asked.

"Because I want the woman who killed my son, and you are my best chance at success."

"You trust me to deliver justice for your son?"

The queen smiled, but it was a cold and lifeless smile. "Of course not," she said to Annja. "But I trust that you will do your utmost to save the lives of your companions. Especially when you know that I will torture them mercilessly if you do not return as promised."

Steel entered Annja's expression, to clash with the iron in the queen's.

"I will be back," she told her. "If a single hair is harmed on any of their heads before I do…"

She left the last bit of it unsaid, confident that the queen had gotten the message.

Satisfied that they both understood each other, the queen took her leave and left Annja with her new guides.

As it turned out, neither of them spoke English. She decided that this would make things difficult but not impossible; she'd worked with non-English-speaking guides before and in this case she had the advantage of having been over the territory once before. At some point, things should start to look familiar.

Her biggest concern was the injury to her head. She'd had a chance to take a look at it since her audience with the king and one thing was certain—she was going to need some medical attention as soon as she got back to the mainland. There was no doubt that she had a concussion—the dizziness, nausea and general difficulty remembering things were proof enough of that—but she was worried she might have a fractured skull, or worse. She wouldn't feel comfortable until she had it checked out.

Nothing to be done about it now. She'd deal with any problems if and when they arose.

She indicated with hand motions that she was ready and her two guides took off at a solid trot. Annja fell in line and followed suit. They took her across the city to the far wall of the cavern, close to where they had entered the first time. Instead of taking the switchbacks up the main wall to the opening high above, the guides stuck to the ground floor, taking an underground tunnel that led them deeper under the side of the mountain.

At any other time she would have been fascinated by the route her guides took her through. It was clear they had been this way before; all of the tunnels and passageways looked the same to her but they had no trouble picking out which branch or turn they should take at any time during their march. Their footfalls were the only sound they made as they moved, and after a while Annja began to feel as if she was following ghosts, so lightly and quietly did they move. Her own steps sounded clunky and loud in comparison.

Time seemed to blur and blend together as they moved through that underground realm. Tunnel after tunnel, chamber after chamber, they ran on. They only stopped for water breaks on rare occasions and even then they were short. The guides had been given orders to get Annja to Chatham Bay as quickly as possible and they had no intentions of letting their queen down.

At one point they came to a section where the tunnel had collapsed and a pile of debris blocked their way forward. After a brief discussion between her guides, Annja was led into a narrower tunnel that she was told should take them around the blockage. The same uneasiness she'd experienced while entering Knowles's dig site a few days ago came over her thanks to the closeness of the walls and ceiling. She just kept telling herself to breathe easy and that got her through.

After descending for quite some time, they began heading back upward, which Annja took to be a good sign. Another long stretch of climbing, and finally Annja could see the sun. Moments later they emerged into the sunlight.

Annja had been on her feet for almost thirty-six hours by the time they emerged from the tunnels. The exit from the cave deposited her on a promontory in the jungle that was part of a north-south ridgeline a few miles away from Chatham Bay. If she'd had a pair of binoculars, she might have been able to make out the *Pride* anchored in the bay, but it was just too far away without them.

She turned to thank her guides and found herself alone, the two Incan warriors having already disappeared back into the tunnels, no doubt on their way home.

If only her job were that easy. Unfortunately, the hard part was still to come.

She sat down and had some water and a couple of pieces of fruit, wanting some energy for the final leg of the trip. If she could reach the bay before the sun set, she'd be in a good position to deal with the others come morning.

When she was finished, she slipped her pack over her shoulders and headed off down the slope in front of her.

She hadn't gone far before she began to run into difficulties.

She was moving through virgin jungle, so her speed was reduced substantially from her travel through the tunnels. What she'd thought would only take a few hours quickly became a half day or more, and Annja wasn't certain that she had that much time. If Claire beat her to the boat…

Annja pushed on.

And on.

And on.

As the sun began to go down in the later afternoon, Annja was barely able to keep her eyes open. One wrong step and she'd stumble off the ledge and break her neck on an outcropping of rock.

She needed to rest.

She spent a few minutes hunting about to find a suitable tree that she could climb into with limited energy expenditure and then lashed herself to the branch with a short piece of rope to keep from falling off in the middle of the night.

The knot on the rope was barely tied before her eyes fluttered shut and she slept.

ANNJA AWOKE TO THE FEELING of being in a bed with clean sheets tucked in tightly on either side. When she tried to move her arms and legs, she found she couldn't do so; she was strapped in as securely as if she were in a straitjacket.

Wait a minute. Strapped in? Straitjacket?

Her eyes snapped open.

A massive snake encircled her, its gold-black scales gleaming wetly in the morning dew.

Anaconda!

The snake had wrapped itself multiple times around her body, from about shin level to just below her neck. Its head slithered back and forth about a foot away from her own, its tongue flicking out repeatedly as if to test the air. Annja had the sense that it was watching her, waiting for that sign of weakness to show that the prey was all but finished.

The coils tightened as the snake pulled its body forward, exerting more crushing force against her own. Some of her air left her in a bit of a rush. Annja knew that all the snake needed to do was tighten itself up a little bit more and she wouldn't have any strength left to fight it off.

The pressure against her body was also starting to cause her head to ache; what started as a low-grade pain would soon spread into a migraine that would be just as debilitating as the coils around her flesh. She needed to get free and she needed to do it quickly.

One of her hands was free. The other was trapped beneath the thick coils of the snake's body. The snake was as wide around as her thigh and had to be at least fifteen feet long. There was no chance she was just going to be able to grab this thing with her free hand and pull it off.

No, more extreme measures were required.

Annja willed her sword into her hand and nearly sighed with relief when it appeared there without a problem. The broadsword was bulky and not all that maneuverable in a tight space, but it was razor sharp and should do the job nicely.

The tricky part was going to be right after she made the first cut. The snake would instinctively tighten up and might even strike at her with its teeth. Short of lopping off its head with a single blow, she was going to have to deal with both attacks at the same time. If she didn't finish the job quickly after that, she was going to be in serious trouble. Nothing to be done for it, though; she had to get free and this was the only method of doing so.

Annja took a deep breath, kept her eyes on the snake's head and then struck with the sword, slashing it against one of the snake's many coils.

The snake's body parted like butter, the sword driving deep into its flesh.

The snake struck in response to the pain, but thankfully, Annja had been waiting for it to do that very thing and she was able to jerk her head out of the way in the last second before the teeth could sink into her face.

It recoiled, preparing to strike again, but so was Annja. Her sword flashed a second time and this time it cut clean through the coil, severing a section from the lower half of its body.

Instantly she could breathe easier and move better.

The great beast hissed in anger and lunged.

It was the move Annja had been waiting for. As the beast's neck extended, Annja used her newfound dexterity to wield the sword with improved accuracy, slashing through the snake's neck and severing its head.

36

Chatham Bay
Cocos Island

After shrugging off the snake's corpse, Annja untied herself from the tree and swung down to the ground. The sun told her it was somewhere around 10:00 a.m., much later than she'd intended to sleep. Another consequence of her head injury, no doubt, and one she hadn't thought to plan for in advance.

She hoped it wouldn't cost her the race.

Annja wolfed down a quick breakfast of dried meat and fruit, followed it with some water and then shouldered her pack and got to her feet. The sleep had done her some good; her thoughts felt clearer and she wasn't having as much difficulty seeing any longer.

None of which will matter if they beat you to the Pride, *so get moving!*

As she drew closer to the coast, the vegetation became a bit less tangled and she was able to make better progress. But she began to worry about running into Claire's little band of thieves unexpectedly; they were all armed and wouldn't think twice about putting a bullet through her head. She began to move more circumspectly and keep her ears and eyes open for any sign of her former comrades.

She came to the river they'd followed upstream and cautiously moved along its bank until she reached the point where Dr. Knowles's Kodiaks had been abandoned. When they'd first encountered them, Annja had thought they'd fallen victim to a crocodile attack. Now that she knew what was happening on the island, she suspected the damage had been done in a more intentional fashion. She just hoped she wouldn't find their motor launches in the same condition.

It didn't take long from that point to reach the beach where they'd started this whole disaster a few days before. Annja hung back in the trees at first, scoping out the beach before moving around to the point where they'd hidden the launches from the *Pride*.

That was when she got her first shock.

One of the launches was missing.

Fear that she was too late tried to overwhelm her, but she fought it down and ignored it. It would only be too late on the day they pried her sword from her cold fingers. Until then, there was always a chance.

She stepped out onto the beach, expecting the sniper's bullet to reach out and touch her instantly, but none came. She hurried over to where the boats had been left and examined the ground. The slide marks indicating where the second boat had been slipped back into the water were partially filled with water but still held a fair bit of their cohesion. That meant they were reasonably new. She was just about to check the remaining launch when the sound of a boat's engine caught her attention.

She looked out into the bay, toward the sound, and

saw with dismay that someone had just fired up the engine to the *Neptune's Pride.*

It wasn't hard to figure out who that someone was.

They had beaten her to the beach.

Not by much, that was clear, but it might be enough.

Might be enough? You've got a functional boat right in front of you that can outrace the Pride *over short distances. Get moving before you miss your shot!*

Her examination of the launch killed that idea before it could get off the ground, however. The launch and the engine seemed intact; Claire was clever enough to know there was no sense in destroying a perfectly good boat when all one had to do was empty the gas tank.

Most of the precious liquid had seeped into the sand, leaving just dregs at the bottom of the tank. Those dregs might be enough to get her out to the *Pride,* but if she needed to do any maneuvering she'd be stranded in the open water.

Think, Annja, think.

Then she had it.

The *Sea Dancer!*

They had left it anchored in Wafer Bay, just around the promontory from Chatham. It wasn't far, especially not by sea, and if the *Dancer* was still there, she shouldn't have any trouble reaching it via the launch. If the *Dancer* wasn't there any longer, she could always row into Wafer Bay and not be stranded out to sea as she might be if she tried to reach the *Pride* with what little gas was left.

Another glance out into the bay showed the *Pride* starting to move and that settled it for her. The *Dancer,* it was.

Annja moved to the prow of the boat and pushed it backward, out into the surf. She kept going until it floated free and then jumped aboard. She used an oar to get it turned in the right direction and then tried to start her up.

The engine coughed and then died.

"Come on, don't do this..." she muttered and then tried again.

The engine coughed once, twice and then roared to life. Annja didn't waste any time, just spun the wheel and headed the launch toward the mouth of the bay as quickly as she could.

She knew the sound of the launch's motor wouldn't be heard over the deeper, louder sound generated by the *Pride*'s diesel engines but she was worried someone might be looking back in her direction as she brought the boat out of the bay. All it would take would be a couple of decently aimed rifle shots and the boat would go from seaworthy to a crumbling wreck in moments. She kept herself down as low as she could, reducing the chance of taking a bullet, and only stood back up in the cockpit when she'd rounded the peninsula separating the two bays.

She had her fingers on both hands crossed as she raced into Wafer Bay, her eyes scanning the water ahead, searching for the *Sea Dancer....*

There she was, right where they'd left her days before. The sight of the expedition vessel bobbing in the gentle surf was one of the most beautiful things she'd seen in a while, Annja thought.

She turned the launch slightly to put it on an intercept course and gave it more gas.

The engine responded by sputtering several times, coughing once and then falling silent.

Annja pounded the instrument panel in frustration.

The boat had been moving at a good clip before the engine died so she let it coast in the proper direction while she tried to restart it. By the third attempt she knew her efforts were futile; the launch was out of gas and wouldn't be going anywhere anytime soon.

Thankfully, the tide was going in and the launch was already moving toward the waiting vessel. With the help of an oar, she managed to get the launch over to the *Sea Dancer* with only a slight delay.

Once aboard, Annja went straight to the bridge and began firing up the engines. She'd been on enough boats of this size that it wasn't long before she was hauling in the anchor in preparation to chase down the *Pride*.

Once that was stowed, Annja brought the *Dancer* about and pointed her at the open water to the east. It was roughly three hundred and thirty kilometers to the coast of Costa Rica. They would start to hit pleasure-boat traffic about one hundred and fifty kilometers offshore, which left her roughly the same amount of distance in which to catch Claire and the others in the *Pride*.

One hundred and fifty kilometers.

Didn't seem like much but Annja was confident that she could do it.

And every passing kilometer brought her closer.

37

Open water
West of Costa Rica

It took her nearly two hours to overcome the *Pride*'s lead and then catch up with the vessel.

They were in international waters at this point, a long way from either Cocos Island or Costa Rica.

Which was good, given what she was going to do next.

She got close enough that she knew the pilot of the other boat, most likely Hugo, had to be aware of her now and so she reached up and flipped on the switch for the loudspeaker.

"*Neptune's Pride,* this is *Sea Dancer.* You are harboring fugitives from justice and are ordered to stop and accept an immediate boarding. I say again, *Neptune's Pride,* this is *Sea Dancer,* over."

Annja began to steer the *Dancer* closer to the other vessel, crowding her, trying to get her to turn and heave to. The pilot of the other vessel recognized her tacti and continually tried to avoid her. They crosse several times and came alarmingly close t along the sides and sterns of the ships but none of that slowed the other vessel down. When such jockeying for position didn't work after nearly ten minutes, the crew of the *Pride* tried something new.

They stuck a rifle barrel out the back window of the bridge and fired upon her.

Annja threw herself to the deck as high-velocity bullets shattered the glass along the front-bridge windows and ricocheted around the command room.

From her spot on the floor, Annja called them a few choice names while the hail of gunfire danced about the room. Thankfully, none of it hit her or any of the important bridge controls. It would be pure luck if it did, but then again, luck hadn't been so kind to her on this trip of late and she fully expected every vital part of the bridge to take at least one, maybe two, bullets right through it.

When the firing slowed, Annja reached up, grabbed the wheel and put the *Dancer* on a forty-five-degree angle relative to the *Pride,* sending the two ships apart from each other.

As the *Dancer* pulled away from the slower and less maneuverable *Pride,* Annja put it on autopilot and went back to dig through some of the gear they had down below. She was specifically looking for something that might help her get the other boat to slow down enough to allow her to board it.

She found what she was looking for in the ship's locker.

It was known as a prop fouler, and devices like it had ~ne popular as antipirate devices following their use by conservationists who used them to jamb up the propellers of the Japanese whaling vessels they were protesting against. It was basically a large weighted net made from Kevlar rope that was thrown into the wake of the propellers where it would be sucked forward into the blades of the ship, effectively jamming them. Earlier versions had been basic nets that were easily unwound from the propellers by simply putting the engines into reverse. The latest versions were not only made out of stronger material, but were weighted like this one to make them much harder to get off the driveshaft and propeller blades.

Annja intended to use it on the *Neptune's Pride*.

In order to do so, however, she was going to have to get close enough to cast it into the prop wash of the boat.

They, of course, would no doubt be shooting at her all the while.

Short of ramming the other vessel, however, she couldn't think of any way to get them to heave to.

And then her gaze fell on the twin speedboats attached to the rear of the *Dancer* and she knew she'd found her solution.

TWENTY MINUTES LATER she added power to the engine and turned the *Dancer* back toward the *Pride*. The current course she'd set would take the *Dancer* right across the bow of the *Pride*.

It was simply intended as a ruse. While Claire's and her cronies' attention was on the *Dancer*, Annja would do a drive-by of the rear of the *Pride* and unleash her prop fouler. Once the boat was dead in the water, she could board when ready, take out Hugo and Marcos, capture Claire and return with them to the Incan city hidden inside Mount Yglesias.

A walk in the park, she thought, but knew it was anything but that simple.

Satisfied the controls were set in the proper sequence and that the ship would respond in the manner she needed it to when she needed it, Annja abandoned the bridge and headed aft. She hadn't taken ten steps before the *Dancer* heaved hard to port and began to speed up. By the time she reached the main deck, the engines were running full tilt and the *Dancer* was cutting through the waves as gracefully as its namesake.

Someone on the *Pride* laid on the ship's horn, firing off a long blast to try to warn the *Dancer* off, and Annja knew that she'd been seen. Things would go more quickly now.

By the time she reached the motor launches at the back of the *Dancer,* her recorded messages began to broadcast from the bridge, adding to the cacophony of sound and motion that she was building to hide her true intention.

"*Sea Dancer* to *Neptune's Pride. Sea Dancer* to *Neptune's Pride.* Heave to and prepare to be boarded. You are in violation of the UN and UNESCO charters on World Heritage artifacts. The captain of this vessel is exercising her right as a…"

The message went on for nearly ten minutes, full of quoted statutes and legalistic phrases. It was all complete garbage; Annja had cobbled it together with the help of the internet not fifteen minutes before. It wasn't

supposed to stand up in court, only distract them with her constantly droning voice. While her recorded words blathered on, Annja fired up the motor launch and disengaged from the *Dancer,* standing in the ship's shadow for the time being to hide her presence.

Annja had hooked the proximity alarm to the intercom as well so that, too, filled the air between the vessels as the *Dancer* bore down on the slower *Pride.* She expected the alarm to cut off when the *Pride* turned out of the *Dancer*'s path, but as it continued Annja realized that the *Pride* wasn't going to turn.

Hugo was playing chicken.

Annja laughed. *Wait until he figures out there's no one in the captain's chair.*

Satisfied that she'd created enough of a distraction to cover her run at the props, Annja eased the motor launch away from the *Dancer* and swung around the stern of the ship, beginning her attack run.

As she came out of the *Dancer*'s shadow, she got her first good look at the *Pride.* It was ahead and to the port of the *Dancer* and it was currently doing everything it could to make an emergency turn in the same direction.

She could clearly see that the captain had waited too long to start his evasive maneuvers and there was little to keep the two ships from colliding. The *Pride* had moved enough to keep the *Dancer* from impaling her on its prow, but it would still do some significant damage to the side of the vessel.

If she timed it right, she might be able to toss the prop fouler right at the moment of maximum confusion, when the two ships bumped into each other.

She just needed to get close enough.

Annja gunned the launch's engine and nearly whooped aloud at the power beneath her feet. She sped toward the rear of the *Pride,* intent on ending this as quickly as she could. All she needed was one good throw....

Annja was expecting to take gunfire from the upper deck of the *Pride,* but no one noticed her kamikaze approach. She was able to steer right up next to the *Pride*'s stern and then throw the fouler with near-perfect accuracy into the churning water above the propeller blades.

As soon as she let the net go, she threw the wheel hard to port, cutting away from the big ship in a wide arc.

Seconds later the engines of the *Pride* went silent as the propellers seized, the fouler's netting wrapping around the blades and driveshaft like a vise.

The larger vessel began to slow almost immediately.

Annja brought the launch around and headed for the side of the ship, intending to climb aboard as quickly as possible to end this fiasco once and for all. She was watching the upper deck of the *Pride* pretty closely as she approached, which was why she saw Hugo the moment he brought his rifle up and over the side of the ship.

Annja knew she was in trouble. She was totally exposed, just as she'd feared. With twenty-five feet to go before she reached the side of the ship, she'd never get there and get aboard before Hugo shot her. Nor could she hit the gas and escape; from his higher vantage point, he'd be able to shoot at her easily.

Hugo apparently assessed the situation in a similar

way, for a wide smile crossed his face as he brought the rifle to his shoulder.

Annja did the only thing she could think of to do.

She dived overboard as the crack of a rifle shot filled the air.

38

Annja heard the bullet zing by her shoulder as she dived into the sea. Images of frenzied sharks and blood in the water flashed through her mind.

She reversed directions as soon as she disappeared beneath the surface, swimming as fast as possible for the safety that the hull of the *Pride* would provide. Dimly she heard more shots being fired and saw darting ghosts whip past her on their way to the depths as Hugo filled the area with gunfire.

Miraculously, none of the bullets hit her and she was able to reach the hull of the *Pride* without injury. That, of course, left her with a new problem—how to surface for more air without getting shot by Hugo.

A problem she needed to solve very quickly.

Her lungs were already screaming at her to open her mouth and breathe, despite the small issue of being submerged. Still, she knew she couldn't hold out much longer. She needed a place she could surface and stay hidden.

But where?

The answer, when it came to her, was perfect. She just hoped she had enough air to make it.

She could hear more shots being fired as she turned and followed the line of the hull toward the rear of the ship, where the *Pride*'s motor launches were kept in hanging berths jutting out over the water.

Only one of the launches was currently aboard the ship—Annja had taken the other one to the *Sea Dancer*—and as she swam for the surface, her lungs screaming for her to breathe, she knew that she could be surfacing right into Hugo's sights if the launch was docked on the other side of the ship.

Please let it be there...please....

Her head broke the surface of the water...and bumped into the underside of the launch hanging six inches above the sea. She opened her mouth and sucked in a great lungful of air.

She clung to the underside of the launch, catching her breath and deciding what to do next. She'd stopped the *Pride* as intended and sent the *Sea Dancer* motoring along. If she could get aboard the ship, she could deal with her three former companions in the manner they deserved.

The best way to do that, it seemed, was to swim for the back of the boat and climb up onto the dive platform, using that as an entryway into the ship. Now that she knew where she was, it should be an easy feat.

Provided Hugo didn't think of the same thing and end up waiting there for her.

She took a deep breath and dived beneath the surface. She kept one hand on the hull of the ship above her head, using the other to help propel her along toward the rear of the vessel. It wasn't far—twenty feet at most.

When she felt the dive platform above her head, she slowly surfaced, doing what she could to not make noise as she broke the plane of the water.

The platform was dimly lit but even in the low light she could see that it was empty.

She grabbed it with two hands, pulled her body up and then stood.

Hugo stepped out from behind the rack holding the scuba tanks and put the barrel of his rifle in the center of her forehead.

"Look what the cat dragged in," he said.

Annja didn't hesitate; she moved her head sharply to one side, getting out of the line of fire, and called her sword at the exact same moment, thrusting it forward even as it emerged from the otherwhere.

Hugo's eyes bulged, his rifle went off and blood poured out of his mouth as three feet of hardened steel punctured his chest just beneath his rib cage, rose diagonally through the body cavity above that point, to emerge from his back just shy of his neckline.

He opened his mouth as if to say something and died.

One down, Annja thought.

She gave a tug, realized she was not going to be getting her sword out that way and simply let it vanish into the otherwhere so that she wouldn't have to spend precious minutes trying to free it from Hugo's corpse.

She brought it back immediately. Feeling as if she'd just been reunited with her better half, Annja moved to go in search of the others and then paused.

She looked back at Hugo's body.

If someone stumbled upon his corpse, it would be immediately obvious that there was an intruder on board, Annja thought. But if he just happened to disappear, they couldn't be sure.

What the enemy thought they knew was often more dangerous and more beneficial to their opponents than they sometimes realized. If she could get Claire and Marcos doubting what Hugo was up to, she would put them off their game and gain an advantage, even a slight one, when the time came.

To that end Annja opened up the dive locker where all the scuba gear was stored and removed two weight belts. One would probably be enough but no sense taking chances.

She slipped the belts around Hugo's waist and secured them both. Satisfied, she dragged the corpse over to the diving pool that provided access to the ocean outside the ship through a narrow vertical tunnel kept at positive pressure, then dumped the corpse into it.

As expected, it sank like a stone and quickly disappeared from sight.

She found a bucket and used some water to sluice away the blood from the deck. It wasn't perfect, but it was a whole sight better than it had been five minutes before. It would have to do.

Satisfied, she turned her attention to locating the other two.

She crept through the lower deck, barely able to hear anything thanks to the proximity of Hugo's last gunshot. She knew her hearing would come back to her, but she didn't know how long it would take and without it she felt like a sitting duck. She couldn't afford to wait it out; she had little doubt that King Tupac would happily slaughter Knowles and any of his team Annja had left behind in retribution for the death of his son.

Annja moved quietly to the middle of the ship, where she found the stairs rising to the next deck. She stopped there, torn with indecision.

Should she continue forward and check the rest of the lower deck, be certain that they weren't down there, or should she continue up to the next level and hunt there? If she did stay on this level, how would she know if they came down and went aft while she was in the forward compartments? And if that happened, what if...?

Don't overthink it. Go forward; clear one deck at a time. Make sure you are not leaving the enemy in your wake with the potential to harm you.

She did so without finding anyone and then returned to the stairs. She stood at the base of the steps and listened, straining to hear anything from above, but she was hampered by the fact that her ears were still ringing from the gunshot.

Unable to make out anything beyond the norm, Annja started up the steps.

She reached the middeck and slowed to look forward and then aft. Most of the aft portion was given over to storage rooms and machinery, everything from the machine shop to the bilge-equipment room. Forward, however, were more of the living spaces for the crew and guests—staterooms, labs, the galley and general wardroom.

Marcos seemed the type who hated the trivialities of day-to-day work, so if he was on this deck he'd most likely be forward rather than aft.

So check the aft compartments, cross them off the list and then move forward. Let's move; time's wasting.

She did just that, moving through the compartments as quietly as possible so as to not give away her position. She kept waiting for someone to discover some evidence that pointed to her battle with Hugo, but so far no alarm had been raised. It helped that there had only been three of them on the ship to start with, now reduced to two.

When she had checked the aft section of the mid-deck without finding anyone, she returned to the stairs and headed forward. For all she knew both Claire and Marcos were holed up in the bridge high above the main deck, but she wasn't going to take the chance of being wrong and allow them to strike at her from behind.

Annja was checking one of the staterooms when she thought she heard something coming from one of the rooms farther along the row. Cautiously, she moved closer.

As she stepped through the door, something came whistling toward her at eye level.

She didn't wait to see what it was, just let her instincts take over, diving forward, underneath the blow, and somersaulted on landing so that she came back up facing the door she'd just left.

Marcos stood to one side, a thick piece of metal with a vicious-looking steel hook on one end, a kind of makeshift fishing gaffer, in his hand.

It had been the end of that hook that she'd heard whistling toward her head just seconds ago.

When Marcos's attention shifted for a split second to pulling his hook free from the wall it had sunken into when it had missed her, Annja called her sword to hand and stood ready.

Marcos looked back at her and blinked. "Where you'd get that pigsticker?" he asked, perhaps even genuinely curious as he hadn't seen her with it just seconds before.

Annja opened her mouth to reply, but Marcos was on her in an instant, trying to use his bigger size to overwhelm her with the sheer ferocity of his attack, his gaff lashing out again and again. Slash and parry, cut and jab. Back and forth they went, neither of them gaining any significant advantage, their weapons ringing every time they came into contact with each other.

They broke apart for a moment, both of them breathing heavily.

Annja tried circling to her right, watching Marcos closely to see if there might be some opening that she could exploit in the midst of their next exchange, but the big warrior had spent too many years in the military to give away a tell like that. He stood his ground, letting her use up her energy while he conserved his own.

Suddenly Marcos exploded toward her, the hook on the end of his gaff swinging in toward Annja's midsection in a vicious strike.

Annja dropped the point of her sword and met the long, narrow arm of the gaff with the edge of her blade, letting the power behind Marcos's strike dissipate elsewhere. Even as she did so, she twisted her own weapon around in an arc that was aimed to gut Marcos where he stood.

But the former soldier was already gone by the time

the blow had landed, dancing back out of range on nimble feet.

Back and forth they went across the wardroom, blow after blow, twisting and turning, each of them striving to gain the upper hand and deliver the winning blow.

So far neither of them came close.

Marcos came in again, swinging the gaff, but something about his tactics was different this time and Annja wouldn't be drawn in so easily. She understood why a moment later when he made a surprise strike with his opposite hand that immediately followed a missed strike with the gaff and a wickedly curved knife narrowly missed her hip.

There was more to his abilities than first appeared, it seemed. She would do well to remember that.

Marcos broke away again, putting some space between them. Annja wasn't completely surprised—she needed a break, too—but then Marcos turned and ran from the room, disappearing into the maze of rooms beyond.

It was going to take some time to flush him out, especially on her own, and time was something she really couldn't spare.

Marcos had headed toward the galley and food storage areas, so there were plenty of hiding places up ahead that she was going to need to be watchful for.

At the door through which Marcos had disappeared, she paused to listen. She didn't hear anything that might give his presence away, so she reached into the room, searching for the light switch.

"Looking for me?" came Marcos's sarcastic voice in

her ear just before he drove his ham-size fist right into the side of her head, concussed only two days before.

Blinding white light filled her senses. Annja's world spun and she was vaguely aware of someone vomiting nearby. It took her several seconds to realize that someone was her and there wasn't anything that she could do about it. Her hands were empty, her sword seeming to have vanished back to the otherwhere.

Marcos seized her by the shoulders, lifted her off the ground and smashed her against a wall.

Even through the pain she knew he was coming for her and she tried to push herself up, tried to get to her feet, but her head was screaming, the pain mesmerizing in its ruthlessness, and all she managed to do was a kind of stumbling half crouch. She tried to summon her sword again, tried to will it back into her hand like she'd done so many times before, but the pain was so intense that she couldn't seem to connect.

This time he grabbed her by the back of her shirt and the waistband of her pants and hurled her across a crowded counter. The sound of metal clanging made her think of her sword again and she tried to call it to hand. She could feel it in the otherwhere, straining to answer her summons, but she was dizzy, and it was like trying to see through cloth, hazy and indistinct.

Had her head injury done something to her? Had it cut off her connection with the sword?

Panic swelled and her hands shuffled fearfully about the countertop, searching for something that she could use to defend herself with as Marcos stalked closer.

"I told you," he mocked as he came toward her. "Told

you that you'd get your own. Now it's time for you to understand just who's in charge of this expedition!"

He grabbed her and spun her to face him, which was precisely the kind of targeting she needed. With him directly in front of her, she couldn't miss.

Her arm came up and the paring knife that she'd scooped up off the counter came thundering down into Marcos's shoulder.

He howled and then backhanded her across the face, sending her stumbling across the room to the launch's industrial-size oven.

His blow had either knocked something into place or else the effects of his original strike were finally wearing off, for the pain in her head began subsiding. The thick blanket that had wrapped itself about her senses was fading, and as she stood there, arms braced on the stove, head hanging down, she realized that she could see. Those scratched and bloody things attached to her arms? Those were her hands. And if she could see her hands...

Behind her, she heard a grunt and then a clatter as Marcos pulled the blade from his shoulder and tossed it aside.

"I'm going to make you suffer for that." He let loose a roar of rage and she could hear him rush toward her.

Not this time....

She stayed where she was, letting him think that nothing had changed, that he was about to vent his fury on a helpless, wounded woman, and then, when he'd committed himself, when he'd generated too much forward momentum to be able to stop, she spun, calling her sword to hand as she did so.

The last thing Marcos saw was the smile on her battered face as her sword appeared, the blade practically humming with eagerness to avenge the wrongs done to her that night.

She had to give him credit—he tried to stop. His mind sent the command to his feet to slow down, turn aside, but his feet never actually received the order because Annja's blade had already slashed through his neck.

Annja completed the turn, stepping out of the way as she did so, so that she could watch Marcos's lifeless body slip to the ground.

The only sounds left in the room were the ticking of the clock on the stove and Annja's breathing.

Annja wiped her blade clean and tossed the bloodied cloth aside when she was finished.

Oh, Claire, come out, come out, wherever you are.

All she could hear was the faint sound of a boat's engine starting up.

The noise was probably louder than she realized, given the messed-up state of her hearing, but nonetheless it was recognizable to her.

Then it hit her—Claire had just fired the engine on the boat's launch.

Her mind flashed with possible actions. There was no way she'd make it down three decks and across half the ship in order to stop Claire before they cast off. Nor did she have a long-range weapon—like Hugo's rifle, which she'd carelessly left behind on the dive platform—that she could bring to bear from a distance. No, this was going to have to be up close and personal, and there was only one way she could think of doing that.

Hopefully it wasn't too late.

She ran for the stairs to the deck above.

Her feet felt clumsy, infinitely too slow, as she threw herself up the stairs hoping that desire alone would make her get there faster. Fifteen steps in all and then she was out on the open deck, turning, turning, searching for the sound, trying to pinpoint its location....

There!

Starboard side, moving stern to bow.

She raced in that direction, cut across the boat to the other side just in time to see the launch headed forward with Claire at the helm.

Claire was too involved in piloting the boat, something she apparently wasn't all that accustomed to, to look up to the deck above and see Annja racing along ahead of her, sword in hand.

You are only gonna get one shot at this....

Don't think, she told herself, *just do.*

Annja raced forward, stepped up onto the gunwale of the ship and threw herself into space without a thought to the consequences.

39

Her fall lasted mere seconds at most, but to Annja it felt like an eternity as her mind tried to calculate trajectories and relative speeds and weight-mass ratios against landing surfaces.

The simple fact of the matter was that she was either going to hit the boat, which would be good, as that was the end result she was hoping for, or she was going to miss and go for a drink in the ocean blue, leaving herself vulnerable to any number of counterattacks—from getting shot by Claire to being run over by the motor launch.

As she dropped unexpectedly out of the sky, Annja really hoped it was the former.

The launch rushed forward, Claire intent at the helm, and Annja saw that she was going to miss her target. Instead of landing in the launch, she crashed down right in the middle of the forward bow, directly in front of the windshield.

And then she bounced.

The speed and forward motion of the boat sent her body soaring right over Claire, where she stood at the controls. Then like a stone skipping off the surface of a lake, she bounced again....

Her sword flashed out, her hands locked on the hilt and the blade buried itself into the deck of the launch, stopping her dead in her tracks the way an ice ax would stop a climber's fall.

Annja had a second to breathe in a sigh of relief and then she released the sword and rolled away from the center of the boat. Just as she did so, Claire turned and put two shots into the very spot where Annja had been.

The muscles in Annja's body ached from the abuse she'd put them through, but she didn't let that stop her as she rolled in the other direction, spoiling Claire's aim another time as she put three more shots into the teak decking.

When Annja discovered the edge of the boat by crashing against the starboard gunwale, she knew she couldn't roll any farther. Claire would have her in her sights in seconds and would be anticipating the move to port. Rolling toward starboard would only put her into the sea, something she'd just worked pretty hard to avoid.

As Claire lined up a final shot, Annja grabbed a metal tool chest and flung it forward, smacking Claire hard enough that she let go of the gun. As the boat tipped and met a strong swell, the gun slid and then disappeared somewhere in the stern of the boat near the engine.

Claire threw herself after it.

Oh, no, you don't, Annja thought and threw herself after Claire.

The two women collided roughly, each trying to gain the upper hand. Claire ended up on top, and she reared back and pummeled Annja with one fist after another.

Annja twisted away. After the beating she'd taken at Marcos's hands, Annja wasn't up for a repeat performance.

Now Claire was off balance and on all fours, trying to fight to get back to her feet. And Annja took advantage of the opportunity to land a massive front kick to the underside of Claire's chin.

The move put Claire flat on her back.

Annja stood over her, hands bunched into fists, waiting for Claire to get up, but the other woman stayed down, unmoving.

Finally! Annja thought.

She stalked over to the stern of the boat, looking for the gun. A sound caught Annja's attention and she turned, straightening up just in time to take a flying kick with both legs right to the chest.

The momentum of the blow carried Annja over the rear gunwale and she scrambled to grab hold of something, anything, as she toppled backward. Her fingers snatched at the edge of the engine cowling and stopped her slide.

With a grin of triumph, Claire scooped up the gun, pointed it at Annja and mouthed, *Goodbye*.

Annja didn't wait around. Staring down the barrel of a .45 was all the motivation she needed to get the heck out of the way as quickly as possible. She let go of the engine cowling, and the wind carried her right off the back of the boat into the water.

The water felt like a brick wall when she hit it, leaving her dazed and confused. Her fingers had a hold of some kind of rope or cord hanging off the back of the boat and she instinctively tightened her grip. The line, whatever it was, unfurled, spooling out behind the boat a short distance before snapping taut with a suddenness that nearly took her arm out of the socket. She held on for dear life, knowing that this one little cord might mean the difference between life and death.

The boat's wake kept trying to force her head under the water and it was all she could do to keep her mouth and nose out of the depths in order to keep breathing.

Annja knew she had to do something. She could already feel her strength starting to wane from the constant battering she was taking behind the boat; if she waited too long she might not have the strength to do anything at all. She needed to get back into the boat.

Fighting against the current, Annja brought her left hand up and put it on the rope. Holding on with her left, she brought her right a bit higher and then repeated the process. Inch by inch, hand over hand, she pulled herself back toward the boat.

She had managed to close about half the distance when the launch hit a particularly bad swell and Annja lost her grip. The launch leaped away from her as if shot from a cannon and only a feverish grab for the very end of the rope saved her from the ocean depths.

Annja hung there, at the very end of the rope, the salt water stinging her eyes, the wind whipping at her face, her arms aching. She was so tired; all she wanted to do was let go.

But then the image of Dr. Knowles and his excavation team rose in her mind and she found a renewed strength.

Hand over hand, she started to inch toward the boat again.

With every passing second Annja thought Claire would look up, see her hanging on and put a bullet through her skull. To her great surprise, it didn't happen. Claire kept the launch on a north-by-northeast heading and was scanning the horizon, obviously looking for something. It wasn't until Annja had dragged herself all the way to the back of the boat that she realized what it was Claire was headed toward.

The *Sea Dancer.*

The jammed controls would have kept the vessel moving in the same direction until it ran out of gas or hit something. With the damage to the *Pride* rendering it inoperable, Claire was searching for a substitute.

Excellent idea, Claire.

The boat was already rocking about because of the speed and the choppiness of the water, so Claire didn't notice Annja standing behind her.

Annja considered calling her sword and using that to subdue Claire, but something just didn't feel right about it. Annja reached up and touched the tender spots on her face where Claire had been wailing away earlier. This was no longer about business; this had become personal.

At that moment, Claire suddenly realized she wasn't alone. Whatever it was she had meant to do, she never got the chance to do it as Annja snaked her forearm around Claire's neck and under her chin, then clamped her arms on her opposite biceps. Claire struggled, but it was over almost before it had begun.

Annja spied a length of rope and used it to bind her captive. Only once Claire was tied hand and foot did

Annja take charge of the launch's engine to chase the distant silhouette of the *Sea Dancer*—the ship she intended to use to transport Claire back to the City of the Sun.

40

Chatham Bay
Cocos Island

The queen was waiting for Annja and her captive as she pulled the launch into Chatham Bay late that afternoon.

Annja hopped out of the launch and dragged it higher onto the beach, where it wouldn't drift away. Claire sat on the floor of the boat. Annja had gagged her earlier, to cut off the endless stream of threats the woman spouted, but all Claire did now was stare in sullen anger.

To think she'd been so swayed by Claire's lies.

Live and learn.

Annja took hold of Claire's arm and helped her stand up, then tried to assist her in getting out of the boat. Claire was unable to walk, or move at all, in fact, so Annja untied the rope from Claire's hands and feet.

Once they were on the sand, they approached the queen, who was flanked by a pair of Incan guards.

The queen was dressed in lightweight robes of bright colors that reminded Annja of Indian sarongs. She sat on a beautiful throne, a woven carpet beneath it, a canopy overhead.

The queen smiled when she saw Annja and her smile grew even wider when she recognized who it was that Annja had with her.

"Well, sword-bearer," the queen said as Annja stepped up and bowed in front of her. "Have you fulfilled the conditions of your debt?"

"I have." Annja gestured at Claire. "Here is your son's killer, as promised."

Claire's eyes grew wide and she fell to her knees, begging the queen for mercy.

The queen watched all this for a moment and then ordered Claire to be quiet, telling her that she could plead for her life later. For once, Claire listened.

"And her companions?" the queen asked.

"They didn't live through the confrontation."

The queen nodded. She watched Annja closely as she asked, "And you?"

Annja raised her eyes to meet the queen's cool gaze. "I am ready to accept the judgment passed upon me in exchange for the lives of my friends, as previously agreed."

Annja refused to let the queen see any emotion other than stoic resolve. There was no other option; she was determined that she and the others were going to get off this island alive.

"By order of Inca Tupac, your death sentence has been commuted. You are free to go, as are your friends. They have been well cared for and are ready to leave."

Annja didn't know what to say. Words escaped her. Annja's selfless act not only saved those under her charge, but ultimately her own life, as well. It was an act worthy of the sword-bearer and Annja felt a fresh sense of pride at having been chosen to carry that burden. She vowed anew to continue to uphold the principles the sword's original bearer had held true.

She looked at Claire, huddled at the feet of the queen, and wasn't sure whether leaving her to her fate was the right thing to do anymore.

Could she make one more deal with this queen?

Claire made the decision for her as she sprang for a dagger on the belt of one of the guards and lunged for the queen.

The queen's face froze in terror, the guards too stunned to react.

Annja, sword in hand now, plunged it swiftly through Claire's truly evil heart.

The queen closed her eyes and bent her head, as if in prayer. Her two guards obeyed her lead.

Annja remained where she was; she couldn't seem to look away from the queen.

Noises in the jungle nearby broke the spell.

This time Annja had no need for her sword, though, as Dr. Knowles and his team, and the rest of the survivors, came into view, flanked by an army of Incan warriors.

Dr. Knowles waved, and many of the others cheered.

Annja smiled.

The queen clapped her hands, and as the guards prepared to escort her back to her mountain sanctuary, she paused and said a strange thing.

"Perhaps one day we will meet again, sword-bearer. And if we do, perhaps you will be willing to tell me the story of how you came to possess that sword of yours."

And without another word, the queen went on her

way, leaving Annja standing there, wondering just what other secrets the woman might be hiding in that mountain sanctuary of hers.

* * * * *

The
Don Pendleton's
Executioner®
BREAKOUT

A secret syndicate profits by freeing ruthless criminals...

When notorious killers and drug lords break out of a maximum-security penitentiary, it soon becomes clear that these weren't escapes; they were highly organized rescues. A covert organization is selling prison "insurance," promising to bust criminals out of jail for a hefty price. With the justice system in shambles, Mack Bolan steps in as an undercover rival insurance salesman, hiring his own team of con men. But he'll need more than his war skills to destroy the operation's kingpin.

GOLD EAGLE®

Available February, wherever books and ebooks are sold.

The Don Pendleton's
Executioner®
HANGING JUDGE

Hell hath no fury like a future scorned…

Justice is a damning word in what used to be called Oklahoma, thanks to a sadistic baron known as the Hanging Judge. Crazy, powerful and backed by a despotic sec crew, the judge drops innocents from the gallows at will. When Jak narrowly escapes, a rift among the companions sends them deep into the wilderness outside the ville. Separated and hurting, time is running out for the survivors to realize they're stronger together than they ever could be alone—before a ruthless madman brings them to the end of their rope.

GOLD EAGLE®

Available in March, wherever books and ebooks are sold.

GDL115

Don Pendleton
PULSE POINT

The U.S. becomes a testing ground for North Korea's latest weapon

From a vessel off the Hawaiian coastline, North Korea launches a test of its latest tech, a nonnuclear electronic pulse weapon, and cripples a U.S. Coast Guard station. Worried the next attack will cover a larger area and put civilians at risk, the President is determined to kill the project before the threat is realized. But the North Koreans aren't fighting fire with fire, and Stony Man must race to uncover and disengage this covert technology…before there's another strike.

STONY MAN®

Available February wherever books and ebooks are sold.